MW01005188

THE MIDNIGHT CALLER

A JACK WIDOW THRILLER

SCOTT BLADE

Black Lion Media

ALSO BY SCOTT BLADE

The Jack Widow Series

Gone Forever

Winter Territory

A Reason to Kill

Without Measure

Once Quiet

Name Not Given

The Midnight Caller

Fire Watch

The Last Rainmaker

The Devil's Stop

Black Daylight

The Standoff

Foreign & Domestic

Patriot Lies

The Double Man

Nothing Left

The Protector

Kill Promise

The Shadow Club

Tom Clancy, in life you were a legend, a master, a true-blue snake eater.

You are missed.

With Admiration,

—Scott Blade

PREFACE

FACT:
The first bricks of the Berlin Wall came down on November 9th, 1989.

1

JOSEPH MCCONNELL, "Jo Jo" to his friends, left the meeting thinking that the right thing to do was to go to the FBI. But they weren't his first choice. His first choice would have been to go to the NCIS. But how could he do that?

He didn't know who to trust. The NCIS was risky. Homeland Security would be monitored. And the FBI?

He just didn't know. He needed time to think.

McConnell was a retired military officer himself. He hadn't retired with the highest rank for a man his age, but high enough. He was satisfied. Having low ambitions helped.

Never had he been anyone important. Nor had he ever aspired to be. He was happy in his former position. He had been satisfied with his accomplishments in the shadow of greater men.

There was nothing to be ashamed of. In the same breath, he also had nothing to be proud of, either. Not really. He lived a mediocre life because he was a mediocre man.

He deserved honorable mentions only for participation, not anything more.

Today, he lived a nice little life in the suburbs outside of Norfolk, Virginia, a well-established neighborhood called Brampton Heights, with sprawling sections of trees surrounding a mid-level golf course. It was quite the place to retire. Mostly, he had retired there not because of his accomplishments in the Navy, but for his silence. He knew things, dark things. And he had been rewarded for keeping his mouth shut.

The thing he knew now that he had learned today was too much, even for him. It was a secret that he couldn't keep.

This neighborhood was far above his pay grade, above his class. Most of his neighbors were well-to-do CEOs, retired congressmen, law partners in international firms, or members of the military who outranked him. Six four-star generals lived there. Soon to be five, because one was on his deathbed, although he had been for six months. Cancer.

Next door to McConnell, there were two retired admirals. He knew them personally. He was proud to have a relationship with each man. They were friendly with him, not in the "come over for cigars and a glass of bourbon every week" kind of way, but casual enough to where he had gotten invites to their homes for big neighborhood parties.

If either admiral had been interrogated, he would have acknowledged that he knew McConnell. And neither would have an opinion of him. He knew that. He had no illusions about that. He was forgettable.

McConnell knew many Navy personnel. That had been his branch of the military.

Not in twenty years of service did he ever stray. Never had he ever betrayed his commander's trust. Even though McConnell's rank wasn't as high as he would have liked, it was still high enough for him to know things. Classified things. Bad things. Sometimes illegal things.

Under normal circumstances, some things he knew would have made the most loyal dog bark. Whenever there had been a delicate mission in the past, he had been the guy to count on to oversee it, or at least to be a part of it.

Good Ole Jo Jo can keep a secret, they would say, or they would think. They must have, because they trusted him with secrets—dirty, dirty secrets.

McConnell stepped out of his town car and shut the door. He left it parked in the driveway because he used the garage to house the ten-foot-by-ten-foot model of the maritime battle of Midway, which he had spent the last six months constructing and piecing together, painstakingly. Many of the pieces had to be specially crafted from a hobby and craft shop on the edge of town. And others had to be ordered off the internet.

Before the meeting that he'd just left, he had gone to the shop and picked up a final piece. It was a model depiction of two fighter planes going up against a Japanese plane.

The piece was still in the box, sealed with plastic wrap. He was eager to pull it out and rig it up to complete the model set.

McConnell didn't know what to do about the subject of his meeting, but he knew that once he took out the set of planes and placed them in just the right place on his model set, he would be in a state of bliss. He could forget for a moment. He could ignore the danger that was coming.

McConnell closed the door to his town car and walked up the driveway. He left the vehicle doors unlocked. He hardly ever locked them because the car was controlled by one of those electric key locks, which he didn't like to use. He preferred regular keys because he considered himself to be old-school. He liked pressing the lock down, but he couldn't in this car because it just popped back up.

At his front door, McConnell paused and switched the brown paper bag containing the airplane models from his right hand to his left. He used his right hand to unlock the front door and push it open. He entered the house.

The outside light switched on automatically at about the same moment.

The house was completely dark except for a lamp that his wife had turned on before she left.

She was out with her friends, probably playing bridge, or mahjong, or some other game where she could lose his money. At least that was the common excuse that she gave him. Like he cared. He didn't. He always pretended to care about where she was and what she was doing to feign interest, usually in front of their children. He couldn't care less. She could leave and never return. He would find a way to live with himself. Of that, he was sure.

Luckily, he didn't have to pretend too often since their two kids were adults who had children of their own and lived in faraway states.

Suddenly, he wondered if that's why they had called him to the meeting. More than his reputation for being trustworthy, and that they needed him to set up contact with the Russian captain. The other thing was that he had no family here to worry about.

He didn't have to worry about what they were planning. He didn't have to worry about his family members being in danger. When the time came and the event that they were planning occurred, he could fly out to Colorado and see his son. He could be far away from the radius of damage that was on its way.

McConnell was all for returning to a better time. That's ultimately what the men in his meeting wanted. They were patriots, and they wanted to return to when the military meant something, when honor was still alive and well, when they had a clear-cut enemy unlike now, where the enemy wasn't a state with a flag.

In the meeting, the Listener had explained to him their plans. The Listener explained everything. And as with his wife, McConnell feigned he was calm and collected, that he could be trusted, but on the inside, he was terrified about what the Listener proposed —terrified.

But he listened and nodded and went along with it all. He acted like he understood, which he did. He was ashamed of the state of today's military.

Today's Navy had invisible enemies, unlike thirty years ago when times had more honor. Back then, they had Russia. They had the Cold War. They knew who their enemy was.

Politicians today used the Navy for spying and intel gathering like it was a spy satellite. And those pinheads at the NSA didn't respect what the Navy was for. They didn't respect the firepower that the Navy had.

What was the Navy doing with all their firepower now? Training exercises. Today's sailors and marines and SEALs hardly got much action. All they ever did was pretend.

It was all hogwash to McConnell and the Listener and the others. A disgrace.

To McConnell and the men in his meeting, the Navy wasn't a library or a tool for spying. It was a broadsword. It wasn't the transportation system that it had become for other branches to sail across seas. The Navy had the nukes. The Navy was the US military's atomic weapon. The Navy was the game-changer.

And now it was all being squandered.

Even though McConnell could agree with the sentiments of the small group of men that he had been speaking with, he wasn't sure about their plan.

He tossed his keys on the kitchen bar top and set the bag down with the models inside, carefully. He shivered a bit because the house was colder than usual.

Probably that time of year, he thought.

He opened the fridge and looked in. He cursed under his breath because his wife had thrown out the leftovers and had cooked nothing for him. Sure, there was food, but it was her duty to cook it, not his. That was how he was raised.

That was another reason he was glad she was out of the house all the time. She had abandoned tradition long ago, the moment the youngest kid was gone.

They were living separate lives. They were roommates more than anything else. She had her room upstairs, and he had his downstairs, which suited him just fine.

It had all started with different drawers in a dresser and then separate closets and then different bathrooms. Before too long, she had taken over the entire second floor of the house, and he was evicted from it.

McConnell closed the refrigerator, went over to a cabinet on the opposite side of the kitchen, and took out a rocks glass. He wanted a snifter, but the only two he had were dirty, still in the sink. Another wifely duty being ignored, in his opinion.

He settled for a clean rocks glass and opened another cabinet above the bar and stovetop. It held a host of different liquor bottles. All dark. All whiskey or bourbon or a blend of the two or cognac, which was his favorite. He only took out the whiskey for special occasions when he wanted to get completely hammered.

He poured the cognac and swished it around in the glass. A strong scent floated out and caressed his sense of smell. He smiled, set the open bottle down on the bar top, and took a sip. Not bad.

He walked to a side door that led to the garage, scooped up the bag with the model planes, and took it with him on his way through the door.

The garage was dark, and colder than the inside of the house, but only by a degree or two.

He walked in, leaving the side door open so that a pool of light crept in enough to illuminate his path.

He set the bag down near the table with the model battle scene and turned to switch on the light. He flipped it, and the overhead light flicked on. The light was a single fixture with two bright bulbs. It didn't matter to him that the light wasn't enough to light up every nook and cranny of the garage. It worked perfectly as a spotlight on the table. Plus, he liked the atmosphere that the lower lighting created. It made the whole room feel like one of those cigar-smoking rooms you see in old movies.

The model table itself was lit perfectly. Shadows crept out and away from the pieces in just the right way.

On the edge of the model table was a glass ashtray, which McConnell was proud of because he had stolen it from the USS Missouri, which he had been stationed on during Desert Storm. Famously, it was the first battleship to launch Tomahawks into Iraqi-held enemy territory. He was always proud of that fact, even though he had absolutely nothing to do with it.

There was a half-smoked cigar resting on the ashtray next to a gold-plated lighter. It was his cigar. He had put it out the night before and saved it.

McConnell stood over the model table and smiled. He was about to complete another masterpiece.

Most of his fellow retired sailors could look back on their careers with great pride. McConnell was only content with his career. But creating these models was something he was proud of. It was sad to think that this was more of his life's work than his military record.

Still, there was one final piece to the puzzle.

He turned, still swallowing cognac, and returned to pick up the model pieces. That's when he came face to face with the man in black and the business end of a silenced SIG Sauer.

The man in black had a name, but McConnell didn't know it. He only knew who he was by reputation. The first time that he'd ever met the guy was over an hour ago at the meeting.

Even then, the man in black was silent.

Now he spoke. His voice was subtle and eerily normal, which was almost more frightening than the gun, strangely. Maybe it was the calmness in it. Or maybe it was the lack of humanity in it.

The man in black asked, "Where's your wife?"

McConnell didn't put his hands up to show surrender. He didn't drop his glass of cognac. He just stayed there, still, and said, "She's out."

"When is she coming back?"

McConnell shrugged.

"Where are your children?"

Without hesitation, he said, "They moved out years ago."

The man in black nodded. He believed him.

Just then, he asked a question that sent fear straight to McConnell's bones. It was the fear you feel the moment you know that you're going to die.

The man in black asked, "She knows about what we're doing?"

2

McConnell's wife drove up and parked on the curb because her husband hadn't pulled in close enough to their garage, again. She had nagged him about that before, many times before. So she knew he did it on purpose.

He did it so that she would have to park her convertible Mazda on the curb. She hated that because it was all white, and the neighborhood kids always stood out near it, every morning, waiting for the school bus. They spat on it and threw rocks at it. She knew it. Even though she couldn't prove it, she knew it in her gut.

And then there was the school bus. Every time that school bus passed, it kicked up dirt or mud or water from rain puddles onto her car. She hated it.

This time she was going to make Jo Jo come back out and move his damn car. She didn't care if he was tired or drunk. She didn't care about his models. She was tired of doing it herself. And she was tired of reminding him about it. She was tired of him.

She should have left him years earlier. She had her chance. Hell, she still could. But at this point in her life, why should she? What would she do?

Her husband was a bastard, but his retirement paid the bills, gave her a roof to sleep under, gave her the car she loved. Where would she go now, at this age?

She could get a job, but that thought made her chuckle.

She had quit her last job decades ago, after her first kid was born. She had done the loyal wife and loving mother thing for years.

No one would hire her. Not now. And even if some company did, what would they pay her?

She could take half of her husband's money, she supposed. But that wasn't much. She knew that. She knew what he took home as a retirement income. Although they had a nice house, there wasn't enough money coming in for her to make a separate life.

If she left now, she would be lucky to end up in a one-bedroom apartment. She would have to give up her car.

Martha McConnell shut the door to the car gently, not slamming it, which was what her instincts wanted to do, but she didn't. She was mad at her husband, not her car. Next, she clicked the button on her key to lock the car doors.

Unlike her husband, she locked her car every time she got out, even if she was only going a few feet away, like at the grocery store whenever she had emptied her shopping cart and had to put it away. She locked the car doors first, and then she pushed the cart to the nearest bin.

The alarm beeped once, and the lights flashed and shut off.

She stomped up the drive in her cheap Friday night pumps that she'd worn to her friend's house. She stopped at her husband's town car and waited for a low burp that passed through her throat and out into the air. She had a slight taste of chardonnay in her mouth.

She continued to the front door and opened it. It was unlocked, as usual. McConnell never seemed to care if their house was ever locked, which was another point that she constantly nagged him about.

Martha stopped in the doorway with the door wide open and reached in to switch the light on. She found the switch and flipped it. Nothing happened. She repeated the process—still nothing.

The lamp that she had left on was off as well. She suspected her husband had turned it off. He hated to leave lights on when no one was home.

Why was the foyer light not working? She wondered.

She tried it again—nothing. She flipped it a fourth time. Same results. Nothing.

The power wasn't out. She knew that because the light from the kitchen was on and working fine. The light was enough for her to see the silhouettes of her living room furniture and the dining room table and chairs beyond.

She cursed under her breath and stepped into the darkness. She closed the front door behind her. Her shoes echoed in the stillness on the tile floor in the foyer.

She dropped her purse on an end table near the door and stopped and took off her coat. She hung it on a hook and brushed their umbrella stand with her knee as she turned around.

Her footsteps were soon soundless as she stepped on the rug just after the foyer at the beginning of the living room.

The house was colder than she expected.

She said, "Jo Jo? Why is the AC running so low?"

No answer.

"Jo Jo, what's wrong with the lights?"

No answer. She walked into the living room.

"Jo? Where the hell are you?"

He must've been in the garage, clowning around with his precious models that she couldn't care less about.

"Jo?" she called out again. She called it out loud enough for him to hear her from the garage.

But there was no answer.

She set her purse on an end table near the door and stopped and took off her coat. She picked up her purse and turned around.

She dug around in her purse to find her cell phone. She swiped up on the screen and turned on the phone's flashlight feature so she could see.

The light was bright, but with a small cone of light that lit up the carpet in front of her first.

She used it to see where she was stepping, not to search the room.

She walked deeper into the living room, passing the TV, the sofa set, and the coffee table. But she stopped short of the armchair just before the kitchen because it looked like someone was sitting in it.

A second later, she was certain that someone was sitting there because she kicked a man's shoe. She twisted and turned to aim the cone of light onto the shoe and kicked it again. There was definitely a foot inside it because it was heavy to her kick, but the person didn't respond. No reflex response at all.

She kicked it again.

"Jo? Is that you?"

No answer.

Abruptly she was attacked by panic and then fear.

The light shook in her hand as she moved it up from a familiar pair of shoes and then a familiar pair of pants and then to a familiar white shirt, only it wasn't white anymore.

She saw his hands. They were duct-taped around the chair. The duct tape reflected the light with a blurry shine. It ran all the way around the man's lap in thick layers of tape.

There were violent waves and ripples in tape like the man had struggled hard to get free.

Martha moved the light upward. Next, she saw trickles of red, dried fluid that were more accurately described as garnet red, and blood.

The garnet-colored blood became more voluminous and syrupy and thicker as the beam of light shook in her hand, moving up from the man's lap to his shirt until there was no more white left in the shirt. That was when she saw only the garnet red color of blood.

Martha gasped at the sight of the neck that was also familiar, and then she saw the face that she knew better than her own. It was her husband.

His neck was well past the point of gushing blood because the blood he had in his body had gushed out much earlier. All that was left was a vicious-looking wound. It looked like someone had tried to decapitate him with a rusty hacksaw. Only he hadn't been decapitated. He had been garroted all the way to the bone.

Martha looked on at her husband's face. While she had known that face for many years, there was something brand new about it. It was his expression. She had never seen that expression on his face before. No one had.

His eyes were wide open, staring into the darkness behind her. Only not staring, because there was no life in them. Not even a sign that life had once occupied his body. There was no sign of anything but utter-terror on his face. It was unlike anything that she had ever seen before.

He was completely stone, like a marble statue made by some twisted sculptor.

The whites in his eyes were completely bloodshot, but not with the garnet color she had seen a second earlier on his shirt. This was a shade of purple that was almost eggplant. They looked like they were about to burst out of their sockets.

It was horrifying.

The phone trembled harder in her hand. She slowly reached out with her free hand. The tips of her fingers touched her dead husband's forehead. Immediately, she recoiled because his skin was so cold that it felt like touching ice.

Martha jumped back, but she was stopped dead in her tracks by a brick wall.

No, not a brick wall, a man. A powerful man.

She heard a subtle voice say, "Where are your children?"

A question that he already knew the answer to, but he liked to be reassured.

As if she were answering a game show question in the lightning round, Martha said, "They don't live here."

The man smiled.

She didn't turn around.

The man behind her asked, "When was the last time you spoke to them?"

Martha trembled even harder, which the man in black knew because the light from her phone danced across the wall, across McConnell's lifeless body.

"It's been at least a week. They're busy."

The man in black smiled in the dark. He didn't really need to ask her that question. He would know soon enough when he checked the phone log on her cell phone.

He liked the feeling that he felt just before she died. The anticipation before he killed her put a smile on his face. It was the best part. Other than the struggle his victims gave him, of course.

In a fast, violent, well-practiced exertion, the man in black whipped out a garrote that he had been holding, pulling it tight until the wire rippled and echoed lightly in the stillness. The wire went over her head to her neck and jerked straight back. The sharp edge of the wire nearly cut through the skin on her neck with little force. A second later, it broke the skin, and blood misted out as she tried to scream.

No sound escaped from her lips. No breath came out of her lungs.

Martha instinctively dropped the phone and grabbed at the wire around her neck with both hands. Desperately.

She fought violently to pull a fraction of slack out of it. But there was none to be had.

The man in black was too strong. He remained still, like a tree planted in the ground with roots dug down deep. Nothing would move him. Nothing would budge him.

She struggled and struggled. When that didn't work, she drummed on his gloved hands. And she gagged and retched and heaved dryly. She made all the faces imaginable under the circumstances, and then she duplicated her husband's dead expression.

The man in black still didn't move. He was much, much stronger than she. He breathed in calmly. This was his favorite part.

She fought and fought until she felt weak and suddenly feeble. She fought until fighting turned into barely moving.

The pain was beyond anything that she could imagine. It was worse than childbirth. It was worse than that time she'd nearly drowned at Lake Mead, a family trip, a better time.

She continued to struggle weakly against him until she was blind, until she could no longer move.

It made no difference.

3

THE MAN in black used his burner phone to call, but first, he dropped his garrote in the McConnells' kitchen sink. He ran cold water over the wire and the dual handles and watched as blood and skin and even bits of sinew washed off the razor-sharp wire.

Plenty of evidence was left all over the living room floor that the McConnells had been brutally murdered. It didn't take a forensic technician to see that, but he wasn't concerned with any of it. None of it would lead to him. And even if it did, it wouldn't matter after Sunday.

One thing that might lead to him, eventually, was the security gate that he had to pass through to get into the neighborhood. They had him on camera at the gate, where he pretended to be visiting someone who lived in the neighborhood.

The man in black had infiltrated maximum-security installations all over the western world. A minimum wage crew of security guards and the low tech of a rising boom gate wouldn't stop him.

The security camera had his face because he had to raise the visor on his helmet so the guard could match the photo on his fake driver's license with his face.

Normally, he would destroy the video from the camera somehow. But that didn't matter.

Once the operation that he was protecting went off, none of it would matter.

The man in black finished cleaning the garrote and then called the Listener, the person who had sent him to kill the McConnells. The Listener was the boss.

After he dialed the number, the phone didn't ring even once. The time counter for the call showed two seconds of connecting on his end, but there was already a voice on the other line.

The man in black said, "He's dead."

The Listener asked, "The wife?"

"Also dead."

"That's a shame."

"You wanted her dead."

"I know."

The man in black said nothing, but wondered how close the Listener had been to the McConnells.

The Listener said, "Get out of there."

"What next? How are we going to get to Karpov?"

"Farmer has found a way."

The man in black had no opinion on the guy named Farmer. He barely knew him. They ran in the same covert circles, with two very different occupations.

The Listener said, "It's quite brilliant. And simple. And a total act of fate."

"How so?"

"We found Karpov's daughter."

"Daughter?"

"She's in New York," the Listener said, and chuckled, which was audible enough for the man in black to hear him.

"Really?"

"And get this. She's a local operator for the FSB. She's been here under our noses."

The Listener had used the word "operator," which didn't mean the telephone kind. He had meant that she was a spy.

The man in black said, "You're kidding?"

He smiled and almost caught himself joining in the chuckle. It was quite a stroke of luck.

"Get to New York. We don't need you here anymore. We might need you there."

"Of course. I'll leave now."

"Good," the Listener said.

"What is Farmer's plan?"

"I'll explain when you get there. You're only going to be there for disposal and backup."

That was exactly what the man in black wanted to hear. Disposal was what he did best. All that espionage, intelligence gathering, and talking to people, making friends, earning trust. He was more than happy to leave that to the career schemers like Farmer. It didn't interest him in the least.

The man in black listened a little longer. The Listener spoke, telling him where to go and what to wait for.

The operation may not even need his services anymore, but it was better to have him around as a backup in case something went wrong.

After the Listener was done explaining things to him, the man in black said goodbye and hung up the phone. He took one more look over the McConnells' house, saw nothing left that needed doing, nothing left that needed his attention, and he walked out, down the drive and down the street to where he had parked his motorcycle.

He looked around casually until he was satisfied that no one was watching him. He slipped on his helmet, lowered the darkened visor, started the engine, and in a burst of exhaust, rode away into the darkening night.

4

The City of New York or New York City?

He wasn't sure.

Jack Widow had heard it called both before. He knew one was the official title of the area that people sometimes simply called New York. With no "City" in the title. As if the state of New York didn't exist. Only the City mattered.

What was the official title of the city again? He couldn't remember, which was a scary prospect for a guy not old enough to have Alzheimer's disease. But grown-up enough to know the name of the City.

He didn't have amnesia. Did he?

No. Not quite. The reason that Widow couldn't recall the name of the City, not at that second, wasn't because of the five guys standing around him. Not all five, anyway.

It was because of only one.

The one that stood directly in front of him. The one with the massive bulk.

He wasn't the biggest of the five guys. But he was the one to worry the most about because he had that look on his face, like he knew how to throw a punch.

More than just the look on his face was his face itself. It wasn't a normal face and far from the kind of face that one would call attractive.

It was the kind of face that showed off the ability to take a punch. It showed that off because it had taken punches. Hundreds. Probably more, Widow figured.

The guy with the face wore a street cap, made from cotton or maybe wool. It was the kind of tattered street cap that looked like it came right out of the nineteen forties, just after the Great Depression.

It was the kind of thing that was cheap to find back then, and it kept the head warm. It was a functional garment. Not now. These days this kind of cap would go for a pretty penny in a department store in New York City.

The guy wasn't wearing it to stay warm. It was a fashion choice.

Times had changed. Certainly. The Great Depression. Another time. The nineteen forties. Or was that the nineteen-thirties?

Widow couldn't remember that, either.

The guy's face was rougher than a four-hundred-year-old map of the world and harder than the side of a tree. Widow saw the advantage of having such a face. On the one hand, it terrified most people, and intimidated even the most capable street fighters, like Widow.

There was a disadvantage about it, which Widow made the mistake of mentioning to the guy.

He said, "With a face like that, you must hear constant laughter from women every time you propose that one of them go to bed with you."

Not the drollest insult that Widow had ever hurled, but not the dumbest either. It did the trick, which was to piss the guy off—not a tactical decision on Widow's part. It was more of a need, the kind of need that Widow liked to have satisfied when he was squaring off with five guys with a woman and a gun present.

After the insult was hurled and the verbal shot was fired, you couldn't take it back. Suddenly Widow wished he could.

The guy with Map Face scoffed with an unintelligible grunt that wasn't even in the realm of sounding like an English word, probably because it was slurred out in a thick Irish accent. Widow didn't get the chance to decipher it because the map-faced guy punched him right in the cheek for the second time.

Hard. It felt like being hit with a battering ram, exerting enough force to bang through the castle doors.

Suddenly, the words "blunt force trauma" sprang to Widow's mind, and he blacked out, standing. It was only a second to the five guys and one woman standing around him. But to Widow, it felt like an eternity of black.

His mind wandered for that long moment. And his long-term memory seemed to work. He thought back to a long military career. Once, he had been undercover, working for the Naval Crime Investigative Services. He had been a Navy SEAL during the last stretch of that career. Although, not really because he was technically an NCIS agent, which is a civilian.

They assigned him to an undercover unit where he went on missions with the SEALs, as one of them. To them, he was one. No one knew he was really an NCIS agent.

He lived a double identity.

Most SEALs knew him as one of them. They trusted him with their lives. They treated him like a brother, but he wasn't one of them. Not really. Not honestly. He had always felt hollow inside knowing that truthfully, he was an undercover cop, sent to spy on his brothers. There was a word for that—rat.

And sometimes he felt like a rat. But only sometimes. Because the truth was ninety-nine point nine percent of SEALs and Marines were heroes—patriots. These were good men. It was lying to them that made him feel like a rat.

But then there was that point one percent. They were the ones who had stepped out of line. He had found that point one percent to be traitors, murderers, terrorist enablers, and even flat-out spies for foreign governments. And then there had been foreign agents who weren't in the US Navy or Marine Corps. Many of them he had to take down in his career. Taking them down was more satisfying because he didn't have to face an American who had gone too far over to the dark side.

At this moment, he couldn't remember any of them, not one face. He couldn't remember the official title of New York, and, for a split second, he couldn't even remember why this guy was punching him in the face.

Widow took the second punch to his right cheek, not as strong as the first one, which he had taken straight to his chin. That was the blow that rocked him.

The jaw and the chin are weak areas of the body. Get punched in the jaw hard enough, and you will go out. Every man has this weakness. It's only a matter of pressure and resistance, but get hit hard enough and it's lights out.

If being punched in the jaw could be measured on a number scale of one to ten, Widow guessed his number might've been a weak eight. But this guy's punches made him believe he had met a guy who could throw a punch that was a ten.

The only reason the guy had hit him in the chin was that, at the last second, Widow moved his face upward to avoid getting hit in the nose. He didn't want to get it broken.

Now he was thinking it might've been better than taking one of Map Face's monster fist punches on the chin.

Map Face had gotten him on the cheek next. A second blow that Widow hadn't agreed to.

* * *

FIVE MINUTES EARLIER, Widow had turned a corner in high spirits until he walked straight into this mess.

He turned the corner of Carbon and Seventy-First Street. It was nighttime. Late. But the city always had enough light that he could still hear baby birds chirping in one of the growing trees planted near the sidewalk.

The leaves were still hanging on in the beautiful fall weather, but they had turned yellow about a week ago. Soon they would turn brown. This was the reason that he had come to New York.

What better place to spend his birthday?

He walked around the corner when he came across a man and a woman standing outside a closing Irish pub, which was abnormal on its own because Irish pubs didn't normally close before sunup, and that was far away.

He had noticed it because he was immediately sucked into the argument in front of him.

The woman was decked out in a leather half jacket, the kind of garment that barely stretched down to the small of her back. She had big brown hair, not in the eighties big perm kind of way, but not far off either.

She might've been about twenty-one years old. Although eighteen wouldn't have surprised him.

She was tall, too. Much taller than the man that she was fighting with. She looked to have an entire foot on him. To his credit, she was in large heels.

She wore a tight skirt, not quite a mini, but Widow figured it wasn't far off either. She held one of those small, shiny purses that were meant only for a cell phone, cash, credit cards, and keys, and nothing else.

Her top was a sequined silver thing. It showed her midriff was the kind that was more out of starvation over exercise. The girl's stomach wasn't the only thing on display. Her cleavage was out, and she wasn't shy about it.

The man had been wearing a three-piece suit, blue and wrinkle-free and dry-cleaned so crisp it looked right out of a flat press.

He wore more rings than he had fingers, which wasn't metaphorical. The guy was missing his pinkie finger on his right hand.

The rings were the size of Super Bowl rings but were more than likely bought from a class ring manufacturer because this guy would've never played in any sport. Ever.

From the looks of him, Widow would've thought he was too small to make it on a JV team in any sport.

The jewelry didn't stop at the rings. The guy had two gaudy necklaces on. They were gold plated, probably plated and thick. Nothing hung from them. He wasn't as blatant as one of those pimps from the seventies. He didn't have his name hanging from the end of one chain. Or anything like that.

Widow heard the guy screaming at the woman. All kinds of expletives and obscenities and invectives. Nothing that he hadn't heard before. And nothing that he had ever stood for before, not when directed at a woman, even if she wasn't dressed in the most innocent way. Not that he didn't approve of how she was dressed. As a man, he certainly liked it. As a citizen of the twenty-first century and America, he believed in *live and let live*. If she wanted to wear a wet trash bag and nothing else, it was none of his business. Naturally, her choice in clothes didn't warrant the kind of treatment that she was getting.

This was New York City, and people were mean to each other in all kinds of horrible ways on the streets and in public.

Widow couldn't stop and reprimand them all. It wasn't his place. He wasn't the manner police.

After turning the corner, his instinct was to assess and move on. No need to make a big deal out of it, as long as the guy wasn't physically abusing the woman or as long as she didn't request help. Then it was none of his business.

She makes her own choices.

Widow kept on walking in the direction that he had planned to walk, which was toward them and past them.

The girl had been standing with her back and left side to him, nearly a profile view.

Her face had pointed toward the man.

The moment that changed Widow's assessment from one of *live and let live* was when the woman's profile changed, and she looked in his direction.

So far, she hadn't said a word back to the gangster-looking wannabe. Instead, she had just taken the verbal abuse, like it was expected of her.

That changed when she heard or felt Widow's presence. She turned and looked right at him.

Her face was a mess of tears, muddy running mascara and bandages and swelling. She had white medical bandages on her nose. Her eyes were puffy, like she had been punched in both eyes. Her cheeks were so veiny that they looked like blue and red and yellow electrical wires running underneath her skin.

There was so much redness in her eyes that Widow wasn't sure if they were red from her crying for a week or if it was blood.

Something told him it was the latter.

Widow had always had a laissez-faire attitude, but there was a limit to that. His attitude had a second phase.

His first phase was to live and let live. His second phase was *do unto others*.

The woman had a face that was virtually broken. Obviously, this current situation had only been a follow-up to a worse situation. That had required her to go to the emergency room for a broken nose and swollen cheeks and probably two bruised eyeballs.

Widow saw this, assessed the situation, and immediately cranked into his second phase, *do unto others*.

The short guy had done something to another. And now it was time for Widow to do back unto him.

The gangster wannabe turned and looked at him and stared.

Widow was a tall man, and a dangerous-looking one at that. He hadn't known low self-esteem since he was in junior high, and back then it was only relative to women. He had never known self-doubt, not in fighting. Not anyone. Not anywhere. Not at any age.

But this guy's self-esteem must've been incredible because he looked up at Widow's face, which must have been ten-plus inches higher than his own.

And he asked, "What the hell you gawking at?"

Widow could've said something witty in return. He could have. But he didn't.

Instead, he stepped right up to the guy and, with his left hand, grabbed the dangling gold chains. He racked them down with enough pressure to hold the guy still, and then he threw a right jab. Hard and fast.

The bones in the guy's face, including his nose and probably his cheeks *cracked!!*

The gangster wannabe let out a cry that was louder than most dying animals.

Widow held onto the gold chains around the guy's neck, tight. He reared his right hand back, slow this time. He wanted the guy to see it coming.

After a calculation of power, because he didn't want to kill the guy or knock him out, Widow threw the second blow to the guy's face. He hadn't really made a plan. There had been no time for that. At that moment, he figured why not make the guy's face look like the girl's?

An eye for an eye was basically the same as *do unto others.*

Before Widow could execute a second horrific blow, the woman screamed, "What the hell are you doing?"

She latched onto his bicep, nearly hanging off it. She had moved so fast that she came out of her shoes.

"Let him go! Let him go!" she begged and pleaded.

Widow let the guy go.

He dropped like a tossed cinder block at a construction site; only he didn't crack open when he hit the sidewalk. That was only because he hadn't been tossed hard enough.

The gangster wannabe said something inaudible because his nose was broken and his cheeks were shattered.

He grabbed at his nose with both hands. Blood seeped out between his fingers and ran over his pale white knuckles.

The woman said, "What the hell are you doing? Why? Why?"

Widow looked at her, confused. It seemed pretty obvious why. This guy was beating on her, treating her like a dog.

He said, "What do you mean?"

"Why are you attacking us?" she shouted at him.

Attacking us? Us?

"I don't like men who beat women."

"He wasn't beating me. We were arguing!"

"What?"

"He didn't beat me!"

"Not this time. But what about in the last twenty-four hours?"

She looked up at Widow as she knelt, rocking the gangster wannabe. He cried like a baby.

"What the hell are you talking about, asshole?"

Widow looked at her. He was so confused. Was she this blind? Did she have Stockholm syndrome or something?

He had heard of abused women like this before. They defended the men who beat them. Some of them even let them do it. But he had never seen a woman who pretended that it wasn't happening, not when there was barefaced physical evidence.

Not like this.

She said, "Well?"

"Your face. Look at your face. You look like he's been beating you with a bat."

The girl stood up, walked right up to Widow.

She said, "These bandages aren't from being beaten! This is from plastic surgery! I'm a model! I had a nose job! And collagen injections!"

Widow looked at her, dumbfounded.

He had made a big mistake, and it was only going to get worse.

Right at that moment, a group of men walked out of the Irish pub. The door shut behind them like it had been attached to a squeaky metal door spring.

The four men who walked out were all big guys. They were dressed almost comically the same. Scruffy, threadbare casual suits. No ties among them. Some had vests. Some had dress shirts and slacks with suspenders.

Then the biggest guy stepped forward. He had been in the back like he was the anchor.

He was the guy with the map for a face.

The woman said, "You just beat up Vinnie, the Irish! Big mistake!"

Widow didn't know Vinnie. He had never heard of him. And Widow wasn't the smartest man who ever lived, but he had better than average common sense.

He knew that this was New York City. He knew he had been strolling through the town's only upper-class Irish neighborhood.

And they were standing in front of an Irish pub that closed early on a Saturday night.

One of the few ways a business like that would close on a Saturday night, early, was if the staff had been given permission to by the owner.

Widow looked up, past the big guys, and stared at the sign.

It read: *Vinnie's Irish Pub.*

His face formed an expression of worry.

It turned out that Vinnie wasn't a gangster wannabe.

He was a gangster.

5

WIDOW FELT bad about his mistake.

The map-faced guy wasn't the spokesman for Vinnie. That job title turned out to belong to the third-biggest guy. He was also the only one who had all of his teeth, Widow had noticed. And he had the best facial features as far as being easiest to look at. He wasn't the ugliest one by far.

He stepped forward and asked, "Irene, what the hell is going on?"

"This idiot knocked Vinnie out. He thought he had been hitting me. 'Cause of the bandages."

The spokesman stepped up to Widow, and two of the other guys stepped around Widow in a circle. They didn't get within grabbing distance, which Widow also noticed. He noticed it because it meant that they weren't amateurs. Like he had assessed them, they had also assessed him. They knew right off the bat that he was no normal guy. He wasn't the kind of guy they usually set out to rough up.

Widow had a lean build, but he was hard as a rock. He had long arms and big hands that had more in common with sledgehammers than human fists.

The four guys all knew to stay out of his reach. Even the map-faced guy stayed clear of it.

They had the number advantage, and by the look of them, they had the experience advantage as well. Especially the map-faced guy. He was the one who worried Widow.

He worried him because not only did he look like he was their best fighter, he also looked a little familiar.

It took Widow a moment, but he was almost positive that he had seen the guy's face before. It was hard to forget, after all. Then it hit him. The map-faced guy was famous. Once the guy had a decent record as an Irish MMA fighter.

But he had retired from fighting in the ring. Widow wasn't sure why. Maybe it was because Vinnie paid more. Then again, maybe it was because he'd nearly killed a guy.

Whatever the reason, Widow didn't want to find out.

The spokesman stepped into Widow's view and asked, "You got a name?"

"Don't you?"

The spokesman smiled and said, "My name is Geoffrey."

He waited, and Widow stayed quiet.

He chuckled and said, "I know. It sounds like the name of an Irish butler. But that's my name. Real name too."

Widow nodded, kept his eyes on Geoffrey, but watched for motions from any of the other guys. If they moved, he moved.

Geoffrey said, "This is Big John. That's Little John."

He pointed at one of the other guys and then the next one. Widow didn't turn to look.

He said, "Guess we know which one is popular with the ladies then, don't we?"

Geoffrey smiled and said, "This one is called Laurie, which is short for Lawrence, which is short for Lawrence Holyfield. No relation to the famous boxer. Obviously."

Widow nodded.

"But you know why people often make that mistake?"

Widow said, "No clue." Although he knew.

"It's not because he's white. Clearly. It's because, like Holyfield, the American boxer, Laurie is a famous boxer. Kickboxer, actually."

Widow stayed quiet.

"Do you know what a kickboxer is?"

"A boxer who kicks?"

Geoffrey smiled and said, "Yes. That's it. But ole Laurie here can't kick for shit!"

Right then, three of them laughed a big, hearty laugh, all except for Laurie. He looked at Widow with a death stare, like he wanted to kill him, which was probably true.

"Know why it doesn't matter that he can't kick?"

Widow said, "No. Why?"

"Because he never had to. He's more into the boxer part. And boy, let me tell ya. He can box."

Widow asked, "Why does it feel like I'm going to find out just how well?"

Geoffrey ignored that. He asked, "Now, what's your name, mate?"

"Tyson. Know what he did to Holyfield?"

Silence.

And then Geoffrey smiled and said, "Funny."

He looked around at the other three and then at Laurie.

"That's funny, Mr. Tyson. That's real funny. I can see that you've got some brains. So, I'm just gonna level with ya. This here is Vinnie the Irish. We're all Irish. Vinnie here isn't the boss or the boss's boss, but he's kin to the boss's boss."

Widow stayed quiet. Kept his fists down by his sides, but ready to go when action was called.

"See. Really, he's a pain in the ass. None of us like him."

Irene said, "What's taking so long? Kill him already!"

Geoffrey turned in a slow movement like he hated being interrupted, and he said, "Shut up, Irene! No one is talking to you!"

She froze like she was more scared of Geoffrey than she was of the others. This told Widow that he had been wrong.

Geoffrey wasn't the spokesman. Vinnie wasn't their boss. They were his babysitters. This meant that Geoffrey was some sort of top lieutenant, since he was the one doing the talking. He was probably charged with protecting Vinnie.

"Now, where was I?"

Widow tried a new approach. The silent stranger act that normally worked for him wouldn't work here. It was going to lead to him beating up four mobsters. And an ungrateful, crazy woman wasn't worth having mobsters on his back while he was in New York to enjoy himself.

He said, "Look, guys. I don't want any trouble. This is obviously a misunderstanding. I thought there was trouble here. Look at her face—simple mistake. I am truly sorry for busting up your friend. You're free to call the police. I'll stick around. Talk to them. I'll explain it to them."

Widow looked down at Vinnie, who was completely passed out at this point.

"And when your friend wakes up. I'll apologize to him. Maybe he'll want to press charges. I'll stick around for that. I am in the wrong here."

"No pigs!" Irene shouted.

Geoffrey shot her a look. Another way of telling her to shut up. And she did.

He said, "Like the girl said, we can't have the police involved. We're not those types of guys. We practice more of a street justice philosophy."

The apologetic approach wouldn't work either; Widow could see that.

Widow said, "Look. I apologized. Admitted fault. What else do you want? I don't have any money, guys."

Either Big John or Little John smirked. Widow wasn't sure which was which.

Geoffrey said, "I think that it's only fair that you take a beating. Like the one you gave Vinnie here."

Widow stared at him blankly.

"I'm sorry. But I can't have word getting back to my boss that we just let you go with anything less."

Widow smiled and said, "There's four of you. And you're all bigger than Vinnie. How am I supposed to fight four of you and call that even?"

"Fight? Oh, no, Mr. Tyson. I'm not saying that you have to fight all four of us."

Widow shrugged, and said, "What then? Just Laurie?"

"No. You're not fighting here. I said: 'take a beating.' I mean exactly that. You're going to stand still and let Laurie break your face. Like Vinnie's."

Widow smiled back at Geoffrey.

"I'm not letting anyone do anything like that. You can all come at me. At the same time. I'm not the type of guy to stand still."

Geoffrey said nothing.

Widow said, "And I've gotta warn you, fellas. You come at me; you're gonna lose a lot more than ears. You're gonna end up with broken bones and shattered faces. Maybe a couple of you will go blind when I mash your eye sockets to mush."

Right then, Geoffrey looked straight at Laurie, and then he looked around the empty street in a quick, scanning motion. He didn't look behind him, just in front, which was behind Widow.

Widow guessed that one of the Johns signaled to him that there were no witnesses on the street in the other direction because Geoffrey did the one thing that he'd need a street with no witnesses on to do.

He pulled out a Glock 19 and jammed it in Widow's face.

He said, "It's not up for debate. You're taking the beating, or you're taking a bullet."

6

"Not here," Geoffrey said, "Around the back. In the alley."

He was speaking to Widow with a Glock 19 pointed at Widow's face. Widow could have taken it away. Easy enough. A twist from the hips. Pivot on the left foot and a hand clamped down tight on the slide and trigger hand. Followed by a fast swipe down and away, jerking Geoffrey off his feet. Maybe he would break Widow's powerful grip and fire a round, but by that time, he would be aiming at the guy behind him. One of the Johns.

Widow thought about it. But in the end, he decided not to because Geoffrey knew enough to show off the gun quick, by pointing it in Widow's face, but then he knew to back away far enough, so Widow wasn't tempted to try a disarm move against him.

Smart guy. Well, smart enough, Widow thought.

Widow turned and looked toward a small street that led into the dimness of a small alley between the buildings.

Before he moved on, he looked left, looked right. Widow surveyed the street, to double-check Geoffrey's assessment that there were no witnesses. And there weren't, not at that exact moment.

But just then, a blue-and-white police cruiser rolled around the corner and slowed. The two cops in the front stared at Widow.

The car was a Nissan Altima model. It was a hybrid—some kind of move by the NYPD to seem more eco-friendly.

Widow wondered if they had to sacrifice speed and maneuverability and power for the PR stunt. Then again, New York traffic was usually too thick to worry about car chases.

Widow said, "Looks like you boys won't get the chance to follow through after all."

Geoffrey said, "Just wait."

Wait for what? Widow thought.

The cops rolled closer and studied Widow's face. They stopped about fifty yards away. Then Widow watched as they brought the car to a full stop and switched on their left turn signal and cut across the road and vanished down another street.

What the hell?

"The cops aren't going to help you. They won't be bothering us. I'm afraid that you're taking that beating whether you like it or not."

These guys were powerful enough to have the cops in their pockets. At least they had the local boys in their pocket.

Widow didn't even realize that the Irish mob had that kind of status in New York.

"Move it!" Geoffrey barked.

Widow moved on. He walked past one of the Johns and then turned the corner.

The other John stepped out in front of him and motioned for him to follow closer, which he did.

They led him halfway down the alley, past the garbage cans, to the back entrance of the pub.

The air smelled of disposed-food and coffee filters and half-empty beer bottles.

Steam drifted up from a grate on the sidewalk. There was one overhead outside light in the alley. It hung from a pole high above them. It buzzed and flickered.

The four guys stopped inside the yellow cone of light.

Vinnie came around the corner with Holyfield holding him up. He was awake.

Like he had done to his girlfriend, Irene, he was muttering expletives, only now they were about Widow. He tried to cut through his babysitters and march over to Widow. Only this didn't happen.

Holyfield picked him up from under his armpits and set him back where he was, like a rag doll.

Geoffrey said, "Shut up, Vinnie!"

Vinnie scuffed and grunted and mumbled, but he stayed where he was.

"Now, Mr. Tyson. This isn't a fight. You raise a fist; I'll kneecap you. Got it?"

Widow stood in the center of the cone of light. The backdoor to the pub was directly behind him, about five feet away. The two Johns stepped into the light. One to his right. One to his left.

Holyfield moved away from Vinnie and stepped up to the center. Geoffrey moved just behind him so that he could have a clear line of sight to Widow.

Vinnie was in the back, still sniveling.

Widow said, "You boys are making a mistake."

"Oh yeah, how's that?" Geoffrey asked.

"I told you I was sorry. I admitted fault. You don't want to make this worse."

"Worse for you. Not us."

"I beg to differ."

"How's that?"

Widow stayed quiet.

"You know what? Never mind. I don't care. Enough of the tough guy act," Geoffrey said, and then he looked at Holyfield. He said, "Do it."

Holyfield stepped closer. The most crooked smile that Widow had ever seen in his life flashed across Holyfield's map face. It was crooked and rigid, like a jagged knife had been used to open his mouth at birth.

Widow said, "I've been all over the world. And without a doubt, you're the ugliest person I've ever seen."

Holyfield's smile changed to an unrecognizable expression because of how uneven his face was.

But Widow recognized the giant fist that swung straight at him.

Don't fight back, or you'll take a bullet, had been the basic warning from Geoffrey.

And he didn't fight back, not at first.

He took the fist straight on the chin. It was hard.

Widow felt his jaw loosen, and his head whipped down in a violent jerk that could've sprained his neck for months. The punch was so powerful that it might've dislocated four of his vertebrae if he had taken it the wrong way.

7

THE SECOND AFTER the punch landed, Widow felt dazed to where he actually forgot things. His mind wondered about the official title of New York City and other things that didn't matter at that moment.

His jaw switched to feeling intense pain from the impact to feeling like his bones were on fire.

Widow had been rocked to the core.

Luckily, his vision was fine, and his mouth seemed to work with no problems because he made a remark back to the map-faced guy about being ugly or about hearing women's laughter. His mouth moved, and the words were coherent. But then he noticed he couldn't quite remember the map-faced guy's name. Not off the bat.

After he made a smart-ass comment about the map-faced guy, he saw another huge fist barreling down on him. He reacted. Fast. He moved his face back and looked right. He took a second punch on the cheek. This one wasn't as bad as the first, because Map Face's knuckles only brushed against his cheek. They didn't quite connect —a combination of a misfire and self-defensive maneuvers.

Although Widow forgot details, he remembered he wasn't supposed to fight back. However, that strategy wasn't working for him. He had enough.

Widow stayed where he was.

He shut his conscious brain off and let his instincts take over.

A flick of his eyes to the right. A flick of his eyes to the left and a quick glance at Geoffrey. No look at Vinnie.

Widow's only two concerns were Map Face and Geoffrey's Glock 19.

He knew that the other guys weren't armed, not with guns. They would've taken them out already. When your squad leader draws his gun, you draw yours—basic tribal gang practice. Widow knew that.

Geoffrey's Glock was the only one.

Map Face didn't have a weapon either. Why would he? He was probably designated by the state of New York as a weapon.

Widow was ordered not to fight back. He was ordered to take a beating, or he would be shot.

So far, he had been doing just that. It looked like he was taking a beating.

But Geoffrey never told him not to move. If a two-hundred-fifty-pound ex-kickboxer punches you, you move. That's a given. Naturally.

Map Face came in at him for the third time. This time he came at Widow from the left, which was what Widow had expected. It's only natural that after two rights, a boxer is going to come in with a left. Mixing it up is a major component of boxing. Any sports fan knows that.

When Geoffrey ordered Widow not to fight back, he meant with fists and kicks. He probably wasn't thinking about the forehead.

The forehead is another weapon that opponents often overlook.

Widow didn't have a forehead made of stone or anything, but he had a thick skull. A lot thicker than most. He knew this because of emergency room visits and numerous field medics and nurses over the years who always gasped at his x-rays and medical charts.

What's one thing that bones have in common with skin?

Bones heal and learn. Skin will heal and scar. Scar tissue is one of the strongest organic external tissues known on humans. Scar tissue can stop a sharp knife if it's bunched up and strong enough.

Widow's bones had built up many, many extra layers of calluses. His bones differed from most of the rest of the human population because he had beaten up a lot of opponents. And he had been hit in the head—a lot.

This had forced his skull to grow thicker and more rigid and tougher.

Widow couldn't remember how good a boxer Map Face had been, but he supposed that the guy's massive fists probably had never punched a forehead like Widow's before.

No one punches the forehead. No point. But Widow had head-butted enough people and been hit in the head enough times to know that his forehead was like a rock.

As Map Face came at him, aiming for his right eye, Widow reared back in a fast, arching motion and catapulted his head straight down.

Map Face was fast and powerful. But he hadn't tried to be fast. He had thought that Widow was standing still like he had been ordered. He hadn't expected that he needed to move fast. This wasn't a fight.

Widow's head moved faster than Map Face's fist, and he broke the arc of the punch.

Widow's cement forehead whipped down and crushed Map Face's left hook. There was no crushing sound, not like Vinnie's face, but Widow felt the fingers dislocate and break and snap under the power and viciousness of his head.

Map Face's expression changed to one that he recognized—panic.

Widow's head wasn't the only thing working overtime. His feet moved and his body twisted.

As Map Face's knuckles were crushed, Widow used the boxer's momentum to shift him between Widow's body and the line of fire from Geoffrey's Glock.

Widow's right foot stopped and planted hard on the concrete, and he shoved the big kickboxer as hard as he could, straight into Geoffrey, straight into the gun.

Widow didn't stay in one place to confirm that his plan worked. He simply reacted as if it had worked.

Move. Shoot. Communicate. That was a SEAL mantra that he knew well.

Widow moved. Shoved. And now communicated that he wasn't going down. They were. He followed behind Map Face as he tumbled into Geoffrey, and the two of them went down. He wanted to stay out of the line of fire. And to control it.

Geoffrey didn't fire the gun. Not out of reflex, as Widow had suspected he might. Instead, he was taken totally by surprise, and he tumbled backward.

The Glock was the only thing that mattered at this point.

Like a football player losing the ball during a tackle, the Glock was out of Geoffrey's hand and sliding across the concrete, open to interception.

Widow wasn't the closest man to it. One of the Johns was.

Widow shifted priorities and ignored the Glock. He ran at John, who was so slow he didn't even go for the gun until Widow was three feet from him, which Widow anticipated.

The Glock had slid behind John, and he had to bend over to scoop it up.

Before his hand could get around the grip, Widow leaped in like a cat and swiped his boot up hard, and kicked John right in the ear.

The John toppled over. When the eardrum is busted or shattered, it's not normal to hear a sound. Not like a breaking bone.

But Widow did hear something come out of the guy's ear. There was a low *crack*. And thick red blood gushed out like a burst hose.

The guy screamed and toppled over and rolled onto his back, which was a mistake.

Widow didn't want to kill anyone, but these guys threatened his life. He didn't have any mercy for them. Not now. Maybe ten minutes ago, he could've let things go. But not now. No way.

He moved over the guy, fast, and stomped a massive boot down onto John's throat. He slowed it at the last second, realizing that death wasn't necessary. No reason to murder the guy. But if he died, no worries there either.

The guy forgot about his ear and started gasping and whishing. Which was good, in Widow's opinion, because if he was whishing, then some kind of air was getting in. He wasn't suffocating. He would need emergency surgery. But he would live if his pals took him to the emergency room fast enough.

Widow forgot about John and reached down for the Glock. But the remaining John intervened and wrapped two big, muscular arms around him. He jerked Widow back in a reverse bear hug. Which Widow thought was just insane. This wasn't a good tactical move, not in a fight against a guy like him.

Then he saw why John did that. The map-faced guy was getting up.

Geoffrey was still down. He was dazed. It looked like his head had hit the cement when he went down.

He probably had blurred vision, Widow presumed.

Widow's toes touched the ground, and he folded them in and pushed off as hard as he could. He launched up into the air a few feet, but a few were enough. He pulled his knees up and used his weight to make himself heavy.

The other John had no choice; he lost balance, and they both fell forward.

Widow tucked in and braced for the impact. It had little effect on him. The other John was mostly just stunned and not harmed.

With his right boot, Widow cracked him right in the face. Easy enough to not break anything, but hard enough to make the point.

John rolled in the other direction and held his face.

Widow didn't wait. He bounced to his feet. He wanted to go for the Glock, but he found that there was no time because Map Face was on him now. He was making his way to his feet, staying steady, standing enough to rush Widow.

Behind Map Face, Widow got another look at Geoffrey. He was scrambling to his feet behind the kickboxer but stumbling. Blood seeped over his left eye from a huge superficial gash across his brow. He clenched the eye closed and gazed around.

Widow ignored him and braced himself for Map Face, who stood up hunched like a linebacker and charged at Widow.

The common weakness of many professional athletes, especially boxers, is their egos. Often, they think because they are paid to play a sport, they can do anything. They think that because they've won a belt, have a crown, wear a gold medal, or hold the title of champion, that they are champions in real life, in the streets.

If Widow had been using his voluntary brain, if it had been working properly, at that moment, he would've recalled recently watching a program on a TV in a sports bar, down the road from a bus station in New Haven, Connecticut, where the Discovery Channel and ESPN were both covering a story about the famous swimmer Michael Phelps who was racing a great white shark in open waters.

To Widow, the whole idea was a ridiculous premise. A cash grab. And a perfect example of champion athletes thinking that they were the best at something just because they had won a competition in a safe, controlled environment.

Of course, the event was staged, and a computer graphic was used instead of a real shark. A real shark wouldn't have raced Phelps to the end. He would've taken a bite out of him instead.

Cage MMA fighting is a little better because at least Map Face had really been in some danger of bodily injury. But even in a cage match, there are rules, and a referee and judges and commentators, and both fighters were evenly matched in terms of weight and class, and they had teams of people behind them.

In the street, there are no rules. No referees. Nothing is balanced, unless by accident.

Plus, in the streets, Widow was fighting for his life, not for a trophy. Whereas Map Face wasn't fighting for his life.

He roared toward Widow, who didn't step right, didn't step left. He figured that Map Face might expect a sidestep. Instead, he stayed completely still until the last moment, and he flogged up his right foot and hurtled it out.

Widow booted Map Face right in the nuts. A hard, devastating attack. The blow hit home like a missile that rocketed straight out of a silo and hit a target seconds later. To Map Face, it felt somewhere between falling ten stories only to land on his groin and a shotgun blast to the crotch of his slacks.

Even though he was temporarily immobilized, Widow wanted to use the opportunity to take him out in a longer-term sense.

Map Face's street cap was dislodged and had slid to the side on his head, which was a bit of a surprise to Widow. Any other, lesser tough guy, and it would've flown off completely.

The guy could take a punch.

Widow scrambled forward to Map Face, who was still holding his groin but still awkwardly standing.

Widow grabbed the street cap and mashed it down over Map Face's eyes with his left hand. He fisted up his right hand and swung in for an uppercut to the guy's chin.

The blow probably wasn't harder or more powerful than Map Face's had been. But it certainly had been better executed and far more precise.

Down from the toes, Widow felt the energy surge up his body, and his fist cracked into Map Face's chin, rocked him, and knocked him straight onto his back.

And like that, his ticket was all but punched.

Widow knew that because Map Face let go of his groin and fell back limp. His mouth was open. His tongue hung out.

And Widow's fist hurt like he had just punched a brick wall, like an oncoming car that sped at top speed, intending to run him over.

His forward brain kicked back on and registered the pain. For a second, he was worried that he had broken the bones in his hand.

No time to speculate, he thought. And his back brain took over again, and he was back on his feet.

Geoffrey was also on him, but still struggling to see what was what. That was obvious because he reached out to Vinnie, who stood off to his right, completely dumbfounded and half terrified by what he was seeing.

Widow registered another thought in his forward brain. He was grateful that Vinnie was a complete idiot. Any other half-competent mobster type would have gone for the gun.

Widow turned and saw that John, whose voice box was nearly crushed, was back on his feet, facing the other direction, but he wasn't going for the Glock either.

In fact, he was doing the only smart thing. He was running away, down into the dark end of the alley.

The girl, Irene, was a different story.

It turned out that she had been the threat that Widow should've kept his eye on because she wasn't just standing near the gun now. She was holding it fifteen feet away and pointing it straight at Widow.

8

"Freeze, asshole!" Irene shouted. Her voice cracked and whined. The New Yorker in her came out in her accent; only it was deeply nasal because of the swollen face and plastic surgery that she had undergone on her nose.

The whole combination made her sound kind of like some actress in a movie who picked up the gun and had zero knowledge of how to use it.

Widow stayed quiet.

Vinnie shouted, also in a nasal voice from his broken nose, "Shoot him, Irene!"

She didn't respond, but Widow could see her irritated with Vinnie bossing her around.

He stood up straight and looked her in the eyes. He held his hand out, palm facing Irene. It was in the gesture for the universal traffic symbol for stop.

He said, "Irene, you don't have to listen to them."

"Shut up!"

"Don't you tire of these guys pushing you around?"

"I'll shoot you!" she said.

She wouldn't shoot, Widow realized. Probably not.

He said, "Irene, you can come with me. I'll get you away from these guys."

"I'm serious!"

Widow saw Vinnie and Geoffrey moving toward her, which wasn't good.

He couldn't let them get to her because they would get the Glock. That was no good for him.

What else could he say? he wondered.

Just then, he got lucky.

The noise and the commotion had obviously been heard from inside the pub because a metal lock racked back, and the alley door swung open. A big Irishman with a hardy voice and an unlit cigarette tucked behind his right ear stepped out into the cone of light.

He said, "What the hell is all the noise back here?"

Sounds of pots and pans and dirty dishes clanking and racking into a sink somewhere echoed out from the open door.

Hot steam and bright light streamed out behind the Irishman.

Widow didn't wait. He took advantage of the surprise and lunged forward, in a half-crouch, with the bright light from the kitchen over his shoulder. He ran at Irene. He darted to the right the second that he knew she had seen him.

She fired the Glock.

The gunshot rang out loud and booming between the alley walls.

Widow didn't stop to check what the bullet hit, but he was sure it wasn't the Irishman, because the sound that Widow heard behind him was like a bullet hitting a brick wall.

He caught Irene completely off guard and knocked her back with a pop from his left hand, straight to her solar plexus. Not a hard hit.

Not a game over knock-out strike. He didn't want to kill her or even hurt her. It was just enough force to drop her and pop the Glock from her hand.

Irene fell back on her butt, and Widow scooped up the Glock from the cracked pavement.

In a fast three-step movement, he backed away from her, swung back to the left, and pointed the Glock at Geoffrey and Vinnie and even the Irishman.

He saw the Irishman was simply a kitchen guy. He was decked out in an all-white, stained, and used uniform like a second-rate chef.

Widow wasn't worried about him, but remained cautious, anyway.

He said, "Listen up! You move; you get shot!"

Silence. They all stood still. The Irishman raised his hands up in the air, followed by Vinnie.

"You too! Hands up!" Widow said to Geoffrey, who paused at first, reluctant, unwilling to give up, unwilling to admit defeat.

Like Vinnie, Geoffrey also reverted to a position of primal submission. He hung his shoulders because he was beaten, and he knew it. But he didn't raise his hands.

Widow was impressed that his sense of pride outweighed the pain of his bleeding brow. But in the end, he submitted and raised his hands.

"All of you. Get on your knees."

They did, including Irene.

Geoffrey was the last to follow, probably because he was afraid of what was coming next. Yet he had no other choice. Widow had the only gun, and he had the distance. Geoffrey knew it wasn't a bluff.

"What are you going to do?" Vinnie asked, still nasally.

"Don't worry about that."

They all stayed on their knees and watched him. All of them trembled out of fear, except Geoffrey.

Widow corrected that.

He pointed the Glock at Geoffrey, made sure that he could see the muzzle pointed at him. He veered it to the right, just a hair, and squeezed the trigger.

Another loud gunshot echoed in the alley.

The bullet shot out and hit the brick wall directly behind Geoffrey. Shards of brick exploded, and a cloud of pebbles and dust hit him in the back of the head.

He flinched and hunched forward.

"Wait! Wait!" he shouted.

"Wait for what?"

"Don't kill us!"

"Why not?"

Geoffrey said nothing.

Irene said, "What are you going to do?"

Good question, Widow thought. He wouldn't kill them. He knew that much.

He said, "Close your eyes. All of you."

They closed their eyes.

"Count to five hundred. Out loud. Keep your eyes shut!"

He heard their voices start at *one.* They weren't in sync, but close enough.

"When you reach five hundred, get John to a hospital."

Widow backed away, slowly, out of the edge of the light. He backed into the darkness. He continued to watch and listen.

He waited for them to get to sixty, and he turned and walked away. He kept the Glock until he was out of the alley. There was a two-way street with a corner and a turn that headed east. He took the turn, kept checking over his shoulder to make sure that the John, who had run away, wasn't on his tail.

There was no one.

He found a dumpster, peeking out behind a green shutter, wrapped around a thin chain-link fence. He took out the Glock, ejected the magazine, and racked the slide. The chambered bullet ejected out. He pocketed the bullets and wiped the gun with the inside of his shirt.

Never letting his fingers touch it again, he reached over the shutter and lifted the lid of the dumpster. He tossed the gun in and dropped the lid.

He walked on and kept the bullets and the magazine for another two streets until he found a sewer drain to drop them in.

He thought about New York City, remembered that its actual title is City of New York.

Widow moved on into the night. He still had a headache from being punched twice, but his memory worked again. And he wondered what time it was.

9

FIVE TIME ZONES ahead of the City of New York, and more than twenty-four hours earlier, north of Greenwich, England, Captain Elon Karpov looked down at the tan line on the ring finger of his right hand, where his naval captain's ring normally was. It was a two-hundred-year-old silver ring, passed down from his great grandfather to his grandfather and to his father until it belonged to him.

By this time, he imagined the ring to be in his daughter's possession in America.

Karpov rubbed his head. It had been days since he shaved it, like he normally did every day.

Karpov had been an admired sailor in the Russian Navy. Not a legend or a famous hero or anything like that, but far from being looked down upon. He'd had a good career. His military records showed him as an above-average officer.

He was respected, but much more than that, he had been trusted. While being the captain of a nuclear submarine meant he had top security clearance and faith, it also meant that he had a background with the Main Directorate of the General Staff of the Russian Armed Forces or better known in English as the GRU or the Main Directorate Intelligence. The Russian version of military intelligence.

Karpov looked away from his ring finger and over at his hat. It rested on a metal panel near one of his crewmen. He felt more than ready to turn over Russia's top-secret billion-dollar submarine technology to the Americans. Like in that American movie he saw, *The Hunt for Red October*. Which made him wonder if the Kremlin had considered that someone might steal that idea from the movie once it was obtainable to the public.

They hadn't taken it too seriously, as he only had to follow the same basic steps as Sean Connery's character had.

He wondered how bent out of shape his superiors had gotten when they learned how accurate the book was when portraying Russian sailors. The Russians still used a political officer as a way of keeping a close eye on their submarine captains, just as they did in the movie.

Karpov had such a political officer on board. Like most of the crew, he was still asleep. But Karpov knew how to deal with him. When the time came, he'd take a page out of Tom Clancy's book and just kill him.

He didn't figure that it would come to that. Most likely, the Americans would return him to the Russian government, like they would the rest of the crew members, who weren't aware of his plans.

Karpov remembered the first time he'd seen that movie. It was nineteen ninety. The Berlin Wall had just come down the year before. The Iron Curtain, as the West called it, was crumbling beneath their feet. Former countries of Eastern Europe were becoming countries of Europe again.

The communist states were falling over like dominoes. The Soviet Union was on its deathbed.

Back then, Captain Karpov wasn't a captain at all. Back then, he was a young man in a Russian state-sponsored university in Moscow. He remembered seeing American movies slowly making their way into his world.

But it was many years before the theatrical release of *The Hunt for Red October* would be available to the Russian population on VHS.

When the wall first fell, the copy that was available to people was edited to make Sean Connery look like the hero, but the defector stuff was all cut out. To most of the Russian viewing public, it appeared to be a story about a Russian captain who had saved the world from nuclear annihilation in the face of US intervention.

Karpov had thought how funny it was that people believed it.

He had seen the movie and realized that it was twisted into state propaganda. He knew that because his father had given him a copy of Tom Clancy's book in English. Luckily, his father had also insisted that he learn English as a boy.

Karpov read Clancy's novel and then watched the fake version of the movie and then sought out the original, which he found and traded a pair of baseball cards with another Russian officer who fancied the sport and had traded something else with a German who had the movie. It came as is. No subtitles.

Karpov watched it.

It was pretty good. Not as good as the book, he had thought.

It was a lot less technical than the book, a trend that he had noticed a lot in American movies. Often, they dumbed down the technical aspects of military movies.

He remembered thinking that Sean Connery played a brave sailor, not unlike himself. But he wasn't brave by fighting for the communist government. He was brave for escaping it.

Like Sean Connery, Karpov dreamed of the American landscape. He dreamed of freedom. He dreamed of escape from the Russian oligarch corruption.

Even though the Iron Curtain had fallen, and Russia was a democracy, he knew better. Russia had only been a democracy for about ten years until the only Russian president in Democratic Russia had turned over power to a young KGB officer and political administrator, Vladimir Putin.

That was when things changed for the country.

Karpov was a submariner by then.

He grew up in a military family. All seafarers. All proud. His father had been a famous Soviet admiral before he had died of pancreatic cancer.

Karpov remembered his father wanting to go to America when Karpov was a kid. An idea that Karpov's father had planted down deep in his mind.

Now, nearly three decades later, Karpov was at the helm of a top-secret fourth-generation Dolgorukiy-class nuclear submarine, known to NATO as a Borei-class nuclear submarine.

This submarine was special. It wasn't just the nuclear payload that was special. There was something else onboard—something more valuable, in certain eyes. That's why the American CIA accepted Karpov's deal. That's why they were going to grant him and his command crew asylum in the US.

In *The Hunt for Red October*, one officer dreamed of living on a Montana ranch. That sounded great to Karpov. He dreamed of owning a ranch and living the American life, far away from the ocean, far away from Putin's Russia.

But most of all, he wanted to achieve the dreams of his father.

"Captain, I see them," his first officer said. He looked through the periscope.

"Mr. Travkin, slow the approach. Ascend. Stay low. Stay quiet."

Travkin nodded and began relaying orders to the bridge crew.

Karpov gazed at his father's wristwatch and noted the time in his head, an occupational hazard more than necessity. He wouldn't document this meeting, not to his commanders. It wasn't a legal mission.

Sean Connery was a rugged Scotsman with a white beard and full head of hair in that movie. But Karpov looked more like Connery in real life. He was completely bald. The last time that he had seen hair on his head was probably nineteen eighty-nine. But he had the same white beard, with tinges of black in it.

Karpov looked at the skeleton bridge crew. The time was late night for them. Most of his crew members were in their quarters, fast asleep. The faces on the bridge were of men he trusted. And even some of them didn't know what his plans were. They trusted him anyway. He knew it.

Like Sean Connery, he had handpicked them.

The submarine hummed and the engines whined briefly and then slowed.

Karpov said, "I'm going up."

Travkin nodded. He knew it was one of Karpov's favorite things about being a submariner. He loved to ascend and stick his head out and watch the boat breach the waves.

Karpov waited to ascend the tower.

The nuclear pack droned, and the propeller slowed. The water rushed around the boat until the bow ripped upward and breached through the waters of the Arctic Ocean.

Karpov went up the tower and opened the hatch. He climbed past the cables connecting to the radio antenna and stepped up onto the tower.

He watched the waves spill over the bow and felt the icy night on his face.

Far off in the distance, blue and white lights lit up the night sky, outlining a vessel that looked like a deep-sea fishing boat.

Karpov smiled, pulled his collar up on his peacoat. He saw the lights of the fishing vessel and then pulled a small flashlight out of his coat pocket. He flicked the switch, and a bright, sharp beam came out.

He pointed the light at the fishing boat and pressed his hand over the beam, shuttered it three times like the CIA had told him to do. He waited a long minute and then got the response, which was four blinks of light back at him. He responded again with two more of his own. They responded again with three.

It was the CIA team that was supposed to take him and his crew from the submarine.

Travkin appeared behind him.

"Is that them, Elon?"

"It is."

"We're really going to do this?"

"There's no turning back now."

"We could."

Karpov said, "You want to?"

"Of course not! I'm with you all the way. I'm just saying that if you've changed your mind, the Americans will understand. I doubt the CIA will start anything."

"I've got no reason to go back."

Travkin nodded.

They stood together on the deck and waited for the CIA boat. They waited to make the transfer.

10

The CIA boat was a deep-sea fishing vessel. It sped onward as the Russian submarine broke waves in the distance.

The man on the deck looked through a pair of binoculars equipped with night vision. He stared through the green colors until he saw the submarine moving toward them.

He called back to the skipper.

"Starboard. They're coming up."

The skipper nodded and ordered one of his men to slow the engine and take their speed down, just above a drift.

The boat had three sailors onboard, counting the skipper. It was a small crew, but all seasoned men. And all trustworthy. They were all glad to be well compensated for their troubles.

From a distance, the boat looked like it had eight crew members, because there were eight men on the deck. Everyone was dressed like a fisherman. They wore fishing waders and gloves and rimmed sea caps. The three real sailors wore similar outfits, only theirs were worn and tattered like they had seen years of sea damage. The other men looked to be wearing brand new fishing clothes, which they were.

They looked brand new because they had never been used before. The men in the new fishing gear had never fished on a commercial vessel in their lives.

The man on the deck holding the binoculars was running the whole show. Technically, the skipper oversaw the vessel, but this guy was the boss over all of them.

The man with the binoculars wasn't the only passenger. The other four men on deck, dressed like commercial fishermen, had been brought with him for this operation. They were four rough Special Forces guys, but not current Special Forces. They were all former operators, but the real fisherman and the skipper didn't need to know that part.

Technically, the man with the binoculars had handpicked them. He used them often enough. They were men he could trust, and this was a delicate operation. It was an off-the-books type of operation.

He looked over at one of them and said, "Get ready."

He saw them adjust their positions.

He said, "Guns low."

Which he hadn't needed to say because they already knew what they were doing. He said it more out of habit. He was used to giving orders.

The closest former Special Forces guy stood tall and lean. He was clean-shaven with short red hair. He didn't look like the kind of guy that a Hollywood casting director would think to audition for a role as a Special Forces operator, but that was one thing that made him deadly.

The other three men looked more like they were serious military types. They all had that rough, Spartan look about them.

They were a tight group. After the last of them retired from the Army, they all banded together for private contracting. They were partners in this endeavor, but the redheaded guy called the shots. He always had. Back in Afghanistan, their last deployment, he had outranked the rest of them.

More than being a tight crew, more than having shared interest in making money, they all had one more thing in common. Back in Afghanistan, something had happened to them. They shared a secret.

The redheaded guy had outranked them, but he wasn't always the team leader. There had been another guy, an officer with that good-hearted quality that none of the rest of them had.

The redheaded guy was his number two until he shot him in the back with a Taliban soldier's commandeered Makarov PM 9mm pistol.

The pistol had belonged to a Taliban prisoner that they were ordered to escort back to a forward operating base. They had two prisoners.

Instead of delivering them, as had been ordered by their actual commanding officer, the redheaded guy had conspired with the other three to shoot him in the back and blame the prisoners for it.

Of course, after they shot the Boy Scout officer in the back, they got to do what they had wanted to do. They tied the two prisoners up to a tree and used them for target practice.

Why not?

They wouldn't get caught. They only had to drag the dead officer's body back to base. No one would think twice if they said they shot the prisoners after they pulled guns on them and murdered their leader.

It all made sense. Simplicity was always key in these kinds of scenarios. The redheaded guy knew that.

The other three never questioned his plan. Not once.

And that had been a wise move on their parts because he had led them out of the Afghan mountains and into a prosperous life of covert operations for hire.

What wasn't to like about that life? They made money, took on contracts for the Pentagon and the CIA, and still got to kill people. It was all good to them.

The redheaded guy looked at the man on deck and nodded and signaled to the others with a half casual salute.

They approached the bow, kept the silenced Heckler and Koch MP5SDs down by their sides and out of sight. They stood in formation.

The air was cold and so crisp that it felt sharp on their skin, like tiny icepicks poking at them.

The regular fishermen were used to the air.

The redheaded guy stepped to the left and dropped to one knee. Slowly, the other three stepped away from the center of the bow and followed suit. They kept the MP4s down and ready.

11

Mr. Travkin stood behind Captain Karpov on the top deck.

"Where will you go first?" Karpov asked.

"What?"

"In America, when we get our freedom. Where will you go first?"

"I don't know," Travkin said.

The wind blew in shards of cold, wet ice around them. Travkin could feel the wetness in his beard. His eyes left the outline of the fishing vessel and broached across the horizon. Everything black in all directions. The moon was nowhere in sight, which gave way to a sky full of stars. The stars lit enough of the black sky to give it a dark blue look.

The water crashed and streamed in steady, rhythmic waves.

Karpov kept his eyes on the fishing vessel.

Never had he and Travkin talked about Tom Clancy's book. He supposed that he'd never wanted to refer to it in front of anyone before. He didn't want to make it seem like he got his ideas from an American novel. It was a little embarrassing and very telling that he was enamored with the American lifestyle.

He thought, *what difference did it make?*

He spoke in English, even pronouncing Travkin's name in the Western version. He asked, "Edward, have you ever read *The Hunt for Red October*?"

Travkin looked back at him. He leaned closer to avoid eye contact with the two other sailors on deck.

He asked, "The American submarine movie?"

"I meant the book, but either. Have you seen it?"

"I saw it once."

"The real version?"

"Of course, not the propaganda one."

"Did you see where the captain said he wanted to go to Montana?"

Travkin said, "That's not what happened."

"It's not?"

"The first mate was the one who wanted to go to Montana."

Karpov tilted his expression and asked, "You sure?"

"Of course. I've seen it many times."

One sailor interrupted. He was a short man, no facial hair and pale white. He held a wired receiver in his hand. The cord stretched down and curled until it attached to a radio on his belt.

In Russian, he said, "The boat is approaching fifty meters, Captain."

Karpov ignored him, asked Travkin, "Why did you see it so many times?"

Travkin didn't respond.

"Captain," the crewmember said.

"Yes?" Karpov answered.

"The fishing vessel, sir. What now?"

"Now, we stop. Order full stop."

The crewmen nodded and called back the instructions into his radio.

They all heard the engine whine, and the propellers hum and the power of the track of waves splashed, and the water spray began dying down.

After several minutes, the submarine slowed to a stabilized drift along the surface of the ocean.

Karpov stopped asking about Clancy's book and said, "Mr. Ivanosky, any noise from the crew?"

He was referring to the sleeping men who didn't know about Karpov's plans to defect. But Ivanosky knew that, really, he was asking about the political officer, who was also asleep and unaware of any change in course.

Ivanosky said, in Russian, "No, sir, the men are still asleep."

Which was what Karpov had figured. Submariners could sleep through anything. Forty-plus days at sea on a huge, steel tube that vibrates everything will do that to a man. It's kind of like learning to sleep in a power plant or a manufacturing plant that runs twenty-four hours a day. At first, it's tough, but after a while, a man learns to sleep to the noise of humming engines and twisting turbines and wheeling cogs and the sporadic spray of steam. Karpov got so used to it he feared that once he was on land in America, he would never have a good night's sleep again without the echoes of machines nearby.

Of course, this was a problem that he looked forward to facing.

The submarine finally slowed until the surf, and the current pushed it along in a peaceful, improvised path.

Karpov smiled and waited. His freedom was only hours away.

12

THE FISHING BOAT approached slowly until the four Russian submariners on the deck were in clear view of the man who had been holding the binoculars.

He set the binoculars down on the roof of the boat and climbed down a ladder from what the skipper had called the bridge. A laughable title, but the man in charge and his Special Forces guys said nothing about it.

He walked up and stayed ten paces behind his guys. He didn't look down at them, but he knew that each had his MP5SD either hidden in one hand or within grabbing distance.

The MP5SD was more than a Special Forces favorite; it was designated with the "SD" in the model number because it stood for silenced. The MP5SD was specially designed to be suppressed. It was better than most suppressed weapons on the market for military units. Better because suppressors never really "silenced" a gunshot. When a suppressed weapon is fired, the gunshot is still loud. Instead of a *boom* it sounds more like a loud *pop!*

The MP5SD has a much-improved suppressor design. Instead of a loud *pop* there is a quiet *PURRRR!*

It is a much better weapon for when you need to kill a handful of Russian military officers onboard a submarine without waking the sleeping crew.

The man in charge looked over at the redheaded guy and nodded.

The redheaded guy said, without turning his head to his men, "Wait till they throw the docking plank down. I shoot first."

The other men all made verbal acknowledgments of the order.

The Russian on the deck waved. The man in charge waved back. He immediately recognized his Russian contact and smiled.

The submarine stopped, and the boat stopped. The Russian captain called out.

He said, "Omaha!"

Which was the city that the American in charge was born.

The American said, "Murmansk!"

The captain smiled. That was the name of the city in Russia where he was born. It was their greeting code to each other.

A moment later, a long, metal grated walkway sprang out of the bow of the submarine. It was a thin, long thing. It was automated and floated on the surface of the waves.

"Wait, behind me," the American said.

He knew Karpov trusted him, but there was no way that Karpov's men would let him walk out onto the bow of the submarine first, not out in the open. So, the American offered goodwill by stepping onto the sub first. He wasn't a seafaring man, so he struggled to balance as he stepped onto the cold, wet steel of the bow.

He was the only member of the fishing boat not wearing the right rubber boots. He had been wearing a pair of loafers, which now seemed the biggest mistake that he had made so far.

Even though the submarine wasn't moving, water still sprayed up over the deck and onto his shoes, making it hard to walk.

He managed and walked halfway up the deck when he realized that his stumbling about made the captain worry he might get swept out to sea.

Captain Karpov ordered something to his men in Russian, which the American knew must've translated as "let me down there. He's going to get blown off the deck." He knew that because the captain and his men were coming down to help the American walk.

He took a dive to play it up. He stumbled right and then left and then slipped completely on the deck.

He cursed as he felt the impact on his chest, which hurt a little. He stayed there and waited for the captain and his men to get to him. As they did, he nodded back to the redheaded guy.

The captain reached one big hand under his arm and helped lift him to his feet.

Their backs were all turned to the men on the fishing boat.

"Are you okay?" Karpov asked.

His English was as good as the American had been told it was. Only his accent was thick. He didn't sound the way the American imagined Russians to sound. He sounded more German. He had a real problem with the "th" sounds. He picked up on that when the captain said, "I thought you were fish meal."

The American realized he must have meant "fish food" and not "meal." Idioms were hard to translate and teach to foreign speakers. And English has tons of idioms.

The American said nothing as he was helped to his feet.

Within seconds, the Special Forces men were directly behind the Russians.

The redheaded guy had his MP5SD aimed right at the captain's head.

"What is the meaning of this?" Karpov demanded.

"Sorry, Captain. It's merely a precaution."

Karpov looked back over his shoulder, saw the silenced barrel inches from his face. He looked back at the American, stared in his eyes.

"It's unnecessary, Omaha."

"It's policy. Just until we make sure that everything is on the up and up."

"Up and up?"

The American said, "Everything is legit."

Karpov nodded.

The redheaded guy walked around, as did one of the other Special Forces guys. He said, "Hand over the gun, Captain."

Karpov was armed. He had a Navy-issued pistol holstered at his side. The American looked at the other three men.

The first mate also had one.

Karpov said, "What the hell is this?"

The American said, "Just do as he says, Captain. It's a precaution."

"We came here to get your help!"

The redheaded guy said, "Your gun, Captain."

Karpov reached for it. But one of the silent Special Forces guys stepped up and stopped him.

"I'll get it," he said, and he reached down and unsnapped the holster and pulled the gun out.

The redheaded guy said, "Take his too."

He pointed at Travkin.

The guy stepped over to him and reached down and repeated the same process, unsnapped the holster, and pulled the weapon out.

"Let's get below, Captain," the American said.

Karpov looked at Travkin and said nothing.

He turned and led the way back to the tower.

"Down that way," he said, and pointed to the hatch leading down to the bridge.

The American said, "Where is it?"

Karpov's face molded into one of confusion.

"Where's what?"

The American said, "Don't play coy, Captain. The thing you promised us."

Karpov looked back at Travkin again.

"It's in my quarters. On a laptop."

"Show me," the American said.

Karpov pointed at the hatch and said something in Russian to one of the crew.

"Stop! What was that?" the American demanded.

"What was what?"

"What did you tell him?"

"I told him to go first."

The American looked at one of the Special Forces guys. He asked, "Is that what he said?"

The guy said, "He told him to go first, quickly, and to lock the hatch behind him. To make sure that we didn't get on board."

Karpov and the first mate stared at the Special Forces guy. They were surprised that he knew Russian. He was always amazed at how often Russians didn't expect him to speak their language, although he shouldn't have been. Most Americans don't learn a foreign language. He knew that.

The American looked at Karpov.

"Is that what you said?"

"You have guns. I can't allow you to board the submarine."

"You don't work for the Russians anymore. Remember? You want asylum in America. It's too late now."

Karpov said nothing.

"Are we going to have any problems when we get down there?"

Karpov said, "Return our guns. Lower yours, and we can board."

The American said, "Okay. Enough of this."

He looked at the redheaded guy, pointed at the first mate.

He said, "Kill him."

Karpov said, "No! Wait!"

It was too late. The redheaded guy squeezed the trigger of his MP5SD. He had the weapon selected for a three-shot burst.

The muzzle whipped up slightly, and the suppressor *PURRED!*

Three bullets surged out and burst into Travkin's chest and neck. Red mist sprayed out into the air.

Travkin never got a chance to speak because the impact made him lose his balance, and the wet steel made him slip. He went flying back off his feet. His head hit the deck and cracked, and his body bounced. Within a second, he slipped off the deck and splashed into the Arctic.

The current took him under, and he was lost in the blackness.

"You son of a bitch!" Karpov screamed.

The American pointed at one of the other crew.

"Him next."

"No!" Karpov shouted.

"Wait!" The American ordered.

The redheaded guy pointed the MP5SD at the other crewman. He didn't fire. A light puff of smoke wafted out of the suppressor.

The American asked, "Are you going to do what you're told now?"

Karpov breathed in and breathed out in heavy breaths. He repeated this process, again and again, didn't answer.

"Are you?"

"Yes. Don't kill us."

The American said, "Good. Now. Do you have any more guns down there?"

"Yes."

"Where?"

"They're locked up in the armory."

"And how many crew are on the bridge?"

"Just three more. Plus, us."

"Good. Good. See? That wasn't so hard."

Karpov had never been the crying type, but Travkin had been his friend for many years. And he had just seen him murdered in a split second.

He felt choked up.

13

WIDOW LIKED the double shot of black espresso he had ordered and consumed within the last thirty minutes, so much that he ordered another. Same amount. Same barista.

The espresso wasn't the only thing that he liked.

A barista named Montana, who might as well have been named Scarlett because she was the doppelgänger of the famous actress, waited on him.

Widow couldn't recall a movie that Scarlett the actress had been in. He didn't watch too many movies. He had no television. But he was sure that he had seen her in one sometime. Certainly, he had seen her in passing, on covers in gas stations or bookstores or somewhere.

Montana was younger than him. He wasn't sure how much. She was far from being a teenager, but under the age of thirty. If he had to guess, he would guess twenty-five, which made him feel a little weird; because today he turned a year older and he was well in his thirties.

Montana had smiled at him more than once. She had taken his order, and with a busy line of people who waited to order and go, she left her station just to bring him his espresso—a special trip.

Widow sat at a little round table near the window. His back wasn't in the corner, but a wall was behind him.

Before Montana returned to her post, she asked, "You sticking around a while?"

With nothing to say, Widow simply nodded.

She looked him up and down, quick. Not a lingering, flirtatious look-over, more like an inspection. She must've been curious, because he had nothing in his hands. He carried no backpack. No books. No smartphone. No laptop.

Obviously, he wasn't there to work on anything.

She said, "We sell newspapers."

"That's okay. I'll just sit."

"With nothing to do?"

Widow shrugged.

"Oh, you're waiting for someone?"

"No. Not waiting for anyone. Just sitting."

She looked at him a second longer and then turned away. Then she stopped and asked, "Sure, you don't want a newspaper? Maybe the *Times*?"

"Got a copy of the *Navy Times*?"

"What's that? Like a paper for the Navy?"

"That's exactly what it is."

"The Army has its own newspaper?"

Widow said, "It does. But the Army has one called the *Army Times*. The Navy is different."

"I know. I was just speaking generically," she said, and she paused a beat and took a breath and asked, "Were you in the Navy?"

"I was."

"Cool."

Silence fell between them for a moment.

Another girl behind the counter shouted, "Montana? Is there a problem?"

Montana turned back and said, "No problem. I'm coming."

She turned back to Widow, said, "I'll be right back with a New York Times."

He smiled. So far, his birthday was going pretty well.

A moment later, Montana had returned with a newspaper folded up, thick and wrinkle-free.

She placed it down in front of him.

"How much?" he asked.

"Don't worry about it."

"It's gotta cost something?"

"Usually, it does."

"What's the price? I'll pay. I insist."

"You don't have to. Don't worry. It's a day old. Can't charge you for a day-old newspaper."

He smiled and nodded—that made sense.

"Let me know if you need anything else. I gotta get back to work."

"Thanks, Montana."

She paused another beat. Widow saw the other two girls working hard behind the counter, and saw one of them look up with a bit of frustration on her face.

Montana asked, "What's your name?"

He looked at her and said, "Widow."

"Widow?"

"Yeah."

"What kind of name is that?"

"It's a name. What kind is Montana?"

She smiled again and said, "That's true. Enjoy your paper and espresso. Widow."

"I will."

She turned and went back to the counter, back to the grind of making coffee for strangers.

Widow picked up the *Times*, opened it, held it in one hand, and took a sip from the espresso in the other.

So far, so good, he thought.

14

THE TOP STORY in the paper was about a New York Stock Exchange Wall Street firm's main office that had been raided by the FBI over embezzlement, bribery charges, and a laundry list of other things.

Widow breezed through it, sipped his espresso. He skipped to the side panels and read a couple of interesting articles unrelated to Wall Street. But it was the second major story that interested him the most. It was given a huge panel underneath the top story, but there wasn't much to it because there wasn't much known about it.

Most of the panel space was the title of the article and two images. The first was an incorrect image of what the story was about. He knew that because the story was about a Russian submarine and the photograph was of an American Sea Wolf class submarine. He knew them all.

But the other photograph was legitimate, he assumed. It was a photograph, in color, of a Russian submarine captain. He looked Russian. But Widow had never heard of him. His name was Karpov.

The title of the article caught his eye. One of Widow's favorite things to do was read paperbacks, and one of his favorite genres was political espionage and mystery.

The title of the article was: *The Hunt for Red October Happens. For Real?*

Widow had read Tom Clancy's book long ago. Although it was fictitious, it remained a favorite of sailors all over the world.

The basic premise of the article was short but frightening.

A Russian nuclear submarine had gone missing somewhere north of Europe in the Arctic, beyond the borders of NATO's defense, but in international waters.

The Cold War was long over, but hard feelings remained. Some in Washington seemed to condemn the actions of the Russians using their stealth technology to subvert NATO radar.

Not to Widow. He saw nothing wrong with it. Sneaking around with submarines was sort of all about what they were built for. What's the point of a military vehicle that submerges underwater, out of sight? Subs are built for stealth operations.

American submarines were fitted with stealth tech. So were the Chinese and probably those of a dozen other countries.

The Russians even came forward and told us the story.

The article named "sources in the Kremlin." Widow knew there were no sources in the Kremlin. In Russia, that meant it came straight from the top. They didn't have a free press.

Widow hadn't read Tom Clancy's book in years, but he recalled the basic premise. A Soviet captain goes rogue, steals a billion-dollar nuclear sub with stealth drive technology, and tries to defect to the United States.

He remembered that in that book; the Russians didn't tell our boys about the missing sub for a long period. At first, they tried to sink it themselves. Then they claimed the captain stole it in order to nuke us, which turned out to be a lie, so that our subs would sink the Red October.

Good book, Widow thought.

The New York Times article painted a completely different picture.

The similarity to the story was that a stealth nuclear Russian submarine went missing more than a day earlier, and they believed the captain might've stolen it.

Those were the only known details. Everything else was fluff.

Widow wondered where it was. That part was a little terrifying.

Apparently, the US was sending much of the Atlantic fleet out to its last known location to find it.

The White House said the whole thing was a recovery operation. They said it appeared to have sunk.

15

THE LINE of people at the counter died down to three—all women. All office workers, obviously. They were talking and laughing, exchanging friendly banter, exchanging inside quips, and sharing in the same events of their day.

New York City lunch hours had ended for most of the suits who worked in the area. The tables emptied, and the people had cleared out, taking their trash to the can just outside the door. A few patrons stayed behind with open laptops and notebooks. Four of them sat together at one of two four-seat tables.

Widow assumed they were local students. They were young, in their early twenties, three young women and one young man. They wore laid-back clothes—baggy sweatshirts for the girls and long sleeves on the guy. They had that no-care attitude that college students often had about their current surroundings.

Widow took another pull from his espresso and found that it was the last. He finished it and set it down and looked out the window.

So far, he had spent his morning walking around Central Park. He rode the subway once, and then he walked the streets.

He would check out the MET later unless something more fun came his way. Maybe tonight he would take in an overpriced dinner and a show.

It was too bad that there was no sports game tonight, or he would see that instead. The two teams that he would like to see were the Yankees and the Knicks. Neither had a home game tonight. And he wasn't staying longer than tonight and Sunday.

Widow reached into his pocket and pulled out cash. He found a five and tossed it on the table for Montana.

Before he could get up, she was walking toward him.

"Widow," she said.

"Yeah? I'm headed out."

"Jack Widow?"

"How did you know that?"

He didn't remember telling her his first name. Then he remembered the first time he paid with his debit card. Maybe she had pulled it off there.

She stared at him and said, "There's someone on the phone for you."

He stared at her blankly.

"What?"

"The phone. At the counter. It's for you."

Widow stood up, took his empty paper cup with him. He walked past her toward the counter. They threaded in between tables and chairs. He stopped in front of the counter, away from a glass display case, on the opposite side of the line and cash register.

"Wait here," she said. Montana walked around to the cash register side of the counter and crossed behind one of her coworkers, who was ringing up a middle-aged man in a tracksuit.

THE MIDNIGHT CALLER 83

Montana stepped out of sight behind a white wall for a moment and then returned with a portable, gray-colored phone that looked more like a remote control than it did a phone. She leaned across a side station, where customers were supposed to pick up their orders, and handed the phone out to him.

"Take it."

Widow took it and brought it up to his ear.

"Hello?"

He heard a voice and recognized it immediately, and smiled.

"Widow?"

"Rachel Cameron."

"Yes."

"What are you doing?"

"Technology is a wonderful thing."

Widow stayed quiet.

"The calendar on my computer popped up. Do you know what it said?"

"Today's my birthday."

Cameron said, "It said that today's your birthday."

Widow stayed quiet.

"Happy birthday, Widow!"

"Thank you."

"Know how I found you?"

"You're looking into my bank records, again? Saw my debit card used?"

"Have I done this to you before?"

"No. Last time you cleared out my account completely to get my attention."

A pause came over the line. He heard what sounded like a chuckle from Cameron.

Rachel Cameron was ten years older than Widow, but that wasn't something that he knew for sure. The only personal information that he knew about her for sure was her name, what she looked like, and that he could trust her. She had never led him astray, not without good intentions, anyway.

Cameron had been in charge of Unit Ten, Widow's old undercover unit with NCIS.

She was the voice in his ear. She was his handler.

"Ancient history now, Widow."

Widow said nothing.

"Got any special plans?"

"Just to walk the city and enjoy my day. Maybe take in a show."

The line cracked in Widow's ear. Another caller.

"Hey, Cameron. This is a business line. Their phone's ringing."

"Well, hey. I got you a present."

Widow paused.

"You did?"

"Yeah."

He looked at Montana. The thought had just occurred to him he had been in the state of Montana the last time that Cameron had interrupted his life.

The irony wasn't lost on him, but the belief of coincidence was. Now a feeling of suspicion crossed over him.

"What is it?"

"It's a surprise."

Widow looked away from Montana, shook off the suspicion. That would've been too much of a coincidence, even for Cameron.

Cameron said, "Go to The Plaza Hotel. Go to the front desk and give them your name. That's where your present is."

"Okay."

"And Widow, happy birthday!"

Cameron hung up the phone.

Widow clicked off and handed the phone to Montana.

"Thanks."

"Who was that?"

"Ancient history."

Montana gazed away from him in a slow movement, like she was searching for what to say next.

"Old girlfriend?"

Widow let out a laugh, just a quick chuckle. He said, "No. Old boss."

"Why's she calling you here?"

"I don't have a phone."

"You don't have a cell phone?"

He shook his head.

"How did she know to call you here?"

"She knows me too well," he said, not wanting to get into the long explanation of it all.

"I suppose you're taking off then?"

"Yeah."

Montana turned, but then she stopped and reached into her pocket and pulled out a folded slip of paper. She reached to Widow to give it to him, her hand trembling.

She said, "Take this. In case you get a phone. I hope you have a good day."

And she turned fast, walked back to the counter, back behind the register and back to work. She never looked up at him again.

Widow already knew what it was. It was obvious.

He didn't look at it. He just kept it in his hand and walked outside. He turned left, headed south.

He stopped in front of a garden supply store, not sure how much business they really had, being in the middle of Manhattan, but he didn't put too much thought into it.

He opened his hand, looked down at the folded piece of paper.

He knew it was Montana's phone number. What else would she give him?

Widow was no saint. He was no kind of idealist or religious man. And he liked women. Especially an attractive one. But Montana was young. *Too young for him*, he thought.

He didn't open the piece of paper because he knew he would memorize the phone number if he saw it.

Throwing it away had crossed his mind, but he wasn't ready to do that either. He wasn't blind.

A taxi blew by and honked its horn, which startled him for a second. It wasn't honking at him. He was on the sidewalk. It honked at a kid on a bicycle—a bike messenger, who flipped back the bird and turned the corner down a one-way street.

Widow stuffed the note into the front pocket of his jeans and tried to remember which way The Plaza Hotel was.

16

STANDING on Fifth and Central Park South, Widow was reminded of *The Great Gatsby*, a novel that he hadn't read in decades. He recalled a scene that had a confrontation between Gatsby and another character, whose name he didn't remember.

The Plaza Hotel was one of the city's oldest hotels and a historical landmark. One of those hotels with a history of celebrities, statesmen, and infamous people all staying there or walking through it at one point or another.

Widow passed through the park and turned on the street. He walked up the sidewalk and past yellowing hedges and huge planters.

There were expensive sedans parked along the street. A doorman stood up a flight of steps to the entrance.

Widow walked up and stopped at the double doors under a black metal awning.

He saw himself in the glass's reflection.

The doorman stayed quiet and looked Widow up and down. At first, Widow thought he was judging him on his attire, which was probably part of the guy's job description—keeping out the undesirables.

For over a year, Widow had lived like a drifter, going nowhere in particular, going everywhere for no reason.

He had often worn modest clothes and gone days without changing them. He got in showers every chance that he could. And sometimes, on the last day of wearing the same clothes, he looked more like a homeless person than he did a former Navy SEAL.

Luckily, this wasn't one of those times.

He wore a day-old set of clothes, including a blue sweater with the sleeves messily pushed up over his forearms, over a collared white button shirt, and a pair of gray chinos. He wore no belt.

The boots on his feet were the oldest part of his ensemble. They were a pair of black, quasi work boots, steel-toed. They reminded him of a pair of combat boots, only more stylish. He walked with the legs of his khaki-colored chinos pulled over them.

Perhaps to someone with fashion sense, they weren't very fashionable, but they were comfortable and clean—no reason to change them out.

The doorman said, "Good afternoon, sir."

He reached up for the door handle and pulled it open in a swift, flawless move like he had done a thousand times a day before.

A rush of warm air brushed across Widow's face. *The Plaza* was running a low heating setting.

It wasn't overly hot. Considering that it was November, the inside temperature felt just right.

Widow passed through the doors and into the lobby, which felt like traversing through a gateway to another dimension.

The word "grand" doesn't do the interior of The Plaza Hotel justice.

Widow had never been inside one of those royal Arabian palaces, but minus the Arabian part, this was probably as close as he would get. There were giant crystal chandeliers, soft pastel tones, a high ostentatious ceiling, and huge pillars stood at the opening to a dining area.

There was a huge skylight in the cathedral-style ceiling, along with good-size antique, Victorian-style tables, and oriental rugs and striking Italian tiles.

The restaurant was steadily full of travelers who were eating late lunches before they headed out.

Widow looked around the lobby, saw the desk to check in or check out. The air warmed up more around him as he approached the desk. To his right, a crowd of people stood around a politician. Must have been someone important too, because Widow noticed the Secret Service agents before he saw the crowd. Sixteen years as a Navy SEAL will do that.

There were only two visible. Maybe there were more hidden in the small crowd. Maybe they were already on the street, waiting with a car to chauffeur the guy around.

One guy stood, obvious, near the politician, facing forward, through the crowd of people. The other was behind him, standing with his back to the wall.

There were lights and a cameraman and a local reporter interviewing the guy.

Widow wondered who it was.

He watched for a moment until he could get a look at the guy. It was some gray-haired man, clean-shaven and polished. He wore a suit with no tie, as did the two Secret Service agents.

The mass of people was on both sides of the journalist and the politician.

After the journalist asked a couple of questions, which Widow couldn't hear, the politician shook her hand and then the hand of the cameraman and then made his way to the exit, shaking hands, waving, and smiling for quick pictures with smartphone cameras.

Widow didn't recognize him. The guy was probably a New York congressman or a senator.

The line to the lobby check-in desk moved up, and Widow was the next person.

A woman who looked more like a girl than a woman, regarding age, waved Widow forward.

The first thing that she looked at, blatantly, were the bottoms of his sleeve tattoos that were visible because of his pushed-up sleeves.

He wasn't sure if she was checking them out because it wasn't normal to see tattoos in a place like *The Plaza*, or if it was because she liked them.

In a polite, slightly automatonic voice, like she had been programmed or something, she said, "Hello, sir."

"Hello."

"Can I help you?"

Widow caught the crowd from the politician scattering, breaking up and moving on.

"Yes."

She smiled and waited.

"I was told that you might have a package for me?"

"What room are you in?" the girl asked and moved her hands into the typing position over a black keyboard resting on a brown, polished countertop behind the lobby desk.

"I don't have a room."

She paused, moved her hands away from the keyboard.

"We only hold packages for guests."

"Can you check anyway? I was told there'd be something here for me?"

"What's your name, sir?"

"Jack Widow."

The clerk moved her hands back over the keyboard and typed in his name. She stared at a computer screen that Widow couldn't see.

After a click of the mouse, a second click, and a pause, she said, "Here it is. Widow. Did you say that you don't have a room?"

"No room."

"It says you do."

Widow looked confused, said, "What?"

"It looks like you have a Terrace Suite."

"I do?"

"Yeah. It was booked for you this morning."

"It was?"

"Is there a mistake?"

Widow didn't know what to say. Rachel Cameron got him a suite at *The Plaza* for his birthday. And it was called the Terrace Suite, which sounded expensive. Then again, all the rooms in *The Plaza* sounded expensive. They could have called it the "Janitor's Closet," and it would have sounded expensive.

"The room is paid for?"

"Yes, sir."

"Then no mistake," he said, and smiled.

The clerk smiled back and returned her gaze to the computer screen. She hit the return key twice and clicked the mouse.

She turned around, walked over to a counter behind her, and opened a drawer. She came out with a key card and turned back to him. She swiped the card through a small black machine and smiled.

She took out a thin cardstock envelope and slipped the key card into a slit, folded it, and took out a black marker. She handwrote something on the side of the envelope and handed it to Widow.

"Take the elevator up to the ninth floor. Follow the signs. This is your room number," she said and pointed to the number that she had written on the envelope.

Widow looked down at the number. It was nine-eleven, which made him think of the terrible terrorist attack that had happened over a decade earlier—a natural thing to think of. In fact, he thought of it often because there had been many, many times that he would look at a watch or a wall clock and see that the current time had been nine eleven. An unfortunate, constant reminder.

He made no remark to her about it. Instead, he reached down and took the envelope and the keycard and thanked her, and turned to the elevators. He walked through the lobby, casually glancing, looking left and looking right, making no clear sign he was interested in anything.

The Secret Service guys and the reporter and the politician, whoever he was, had gone. But there was still a pair of guys left, sitting on a pair of expensive, antique leather chairs. They sat facing the entrance and the lobby front desk.

They wore similar clothes. Expensive Oxford shoes. Expensive chinos, one brown, one black. The guy on the left had a black knit sweater, sleeves pushed up like Widow's. The other guy had a white polo shirt under a black blazer; both looked expensive.

They wore silver watches, one with a traditional face, and the other with a digital face and loaded with buttons and probably diver features that were completely useless to the guy in real life.

Both guys were built a lot better than most of the men who walked through the lobby.

They spoke casually to each other, looking around, checking the entrance, and checking the elevators, and checking the fire door.

These guys were staking out the place. Widow knew that for sure.

They obviously weren't Secret Service, nor were they FBI or NYPD. Their outfits were too expensive for NYPD. And the FBI wouldn't stick two guys in the lobby, not so obvious. Not so close to each other. They would've had only one in the lobby, if that. Maybe they would've had a whole team outside, on the street. That would've made sense. They would've surveilled from a fake utility truck or a delivery van. They would've had a chopper in the air for a serious bust.

These guys looked government or former government. Widow considered CIA or NSA, which didn't seem legal since neither is supposed to operate on American soil, not in the stake-out sense.

And these guys weren't street thugs. Not in here. Not like the Irish guys that he'd already run into. No way.

They would never come into a place like this. Not in a million years.

The only other option remaining was private security, which made sense to Widow. A couple of clean-cut rough guys with blatant military backgrounds. That was a high probability.

Then again, maybe they were just a pair of veteran army buddies on vacation, hanging out in the lobby of a hotel in New York City, waiting for their wives. It could be true. Maybe the wives ran off to a local spa. Maybe they were getting their nails done, getting back massages, doing vacation things.

Widow was in *The Plaza*, led there by his former boss. She had led him astray before. She had manipulated him to do work for his old unit before. Had she sent him here for something other than a friendly birthday gift?

That was highly plausible.

And what were the odds that he had seen Secret Service in the lobby and now a pair of private-looking security guys, trying to blend in. Coincidence?

Could be. Stranger things had happened.

And really, was it that unusual? New York City is a major hub of all kinds of activity in North America. Just this summer, he had been there. He had been to the FBI headquarters.

Anything was possible.

Widow glanced at the two former military guys. If these two were some kind of private security, they weren't armed. Not that he could see.

There were no visible gun bulges in their waistbands. Not at their ankles. Not their pockets. No signs of holsters. No signs of handguns.

The one guy wearing the blazer might've had a gun tucked into his inside pocket. There was definitely no shoulder rig. Widow would've seen it because of the way the guy moved, checked his watch.

Widow's best guess was that they might have been sitting on their guns. They could have been tucked neatly away behind them at the smalls of their backs. Might have been carrying small handguns, the easily concealable kind.

Widow looked forward at the elevators. He reached them, stopped in front, and pressed the button, and waited.

He didn't look back at the lobby.

After a long moment, the right-side elevator came down to the first floor and stopped. The doors sucked open, and Widow waited for the occupants to unload.

Two young ladies stepped off.

Widow stepped on.

The elevator smelled of fresh daisies and perfume, and maybe a little cologne mixed in. That likely cost more than his whole wardrobe, not that expensive, because he had spent less than fifty bucks on his whole outfit.

Back in the United Kingdom, a long, long time ago, Widow had dated a Dutch model. Not of the Victoria's Secret, famous runway variety, but certainly on her way. And she had tons of perfume. Most of it was probably free to her. A perk of the industry, Widow supposed. Kind of like how he got free bullets for being on a SEAL team.

Even though the stuff came to her free to use, Widow had looked at the price stickers, slapped on the boxes that the bottles came in, a force of habit.

Some of the prices on the perfume boxes were frightening.

Widow had never really been a man with low self-esteem. Life had enough tribulations without walking around feeling bad about yourself. But having seen the prices of things that model was used to getting for free sure made him feel like he had been put in his place.

He and the model were basically just having fun. But there was no future between them. He could never provide her with the luxuries that she had grown accustomed to.

He remembered having those kinds of doubts. The right thing to have done would have been to talk to her about them. Maybe she was above all that. Maybe she would have told him he was crazy for thinking she only cared about her lifestyle.

He never talked to her about it.

It turned out it wouldn't have made a bit of difference, anyway.

One day she had told him she was going to Paris for work. She never came back. He remembered reading about her later on. She had married some rich German guy with a famous last name. Not a celebrity name in the Hollywood sense, but in a wealthy family sense. They had old money, a lot. And this guy stood to inherit all of it.

Widow pressed the button for the ninth floor.

The doors paused for a long second and then closed.

17

THE HOTEL SUITE had a set of French doors that faced out over a courtyard. Not a Central Park view, but not bad either.

Soft music played low from the speakers of a smart television. Widow had searched for the music channels and left it on the first thing that he found, which was a station that catered to the light jazz crowd or simply the softer music people. He wasn't sure.

He wasn't an expert on music. Jazz was a type of music that no one claimed to like because most of the people who "liked" jazz always said that they "loved" it.

Jazz fans were mostly collectors and zealots. To Widow, it was okay.

The music might've been soft lounge music as well.

Whatever, he let it play. It was perfect for a quiet, tranquil mood.

He opened a French door and looked out at the balcony. There were two chairs and a little patio table.

He stepped outside with a bottle of champagne that he took from a small refrigerator and a rocks glass. No ice.

He popped the cork and poured a nice glass, stared out over the interior courtyard and the reflecting pool, left the bottle out on the tabletop. He didn't use the ice bucket.

It had been a long couple of days. Except for his run-in with the Irish mob wannabes, it had been a great two days. He had actually enjoyed himself.

The thought of going out for his birthday had occurred to him. He'd had nothing to eat since breakfast. He should have gone out to eat since a birthday only comes once a year. But he wasn't hungry. He felt more tired than anything.

Widow drank a glass of champagne and people-watched.

Across the courtyard, four floors down, he saw a handsome couple. They drank a bottle of red wine to the bottom and laughed and kissed every few minutes. They exchanged loving, soft touches and looks with each other between kisses.

The whole affair made Widow experience a sensation that he hadn't felt in a long, long time—loneliness. His was a life of solitude, a life uninterrupted. He couldn't imagine feeling beholden to someone else.

Widow enjoyed the company of other people. Especially the fairer sex. But he had never felt that *need* that he saw in couples from time to time. It was that obvious bond that lovers had; the kind of can't-live-without-someone sort of thing.

It was a beautiful thing. He admired it as much as any other lonely person did.

It was that thing called *love*.

On the flip side, that kind of thing was fleeting. He saw it every day, on trains, on buses, in parks, on the sidewalks, even in the company of the drivers who picked him up from the sides of American interstates.

The commonality of the thing called *love* that he saw in each one of them, and in the couple across from him, was that they were almost always in a honeymoon phase with another person.

Widow had never really been in love, not the imagined storybook version of the concept. Not the kind of thing where two people meet, fall in love, and wind up staying married until they grow old and die.

That sort of thing seemed almost impossible nowadays because of technology and culture. Widow knew that.

Still, seeing this couple made him a little envious.

Widow looked away from them and stared around the interior of the hotel.

He saw two men sitting a couple of rooms down from him. They too were on a romantic weekend in New York City. He saw that right off the bat. They kissed each other on the lips, not a loving, lustful, romantic embrace, like the two lovers across from him. It was more of the traditional *they had been together for a long time* kind of kiss.

Afterward, they peeked over at him. He nodded at them in a quick, polite gesture and turned his attention back to gazing around.

He drank half of another glass of champagne and started in to head to bed.

Widow got up from the chair, grabbed the half-empty bottle, and reentered the room. He slid the bottle back into the door shelf of the mini-fridge and left the glass on top. There was no sink or kitchenette in the room.

He left the window open because he liked the breeze that swept in. It was gentle, but enough to blow the curtains around in a slow-moving wave.

Widow turned down the bed, which was tucked tight. He stripped off his clothes and switched off the lights and dumped himself down.

In seconds, he was fast asleep.

18

HER WRISTS WERE bloody and bruised and hurt like hell. They would be black and red for days, maybe weeks, after she got free. If she ever got free.

Her vision was blurry, and she was dazed. It wasn't from being slugged in the face, but she had been twice.

She was dazed because they had injected her with something. She remembered that.

They had only gotten her twice, two days ago, and last night. Both times were around midnight, but she didn't know that. She only knew the first night was midnight.

They had ambushed her in her hotel.

She had checked into the hotel under a fake name, one of many that she had been assigned.

She wasn't sure what was going on. The only thing that she knew for sure was that she had been betrayed. Had to have been.

No one else knew where she was.

There was a slim possibility that her kidnappers were her own countrymen, dangerous guys from the agency that sent her, but she doubted that.

They wouldn't have ambushed her like this. Certainly, they wouldn't have locked her up in the bathroom of her hotel room.

And that was where she was. She was sure. Even with blurred vision and devastatingly disoriented, she knew where she was because she was lying in a spacious claw bathtub. It was unmistakable.

She knew they wouldn't move her from the hotel. One reason she had checked into it was because it was a popular destination—lots of witnesses.

That was the only way that she would meet with them. What she didn't understand was why they ambushed her. She thought her contact had good intentions. Her contact was a lot more than she bargained for. His intentions were less than honorable.

The woman in the bathtub was tall, five foot ten, and thin, which made her good for the spycraft because she was supposed to play the part of a model, living in New York, rubbing elbows with political leaders and people in the know.

She had been good at this assignment, another reason she doubted it was her own government that had ambushed her in her room.

The bad thing about being tall was that she was gangly, which made moving around in the tub very difficult. They had used zip-ties to restrain her hands behind her and tie her ankles together.

Then there was the headache, which felt more like a migraine. Her head pounded.

Every time that she fought or squirmed or shifted around, trying to escape her wrist or leg fetters, a sharp pain discharged through her head. It felt like fire. She didn't remember her attackers hitting her over the head. Why would they, when they had drugs to put her out?

The headache was probably a side effect of the sedative.

Her abductors had left the light on in the bathroom. She stared up at it and saw only the bright whiteness and fuzzy details of the ceiling.

She closed her eyes and tried to remember what had happened.

The first thing she remembered was checking into the hotel. Plenty of witnesses saw her. The hotel had been busy, a good sign. However, it also meant that she was forgettable among the crowd of tourists coming into New York.

She remembered going up in the elevator.

The woman in the tub paused, tried to remember anything before the elevator.

There were small crowds of people in the lobby and a line at the check-in counter, but there was one guy in particular she remembered sitting in the lobby. He was alone.

She remembered he was plain American, that was obvious, and had a demeanor of former military about him; only it was bred out. That was the first thing about him that stuck out to her. He looked not just former military, but like he had tried to lose the look.

He had brown hair, and a trimmed beard. He wore a sweater, sleeves shoved up, with sleeve tattoos. That was the sign that made her think he was former military. Not a guarantee, but a sign in the right direction.

The other thing that really stood out to her happened when she walked by him and pretended to be lost. Like she was headed for the elevator, only she went the wrong way.

She walked past him, stopped at the entrance to the restaurant, and looked around like she was searching. Then she asked one of the restaurant workers to point out the elevators. She even spoke in her accent, which she had found American men loved.

The employee pointed out the elevators, saying she had passed them.

She thanked him, turned, and walked back.

Both times that she passed the guy sitting in the chair, not once did he ever look at her. Not a glance. Not a quick peek. Nothing. And that wasn't normal.

He made no attempt to look at her backside, which never happened. Not in the tight dress that she was wearing.

She knew something was up with him.

She should never have gotten in that elevator.

She remembered opening the door to her hotel room. Then she remembered a gigantic, gloved hand swiping over her head and around her mouth and a muscular arm squeezing around her neck from behind.

One guy jumped her from behind, and the second stormed into the room after both of them. Within a few seconds, he had injected something into her arm. And then she was out like a light.

* * *

The woman in the bathtub opened her eyes and stared through the haziness and the mental fog at the ceiling and bright lights again.

How she got here didn't matter anymore. How she was going to get free was all that mattered.

She focused on nothing else.

She remembered that one of them, the second guy to enter her room, she figured, had injected her twice with the same sedative. The second time had been when she was confined in the bathtub. It had been around midnight; she figured, but wasn't sure.

She pushed off the tub with her butt and strained to see over the lip. Her sense of balance was off. Her brow barely cleared the lip.

There was a vanity counter, with a sink, crystal faucet, expensive-looking wallpaper and tiles, and a toilet.

She stared in the door's direction. She could see the basic outline and shade of off-white. The details of the hinges and the knob were still fuzzy.

It was shut.

A mistake, she thought. The proper thing to do would have been to leave it open so they could at least hear her in case she made noise, or be able to peek in with no trouble to make sure that she was still sedated.

Leaving the door closed left her with freedom of movement. At least it would if she could move.

The muscles in her lower back hurt and felt weak. There was a stinging sensation in her legs. A side effect of whatever drug they were sticking her with. She let go and slipped back down into the tub. Her skin squeaked against the interior.

She lay back, panting for a long second. It took a lot out of her just to make that little of movement.

She tried to relax, letting her lungs fill and expand. Then she let out each deep breath, slow and relaxed. Taking in one slow breath at a time and then repeating the process.

How the hell was she supposed to get out of this?

She had to figure it out, and there wasn't much time left. She had to get free before the guy came back in to inject her again.

There was no way of knowing the exact time in her head, not from waking up in a closed bathroom in a tub, but she figured it was around midnight. The guy had injected her with a sedative twice. She woke up groggy, which meant that she had slept a long time.

If they were using the same sedative, the same amount each time, then she probably woke up each time at the same hour. Maybe not dead on the minute, but close enough.

The woman in the tub concentrated. She didn't need to be calm, not in the Zen sense of the word. What she needed was her adrenaline to kick in.

Every day, every week, there were countless stories of women who looked like her being kidnapped, abducted by strangers. These women almost always ended up on the local news stations a couple of weeks after disappearing. Usually they had been tortured and raped, and were almost always dead.

Luckily, she was no ordinary woman. She had been trained. And she had been trained for this very situation.

She thought back to her training. The thought of suicide came to mind first. This wasn't her training, but she had learned that it had been the training of her predecessors from sixty years earlier.

The long list of women who came before her had been given cyanide capsules embedded in one of their back molars. This was the "way out" that they were trained to take.

Nowadays, this wasn't the answer for most of the women in her line of work. The institution she came from no longer cared if an agent was captured and tortured.

They didn't care because their agents weren't told anything. Secrets were typically kept away from agents like her.

Why should they care if she was captured?

If they found out that she had been taken, they would simply delete her records and disavow her status. She would be swept under the rug and forgotten.

And that was under the worst circumstances. Being captured in the United States by an American agency was a cakewalk for her. Her government knew that she would simply be returned to them.

No harm. No foul.

However, none of this was a comfort to her. It meant that her government didn't give a rat's ass if she lived or died. And for another, she wasn't sure who the hell these guys were.

The only thing she knew was that it wasn't typical of American agents to tie a woman up and dump her in a tub.

Her American counterparts were notorious for being more humane. Again, she doubted that these were American spies.

She closed her eyes tight, felt the adrenaline surge through her as much as it was going to, and popped her eyes open. She rocked up and then back on her butt and repeated it three more times until she could tuck in her knees and swing her hands up and underneath her. They brushed up her thighs and under the backs of her knees. Then she pulled them past her feet, and the zip-ties around her ankles until they were out in front of her.

Pain rushed through her shoulders from the fastness of it all.

She fell back and took a couple more deep breaths.

Then she rocked again as she had before, only this time it was to get on her feet. She finally stood up, reaching forward and grabbing the nozzle to the shower for balance.

She looked toward the door. She heard voices on the other side, distant, but in the hotel suite somewhere.

No one came, but she knew that soon one of them would come to check on her, probably with the needle in hand.

She waited another couple of long moments because she wanted to let her balance return for the next part.

After she felt confident that she could stand without falling over, she reached her bound wrists straight up in the air above her head, stretching them all the way out. Next, like a wild stallion's kick, she jerked them down as fast and as hard as she could.

It was one lesson that she was taught in her training.

The force and the speed of her action broke the zip-tie apart, and her hands were free.

* * *

It took several more breaths before the woman in the bathtub was ready to make another move after getting free from the hand restraints.

When she finally had her balance, she sat on the edge of the tub and draped her legs out and over the edge. She sat there for another minute, hoping that her vision would get better, but it didn't.

The little trick of getting out of zip-ties only worked on hands. Human legs aren't attached correctly for this to work. There was a method to do it, using the same properties of physics, same sort of movements, where the prisoner lies on her back and pulls her feet all the way back to her face, and then kicks straight up with both feet and jerks back at the end. But this method required tremendous strength and flexibility.

She had the flexibility part—that came from yoga twice a week—but the remains of the sedative coursing through her veins killed the chances of having the right amount of strength.

Besides, she was running out of time.

She stood up slowly. Blood rushed to her head, and she felt it. But she pressed on. Half-hopping, half-scooting, she made her way to the bathroom door.

She hadn't seen the suite, nor had she ever stayed in *The Plaza* before, but she had been trained well. Before she even checked in, she had memorized the layout of the Terrace Suite.

She was on the ninth floor. There was a balcony and a window overlooking an interior courtyard.

She closed her eyes and tried to picture the room next to the bathroom. It was a bedroom. There should be a king-sized bed on the other side of the door.

There was a table with a lamp and an armchair. The next room after that was a living room, furnished with a television and a mini-fridge and hotel furniture.

Hopefully, the kidnappers would be in the living room. She knew that there were at least two guys. Maybe more.

She wouldn't get a better chance to make an escape.

She looked around the bathroom one final time. She had hoped that there might be a sharp object in there to cut through the zip-ties on her ankles, but she had no such luck.

No scissors left behind by the previous occupants—nothing in the trash.

Even if the previous tenant had left a pair of scissors or a nail file behind, the Plaza's housekeeping department was on the ball. They would have picked it up.

She reached out, grabbed the doorknob, and gently turned it. She peeked out.

No one was there.

She opened the door a little farther—nobody on the bed. No one sat on the chair.

She still heard voices. Then she squinted and looked into the next room.

The voices that she heard weren't her kidnappers. The television was on.

She couldn't make out the screen, but she could see the colors and hear the actors on TV talking.

It was a late-night talk show; she figured. Sounds of an audience laughing and a host telling jokes filled the room. It was turned up fairly loud, not enough to bother the neighbors, but enough to fill the suite.

At first, she thought that was a mistake because it might draw unwanted attention. It might have been because they were using a small crew to guard her and needed the noise to stay alert.

She couldn't see who was watching the TV. The sofa was out of her line of sight.

She ignored that and turned to the bed. She hopped over to it and used one hand to steady herself, and hopped as quietly as she could. She plopped down on the bed, partially because she'd lost the strength in her legs to sit down slowly.

She looked over at the open doorway. No one came.

She turned back to the bed and looked at the nightstand next to it.

On the nightstand, next to a thin gold-trimmed lamp, was exactly what she was looking for. She didn't find the number one thing on her list of items that she could really use right now. Nor was it the number two item. Number one would have been a loaded gun, and number two would have been a knife to both cut through her zip-tie and use as a weapon.

Instead, she had to settle for number three, which was a telephone.

A small digital clock sat next to it on the table.

She was close enough to see the time, blurry or not. She watched as three of the four displayed numbers changed over to the time. They went from eleven fifty-nine to midnight.

Her government trainers had taught her numbers to remember. One of them had been a local New York number to use in case of emergency, which this was, but the problem was that she couldn't call her contacts.

She was on a mission that wasn't sanctioned by her government. In fact, they would see her as a traitor for it. She was on her own.

The only thing that she could think to do was to call the local police. At least they would come for her. She could figure out how to get away from them later.

Chances were that her kidnappers didn't plan to let her live. At least the police wouldn't kill her.

The number for police in America was a short, three-digit number. That was one of the great things about Americans. They were good at streamlining things like that.

She scooped up the phone and put it to her ear. She dialed nine-one-one on the number pad, and the phone rang.

19

THE PLAZA HOTEL was an old hotel. They had old phone lines and old landline telephones in the rooms. Not rotary phones. They had push-buttons, but they were old. The phones were polished and kept clean. They looked like the original, out-of-the-box condition they were in the day they were all purchased.

Somewhere inside The Plaza Hotel, some years ago, it was determined that the phones would be maintained and kept for as long as they worked. It was a way of keeping a classy, uniform, antique look, which worked well with the motifs and the look of the hotel.

Back years and years ago, it was determined in the hotel industry that having a nine-eleven room was bad when most hotels have both an internal and external phone line system.

A person needs help. They dial nine-one-one, and instead of getting the police, they get the person staying in room nine-eleven.

To dial out, one must first dial nine—a universally known quantity.

The thing *The Plaza* did, instead of changing the room numbers and telephones, was they posted a card on the base of the phone that instructed the guests needing emergency services to dial nine-nine-one-one. A quick extra number, no big deal.

When this woman needing the police dialed nine-one-one, she got the room instead of the police.

* * *

Widow was sound asleep when suddenly his phone rang.

Widow opened his eyes abruptly, like he was way back in SEAL training and the instructors had just barged in, ringing dinner bells and sounding bullhorns in his ear.

He was facing away from the telephone, sleeping on his side.

He flipped over and grabbed the phone, nearly knocking over the lamp.

"What!" he said.

A pause. No one spoke. He heard breathing.

"Hello?" he said.

A low, sultry voice with a foreign accent said, "Help," in a whisper.

"Hello? Who is this?"

"Can you help me?"

"Who is this?"

"Are you police?"

Widow sat up and looked at the clock, saw the late hour, and asked, "Who the hell is this?"

"I need help."

"Where are you?"

"Are you police?"

"No. You dialed my room number," Widow said. He looked down at the base of the phone, read the note about emergency calls.

"You gotta dial nine-nine-one-one. Not nine-one-one."

He realized that was idiotic.

They should change his room number, he thought. He guessed even *The Plaza* was too cheap to change all the room numbers just to get rid of nine-eleven. He supposed they could have simply made a nine-twelve A or something.

"Help me," the woman's voice whispered.

Widow used his free hand and slapped it to his forehead, easy, and rubbed his forehead.

"Where are you?" he asked.

"I'm in the hotel."

"What room are you in?"

She paused a long beat.

Her accent, he thought, sounded Russian, or maybe Ukrainian.

"I cannot remember."

"Step outside and look at the number on the door."

"No. No. I cannot do this. No way."

"How can I help you if I don't know what room you're in?"

Silence.

"Ma'am?"

"I need help."

"Okay. Tell me what's going on?"

Silence again. Then she came back on the line.

"There're men. They kidnapped me."

"Kidnapped you?"

"Da. Da."

Widow automatically recognized the word as Russian for "yes," said twice.

"Okay. I can call the police for you."

"No! No!"

"Why not? You need the cops."

"No police. Please. You help me."

No police?

This sounded dubious.

Widow ignored that part, and he asked, "How many guys?"

"I don't know. Maybe two?"

"Okay. Did you get a look at them? They hurt you?"

"No. No look. Not really. They not hurt me so far."

"What have they done?"

"Just inject me with a drug."

Silence.

Widow asked, "They injected you?"

"Da. I mean, yes. Some kind of sedative."

Two guys kidnap a woman, in The Plaza Hotel, they inject her with a sedative, and they have not hurt her?

Sounded risky, Widow thought.

"Who are you?"

She answered, but then she said, "I cannot tell you."

"Why not?"

"Please. Just come help me?"

"Listen, ma'am; you need the cops. I'm just a guest."

"No! No! Police will be bad for me. Please, you help?"

Widow paused a moment.

Before he could answer, he heard a man's voice in the background.

The words were loud, short, and the accent was unmistakably American. Not Russian.

The man said, "What the hell are you doing?"

Then he heard another male voice. Far away, in the next room, maybe.

The second voice said, "How did you get free?"

"Ma'am?" Widow asked—a reaction.

"Help me!" she shouted.

He kept listening, didn't react.

He heard a scuffle. The woman attempted to scream, but it was cut short by a loud smacking sound.

One guy punched her in the face, Widow figured.

With his free ear, he had hoped that he would hear her scream, but she hadn't been loud or long enough to be heard. Plus, she could have been on any floor in the hotel.

Widow waited, listened.

The scuffle was over quick, but he still could hear voices, too low to be understood this time.

Then he heard scratching sounds like someone was picking up the telephone.

A brief silence and he heard nothing, and then a low sound that was unmistakably someone panting. Probably one of her kidnappers, listening for Widow to speak and trying to keep his loud breathing away from the phone.

Widow spoke first.

"Hello?"

No response.

"Hello?" he repeated.

The American voice, with low panting, said, "Sorry for disturbing you, sir."

"What's going on?"

"It's not your concern. It's my wife. She's had too much to drink. She gets like this sometimes. I apologize. Please, have a nice night."

The guy hung up.

Widow stayed where he was. He kept the phone to his ear and listened to the dial tone.

Was she telling the truth?

He was almost certain that she had been. Widow had heard a lot of lies in his life, and he had told a lot in his old life. The undercover cop life required lies.

This woman was telling the truth.

He should have called the police. She had begged him not to.

Why?

Widow hung up the phone and sat there for a long minute, trying to figure out what to do.

If she was telling the truth, then these guys wouldn't kill her. Not because she had gotten ahold of the phone. They hadn't gone through all the trouble of keeping her alive and sedated just to kill her for trying to escape.

Also, if these guys had access to sedatives that required injections as a delivery system, then they were more than just random street thugs.

Getting chloroform was a hell of a lot easier than getting expensive, fast-acting sedatives that required prescriptions.

Something bad was going on.

Widow stood up, still naked. He rushed over to the armchair and picked up his pants, slipped them on.

He walked into the living room. Left the lights off in case they were in a room across the courtyard and could see him.

He stood out of sight of the window and leaned just enough to peek out.

He saw nothing unusual.

The couple across from him was gone. There was only one woman sitting out on her balcony, smoking a cigarette, which Widow wasn't sure was allowed in the hotel or not.

He ignored her and returned to the bed, dumped himself down, and picked up the phone.

He dialed zero, listened to a whirring sound, and heard a click.

A hotel operator picked up and said, "Front desk, how can I help you?"

"Can you tell me what room just called me?"

"Is there a problem, sir? Someone bother you?"

"No. Nothing like that. Just a friend of mine. I forgot to get her room number from her."

"Would you like for me to reconnect you?"

"No. Just give me the room number."

Silence fell over the line.

Widow suspected the operator was reluctant. Maybe she wasn't sure if she could give out a guest's room number that easily.

"Look," Widow said, "The truth is kinda embarrassing."

The operator didn't answer.

"The woman who called, I met her tonight at the bar downstairs. She just called and asked me to come to her room to...finish our conversation. But like an idiot, I forgot her room number. I really wanna go visit her."

"I don't know," the operator finally said.

"Come on. It's my birthday. You'll really be helping me out here."

The operator clicked on the keyboard; Widow heard the punching of the keys.

"Happy birthday, sir. I guess I can do this for you. No problem."

Widow smiled.

She said, "You're in luck. The room is right around the hall from you. It's nine-twenty-one."

"Thank you so very much."

"No problem, sir. Anything else I can help you with?"

"You've done enough. Thank you," Widow said, and hung up the phone.

Nine-twenty-one was close.

He got up and jogged into the bathroom, turned on the sink, and ran water over his face, slicked his hair back.

Then he put his T-shirt on, left off the sweater. He put on his shoes, laced them up, left off the socks.

Looked around the room for a weapon to use in case he needed one.

There wasn't much that looked like it would be useful.

He opened the mini-fridge. There were bottles of beer. He considered emptying one, breaking off the neck, and using it as a stabbing weapon, but that seemed extreme. Besides, he didn't want to walk down the hallway carrying a broken bottle.

He'd already opened the champagne bottle, or he could have used it as a club.

Widow searched the drawers in the dresser. Nothing.

Then he looked in the drawers in the nightstands. He found a Bible. It was an old, thick hardcover, which was difficult to find. It must have been in the hotel room for ages.

The first question that he asked himself was, *Did they still keep Bibles?*

He flipped it open to a bookmarked page and looked at the bookmark. It was one of those Christian bookmarks offering a declaration of why he should immediately convert over. Then he stuck it back into the pages of the book at random and flipped back to the inside cover. The book wasn't stamped by The Plaza Hotel. It was stamped by a church on Fifth Avenue. Someone had left it. Probably someone from out of town, passing through and stopped at the church for a Sunday sermon.

Widow wondered if the church considered it *stealing*; if you take a Bible and leave it with the intention of someone else finding solace in it?

He closed it and shook it in his hand, slow, up and down, like a playground seesaw, and felt the weight. It was heavy and hard. As reading material, he wasn't interested. He had already read it before. But as a club, it would do nicely.

Widow took it and his keycard and left the room.

20

WHOEVER WAS WATCHING the girl with the Russian accent, whoever the kidnappers were, professional or not, they would wait for someone to come snooping around.

The girl had broken free and had dialed Widow's room. They may not have known whose room number had been dialed, but they would be cautious enough to expect him to come looking.

It was stupid to go straight for their room. An amateur would go there first. No, the right approach was to go to the elevator first. He wanted to check to see if one of them was watching the elevator.

It made sense to Widow that the two guys he'd seen in the lobby earlier might be related, somehow.

Maybe the guys in the room called down to the guys in the lobby. There might be two of them coming up. They might be armed.

Widow walked casually to the elevator. He held the Bible open and pretended to be reading the Book of Job.

As he turned the corner, he saw the elevator stop. The bell dinged. The doors opened. As he had expected, the two guys from the lobby stepped off, and the doors shut behind them. The elevator moved on.

They turned and looked left and looked right. The guy in the polo shirt and the blazer stepped to Widow's right. The other one followed suit and stepped back to Widow's left.

Widow ignored them, kept his face down, looking over the Bible. He kept his walk casual. At fifteen paces from them, he reached up and licked his finger and turned the page.

He noticed that both of them slowly moved their hands behind them. Both right hands. Both in the universal gesture that everyone understood as two guys with guns holstered behind them.

Widow walked forward, acting unshaken and unimportant, which was what he hoped they would see and back off.

Once he got within ten feet of them, he was at the elevator. He turned, reached out, and pressed the down button. He lifted his head from the Bible and acted like he hadn't even noticed them before.

"Oh. Hello, guys. Having a good night?"

The guy in the blazer stepped in closer, but stayed out of striking distance. He looked at Widow suspiciously.

He asked, "You staying here, sir?"

"Oh, yes. But I didn't pay for the room or anything. Can't afford it. I'm in town for a convention. Here in the hotel."

"A convention?"

"Yes. I represent the First Catholic Church of New Jersey," he said and showed them the Bible.

The two guys looked at each other blankly, almost dumbfounded.

Widow stepped closer, striking distance, and showed them the Bible's cover.

"This was my father's Bible. Are you guys religious?"

They shook their heads.

The other one, without the blazer, moved in two paces closer and stared at the inside pages of the Bible like he suspected it having a hollowed-out center where Widow was smuggling a gun.

He asked, "You're walking down the hallway, in the middle of the night, reading a Bible?"

"A Friday night," the guy in the blazer added.

"Of course. It never matters when you read the Bible. God's message is always welcomed."

They looked at each other again, a quick glance, speechless and obviously not buying it.

Widow determined within seconds that neither of these two was the leader. The one in the blazer was doing more of the talking, but he had also made more mistakes than the other guy.

It was common practice for Widow to take out the leader first, but in this case, both men were matched.

The one without the blazer was a little closer now, which made him a volunteer.

The one without the blazer asked, "What message is that?"

Widow could see his forearm muscles twitch and his veins pop. He was gripping and un-holstering his gun.

Right then, at the moment that Widow was calculating, the bell on the elevator dinged.

Both men glanced up and looked behind Widow, a fast set of glances, but slow enough for Widow to make his move.

He held his breath, pivoted from his left foot, and slammed the spine end of the Bible straight into the voice box of the guy in the black sweater.

It was a vicious blow, a little too vicious. A part of him hoped it wasn't enough to kill the guy. There was no need for that, not when he hadn't fully vetted them as bad guys just yet. He knew they weren't FBI or police, but they could have been CIA. That would have been highly unlikely and illegal, not that that had ever stopped them before.

The guy in the black sweater let go of his gun and tumbled back against the wall, wheezing. Which reminded Widow of the Irish John from the day before.

He was distracted for a split second by the thought.

The guy in the blazer was a lot faster than Widow had hoped. He didn't waste time trying to draw his gun. Instead, he rushed forward and pushed Widow straight back into the elevator.

The blow didn't cause any damage to Widow, but it got him off guard, and he went off his feet.

He was lucky enough to grab a quick handful of the man's blazer, and they both ended up hitting half of the elevator floor, half of the hallway carpet.

Widow kept the Bible in his other hand on the way down.

The two men hit hard. Widow took the brunt of it. He ignored the sudden pain because acknowledging it would give the other guy a second of advantage, which the other guy was expecting because he went for a gun with his right hand. Widow held the Bible in his right. He slammed his left hand, hard, and clamped down on the guy's forearm, holding his arm and gun hand locked behind him.

Instead of changing his tactics, the guy did exactly what he had expected Widow to do; he flinched, dwelled on his stuck hand.

Widow whipped his right shoulder back and up, flinging his arm as far back and as fast upward as it would go in the short distance between his elbow and the floor. He threw a short, but powerful right jab, using the spine of the Bible as a pair of knuckledusters.

The book hit the guy square on the bridge of his nose, cracking it, breaking it, making an obvious hole in the guy's face.

Blood gushed out like a runaway fire hose, like a cracked-open hydrant on a hot day.

Within seconds, enough blood sprayed out onto Widow's face to blind him if it had sprayed in his eyes, which didn't happen because he'd turned his face away enough.

The guy's right hand went limp for a split second and then jolted back to life and the guy fought to pull it away. Widow released it, and the guy grabbed at his broken nose or broken face. However he wanted to look at it.

Widow rolled him off and scrambled to his feet.

He kicked the guy over on his side and jerked the gun out.

It was an unusual handgun. He recognized it as a Maxim 9, which was a futuristic-looking gun because half of it, from the handle past the trigger, resembled a SIG Sauer Special Forces handgun, and the muzzle looked like a pulse phaser from Captain Kirk's personal arsenal.

He had never held one or seen one before in real life, only read about them in Forbes, as a new, expensive toy for collectors. The problem with that statement was that it wasn't available to the public, not as far as Widow knew.

The reason it wasn't available was that the boxy end part was a built-in silencer.

From what he could remember reading, it was whisper quiet, a great noise suppressor. Normally, they aren't silent at all. Normally, a .45 handgun like this, equipped with a suppressor, would sound like a loud cough when it was fired inside a place like The Plaza Hotel.

Not the Maxim 9. If the claims in the article by the manufacturer were true, then it was more like a quick hiccup.

The other thing that stuck out to Widow was the "unavailable to the public" piece of the article. So far, there had been only one buyer of this weapon that he knew of, and it was the CIA. The rumor, not mentioned in the article, was that it was being tested for wet work teams, which are essentially death squads run by the agency. These were Special Forces guys, with a little more bloodlust than the average soldier. And they were no longer military. These were guys who were privately contracted by the Pentagon, CIA, or held as exclusive employees, without the paperwork attaching them to the government.

The whole thing only meant that they weren't to be trifled with.

What the hell are they doing kidnapping a foreigner on American soil?

Widow didn't want to kill them, not without some answers.

Suddenly, he noticed the wheezing from the other guy had stopped. He turned to look and saw the guy was half-standing, his back to Widow.

The windpipe must have been okay, after all.

He reached for his gun and slowly drew it.

It was the same Maxim 9 handgun.

Widow could have shot him in the back, or even the leg. That would have put him down long enough for Widow to disarm him.

Instead, Widow hurtled the hardcover Bible at him like a major league pitcher. The book smacked the guy clear in the back of the head and hard. It was as hard as Widow could throw. If it had been a large rock, the guy would be dead from a crushed skull. But it was only a book.

The Bible bounced off his head and landed on the floor.

The guy tumbled forward and crashed first into the wall and then slid down to a cushioned bench. He didn't get back up.

Widow looked both ways up and then down the hallway, in case someone came out of a room to investigate the ruckus. No one came out.

Then he stuffed the Maxim 9 into the back of his chinos. It was a little loose because he wasn't wearing a belt, but it stayed put well enough.

He reached down and grabbed a handful of the trouser leg of the guy in the blazer and dragged him out of the elevator.

The guy squirmed and fidgeted like a snake, but with less power.

Widow dragged him over to the other guy. He stopped and reached down to check the guy's pulse. It was weak, but it was there. He was breathing, but he wasn't conscious.

Widow took his gun too and stuffed it into his front pocket. Then he hauled the first guy up by the arms and held him there by his collar.

"Who the hell are you?" the guy asked nasally, with a defeated tone.

"How many are in the room?"

"What?"

"How many guys are left in the room? With the girl?"

The guy paused a beat.

"You're the one she called? Staying in nine-eleven?"

Widow nodded.

"Just you?"

"I asked how many are in the room."

The guy didn't answer.

Widow reached up with one hand and grabbed the guy's nose over his hand, and pulled down on it.

The guy let out a nasal, pathetic screech.

"Wait! Wait!" he shouted.

"How many?"

"Two. There's two other guys."

"Thank you," Widow said. Before the guy could protest, he whipped his head forward in a violent arc and head-butted the guy right in the face. It wasn't the hardest that he could do, but enough to put the guy out, which it did.

One minute there had been somebody home, and the next there was not.

Widow lowered the guy to his butt and looked around once more—no sign of anyone coming out.

The elevator doors sucked shut, and he heard the low rolling sound of the cables. The elevator had been called and was on its way to another floor above him.

Widow saw a door marked as the fire stairwell.

He dragged the guy in the blazer across the floor and pulled open the door, hauled the guy through it, and tucked him away in the corner behind the door.

He went back into the hall and repeated the process with the other guy. In their pockets, he found wallets and IDs that looked fake, professionally done, but fake. He also found cellphones and cash.

Widow left the wallets, took the cash and the phones, left the Bible in the stairwell with them, and left both men behind.

He took the Maxim 9 from out of his front pocket and ejected the magazine, emptied the chambered round, and dry fired it at the floor. It worked.

He reinserted the magazine and scooped up the bullet that had ejected. He slid the bullet into his pocket and kept the gun out, ready to use.

Widow continued toward room nine-twenty-one.

21

ONE PHONE WAS PASSCODED, but the other was not. He tossed the passcoded one into a wastebasket in the hall and stuffed the cash into his pocket. A bonus.

He opened the home screen of the cellphone and pulled up the internet, searched for The Plaza Hotel. He found it and clicked the contact button, and waited. He saw the house phone number and clicked on it. The phone asked if he would like to call it. He clicked the yes button and waited. The phone dialed and rang.

"Hello, The Plaza Hotel?" a voice said.

Widow said, "Can you connect me to room nine-twenty-one?"

"One moment, sir."

There was another click and a dial tone.

Widow picked up the pace and walked on until he was standing outside room nine-twenty-one. He stayed out of sight of the peephole.

He moved the phone away from his ear, and slid it into his pocket, left it on speakerphone.

He heard the ringing on the other side of the door, and then it stopped. He heard a voice say, "Hello?"

In a wild, mad-dash scramble, he stepped out in the middle of the hall and charged forward and kicked the door as hard as he could. A lot of times, hotel doors are made hard enough to withstand the brute force of unwanted intruders' attempts to break-in.

Luckily, Widow applied the right amount of force, and the door wasn't deadbolted.

It slammed inward in a heavy swing.

One guy stood on the opposite side of it, looking through the peep-hole. The force of the kick and the blow sent him tumbling back onto the floor.

Widow barged into the room and pistol-whipped the guy square in the mouth, which had been a miscalculation. He had meant to hit the guy in the forehead, hoping to knock him out. Instead, he heard a tooth chip and crack, and the guy yelped.

The back of his head hit the carpet, hard, but not enough to knock him into unconsciousness.

Widow didn't go for a second punch; he didn't want to give the guy answering the phone time to react.

He pointed the gun at the guy and shouted, "FREEZE! FREEZE!"

The old cop voice came back like he had used it yesterday.

The guy froze. His gun was out, but it was on the tabletop. The room phone was in his hand, near his face, and his other hand was holding a corked syringe. The contents were clear and filled up to the halfway mark.

They had been about to sedate the woman, Widow figured.

There was something sickening to him about that kind of procedure versus the old-fashioned way of keeping a prisoner. Injections and sedatives and drugging and tranquilizing seemed clinical to him, almost inhumane.

It also confirmed in his mind that he was dealing with a group of bad guys who had some government ties or even backing.

He said, "Slow, stand up."

The guy stood up.

Widow stepped forward into the room and reached back with his free hand, shut the door. Only it wouldn't close. The inside door latch was cracked and splintered.

Keeping his eye on the guy by the phone, he used his foot to push it shut as much as it would go.

He stepped forward, stopped at the guy on the floor.

He was holding onto his mouth. Widow could see trickles of blood seeping out of his fingers, but nothing like the guy from the hall.

Widow looked down at him quickly, took aim, and said, "Sorry."

The guy's eyes looked up, wide.

Widow stomped down on his forehead with a heavy boot—another lights-out blow to the head, which worked like a charm. The guy's eyes closed, and he went to sleep.

Widow turned back to the guy in the chair next to the phone.

"Hang it up," he said.

The guy hung it up.

"Who are you?" the guy asked.

"Not important. Who are you?"

"Can't tell you that."

"Wrong answer," Widow said, and he squeezed the trigger of the Maxim 9.

It worked as advertised, almost. A bullet fired out and hit the telephone inches from the guy's hand.

The phone actually dinged once, like it had an actual bell inside, which it probably did. Expensive plastic cracked and shattered into small pieces, exploding all over the tabletop.

The guy flinched, covered his face with the hands.

"Okay! Okay!"

Widow waited, aimed the gun at the guy's center mass.

"We're a paramilitary group."

"Private?"

The guy nodded, which was exactly what Widow had suspected and also what he didn't want to hear.

"Government contract?"

The guy said nothing.

Widow closed the distance between them, stopped right in front of the guy, who had to look up to see him.

Widow lowered the gun, pushing the muzzle right on the guy's right kneecap.

"Are you working for the Pentagon?" he asked.

"No! No!" the guy said, trembling.

"Who then?"

"I don't know! I swear!"

Widow leaned his weight forward, intensifying the pressure from the gun down on the guy's knee.

"I'm telling you the truth! I don't know! I'm not in charge! I just take orders! We all do!"

"Who is in charge?"

The guy stayed quiet.

Widow said, "I'm not bluffing. Don't make me shoot you to prove it."

The guy trembled some more. His eyes darted back and forth. He looked at the guy on the floor and looked back at Widow.

"His name is Connors."

"Got a first name?"

"Danny Connors."

"He's in charge of your crew?"

"Yes!"

"He'll know the name of your contractor?"

"Of course! He pays us! He tells us what to do!"

Widow stepped back, moved the gun away from the guy's knees, and pointed it back at his center mass.

"What did he have you do here?"

"Babysit!"

"Where is she?"

"Bathtub!"

"Why her?"

"I don't know! I done told you that! We just are told what, not why!"

Widow nodded. He believed him. The guy was telling the truth. The good news was that these guys weren't CIA or contracted by the Pentagon. They were too much of an unknown, untested bunch. Widow could see that.

They weren't unqualified, just not professional enough.

They were good, but not good enough. Certainly not better than he was. Which was a high bar to reach, but the Pentagon would expect nothing less.

Out of all the contracts that private military groups could get, the US government was the best because they paid the best.

Someone else hired these guys.

"What's in the syringe?"

"I don't know," the guy said.

"You don't know?"

"I mean, I don't know how to pronounce it. It's written on the bottle," the guy said and gestured with his head where it was kept.

Widow didn't look.

"You think I'm stupid?" he said.

"What?"

"You think I'll look so you can charge at me?"

"No! I swear! I'm just telling you where it is!"

"Stand up!" Widow said, and he stepped back a couple of paces out of the guy's reach.

The guy looked puzzled, but stood up as ordered.

"Turn around!"

The guy slowly turned around.

Widow moved forward and switched the gun to his left hand while he scooped up the syringe with his right.

He pressed the plunger, squirting out a short spray of the contents.

He said, "Bend over.'

"What?"

"You heard me!"

The guy didn't turn around. He bent over as ordered, grabbed the rests on the chair to steady himself.

Widow stabbed the syringe into the guy's butt and pressed the plunger, emptied most of the contents into the guy's fatty tissue.

The sedative worked fast too because, within a minute, the guy was out. He toppled forward over the chair and sank forward in an uncomfortable position.

A few seconds later, he was actually snoring, in a cartoonish tempo.

Whatever was in the needle, it was powerful.

Widow used the rest on the guy on the floor—no reason to leave him to wake up before the other guy.

Widow tossed the syringe onto the floor and lowered the gun. He walked to the bathroom and opened the door.

Inside, he found the lights were already on, and he saw a woman's leg dangling over the edge of a claw tub.

He walked over and looked down.

Looking up at him was a beautiful Russian woman. She wore a tight, red dress, which was tousled and dirtied up a bit, but still on her body. Her shoes were at the bottom of the tub and off her feet.

She had long, dark brown hair that was disheveled and all over the place. It was thick enough to reject a motorcycle helmet.

Widow saw that her wrists had been double zip-tied. Which was overkill, he thought. And her feet were also zip-tied, but she hadn't been sedated yet. Her eyes were wide open and alert.

What he also saw was that she was stunningly beautiful, only with a look of terror on her face that would have made a cold-blooded killer uncomfortable. Which he realized was because there was a blood-covered giant standing over her, holding the same gun that the guys who had done this to her had been armed with.

22

WIDOW TUCKED the gun away and reached down to grab the woman by her wrists. She fought back and squirmed and kicked.

"Calm down," he said. "I'm here to help."

She stopped fighting and mumbled something that he couldn't understand because they had stuffed and duct-taped a rag in her mouth.

Widow said, "Hold on a minute."

He scooped her up, and out of the tub, sat her down on the toilet.

"This might hurt," he said. He grabbed the tape over her mouth and paused.

She closed her eyes shut like she was ready.

In one fast act, he ripped the tape off.

She didn't make a noise, but her expression turned to a quick, painful one. Then she spat out the rag.

"Who are you?" she asked.

"Not important right now. I'm the guy you called."

She nodded.

"Is there a knife here somewhere?"

She didn't answer.

"For the zip-ties."

She shook her head and said, "I don't know."

Widow stayed quiet.

She said, "Take me out of here first. We can find a knife later."

"Don't worry. I made a good amount of noise, busting through the door. Someone probably called hotel security by now. They can get you out when they get here."

"No! No! I can't be found by security or police. You must take me out of here."

"Take you out? Why no police?"

"Please! You must!"

Widow asked, "Where?"

"To your room. Let's go there first. Then we get me out of these, and then I go. No trouble."

Widow thought for a moment. Normally, he would just call the cops, but considering he beat up four guys who may or may not have ties to the Pentagon and his past, the last thing he wanted was to be involved at any official level.

He shrugged and agreed.

"How do we get back there? Are you going to hop there?"

She paused and looked him over from his ankles back up his torso.

"You are a big guy. Carry me."

"What?"

"Pick me up."

"Like over my shoulder?"

"Yes. Like caveman," she said and smiled, which made the terror that had been on her face sweep away at light speed, replaced by warmth.

Suddenly, Widow realized that the last time a warm-blooded, straight man had ever told her no was probably a decade in the past, more even. The last time that had happened was probably when she wasn't even a teenager, before her body was more developed.

As far as he could see, she had been blessed with the right amount of curves for a woman as thin and lean as she was. A second look at her told him that those curves were worked on. Her legs were muscular things, like a dancer's who did two shows a day, meaning that she probably incorporated squats into her daily workouts.

"Well?" she interrupted his boyish contemplations.

"Sorry. Yes. Let's go."

He knelt down and reached around her thighs, above her knees, and hauled her up over his shoulder carefully.

He walked to the door and opened it, peeked out into the hall. No one was there—no security guard.

Quickly, he took her out and shut the door behind him.

He walked at a fast pace, but not running or jogging, with her over his shoulder.

They passed the elevator just as it dinged, and the doors opened behind them, but they were well out of sight.

They made it back to his room. He set her down and opened the door with the keycard, and stepped in. He helped her hop in behind him.

The door shut, and he watched her hop over to the table where his hotel phone had been, and then she plopped herself down on the chair next to it.

"Let's get these off, please," she said.

And once again, he didn't say no.

23

THE LAST THING that Widow had expected to feel was hungover. But suddenly he did. He figured it wasn't the glass of champagne that he drank, but that he had been woken up from a deep sleep, had dredged up adrenaline and then had taken out four armed guys that caused his body to crash from the high. And now he felt hungover.

He opened the minibar and pulled out a couple of protein bars, offered one to the Russian woman, tied up, and sitting in his hotel room.

That thought made him smile.

"What's funny?"

She noticed.

"Oh, nothing. I'm not laughing."

"Why smile? This is serious situation."

"Sorry, it was just a thought I had from earlier. I was half asleep when you called. Still trying to get acclimated."

"Acclimated?"

"Reoriented."

She nodded.

Silence.

Widow asked, "You're Russian?"

She nodded.

"My name is Jack Widow."

"Anna Johannsen," she said.

"Johannsen? Is that Russian?"

She looked at him and smiled.

"Sorry, I meant Eva Karpov. That's my true name."

Widow nodded. She used an alias. Interesting.

"What the hell is going on?"

"First, get me out of these?" she asked, and gestured to the restraints.

"Of course," he said. He set the protein bars down on the table.

Widow looked around the hotel for a moment and then used the half-empty champagne bottle. He took it into the bathroom and over the sink, and considered breaking it on the countertop, but then thought about how expensive that looked.

He turned to the tub, dumped out the rest of the champagne, and used minimal force to break off the bottom of the bottle. One good, hard whack, and he had several fragments of sharp green glass and a whole bottleneck, still intact.

Widow dropped the neck into a wastebasket and picked up a sharp piece of glass.

He returned to her.

"This is all I can find."

She shrugged and gave him her wrists.

He sawed and tried to stay as far away from her skin as he could. The last thing he needed to do was cut her wrists.

After a lot of effort, the first zip-tie popped off.

"Stop."

She stopped him and motioned for him to back off. Then she repeated the same escape technique that she had done back in the other hotel room, the first time she got free from her zip-ties.

He was impressed.

"Where did you learn that?"

She didn't answer. She held her hand out and took the sharp glass fragment. She relaxed in the chair and pulled her feet up, and reached forward and started sawing the zip-tie binding her ankles.

"I learned it in the service."

Widow stepped away, picked up a protein bar, and sat in the other chair across from her.

"What about you?" she asked.

He stayed quiet.

"Where did you learn to take out armed professionals like that?"

"They weren't professional. Not really. More like semi-professional."

Karpov said, "I thought so. You are military?"

"No. Not anymore. Once."

"Thank you for helping me."

Widow nodded.

"I'll be out of your hair soon."

"Not so fast."

She finished cutting her feet free and then lowered them to the floor. Widow realized that he should have brought her shoes, too.

"What the hell is going on?" he asked.

She scooped up the protein bar, ripped off the paper like she was angry at it, and stuffed her mouth full. Apparently, her kidnappers hadn't fed her much.

She chewed and swallowed the first bite and put her hand over her mouth to cover her animal-like consumption.

"My name is Eva Karpov," she repeated. "I'm a rezidentura."

Which Widow recognized to mean resident. That's what the Russians called a spy who lived in a foreign country, a resident.

"You work for the SVR?"

"You know what that is?" she asked.

"It's the Russian Foreign Intelligence Service."

She nodded.

"I'm an agent."

"A spy?"

"Yes, but not anymore."

"What do you mean?"

"I quit."

"Quit? They let you do that and stay in America?"

"They don't know. Not yet."

"So, who are these guys? They're American."

"Yes. I don't know who they are."

Widow wasn't sure if she was lying or not. Normal people emit tell-tale signs that they are lying. We all do it. It's human nature. No one is immune, but some are better at hiding most of these signs than others. Especially a beautiful Russian agent with spycraft training. Widow had never known a Russian agent before, not a beautiful woman, anyway.

He had heard of them. They were legends in the intelligence world, myths. He had always thought that they were more myth than legend, more legend than fact. But there was one sitting in front of him.

"Sorry, but I'm starving," she said.

"Go ahead. That's yours," he said and pointed at the remains of his protein bar.

She didn't say another word. She scooped it up and devoured the bar like she hadn't eaten in days, which Widow realized she probably hadn't.

"Want something else?"

"Yes."

He returned to the minibar and opened it, and peeked in.

"What would you like?"

"Something big."

Most of the options were junk food.

He pulled out a bag of nuts, figuring that she needed the salt and the protein more than sugar from anything else that was there.

He handed it to her. She took the bag and started devouring them, too.

With her mouth half-full, she said, "Thank you so much for your help, Mr. Widow."

"Tell me what is going on."

"I don't think I should."

"Why not?"

"You could be in danger."

"I'm already involved."

She stayed quiet.

"None of those guys are going to forget me. When they wake up, they'll remember who did this to them."

She nodded and said, "We should leave the hotel too."

"Let's wait and see."

"Wait for what?"

"So far, no one has come to our door. No security. Which is usually what would happen. If we can stay the night here, that would be best. We could leave at first light."

"What if someone called the police?"

"We'll know that soon enough. NYPD is fast. If the hotel called them, they'll be here in the next ten minutes, I would think."

"What about the others?"

"What others?"

"You only knocked out two in my room. There are two others. In the lobby."

Widow smiled and said, "No, they're not. They're in the stairwell."

Eva smiled and asked, "Who the hell are you?"

"I told you. My name is Jack Widow."

"I mean, where did you come from?"

"I came from this room."

"What kind of soldier were you in the military?"

"I wasn't a soldier."

"I thought you said you were ex-military?"

"I was. I wasn't a soldier. I was a sailor."

Eva nodded, said, "You were Special Forces?"

"SEAL," Widow answered.

Her eyes lit up.

"I see. No wonder you can fight like that."

Widow stayed quiet.

Silence fell between them, and Eva ate the last of the nuts. She wiped her lips in a sultry way that Widow wondered was just second nature to her, because of the kind of training she must've gone through. He didn't want to bring it up, but he had heard that female agents were trained much, much differently from males.

Russians taught them to use all the wiles available to them. There are countless stories of Western politicians, generals, and even heads of state falling to the wiles of a Russian woman.

24

WIDOW WAITED another ten minutes on top of the first ten, making an even twenty, just to be safe. No one came to the door—no hotel security. No police.

Widow opened the door twice and peeked his head out into the hall.

He heard no commotion—no signs of police.

"That's weird. Right?" Eva asked.

He shook his head.

"Not really. It is a Saturday night, in New York City, and it's after midnight. Likely that whoever is staying in the rooms near nine-twenty-one is still out on the town somewhere. Either that or drunk and passed out in their beds, sound asleep."

He kept the door ajar and looked back at her.

She said, "Okay. But what about those men? They won't stay knocked out for long?"

"Except for the ones I injected."

"The other two in the stairs?"

"Yeah?"

"There's more of that stuff—the drug. There must be. You could knock them all out for the next twenty-four hours."

Widow said, "That's a good idea."

"I'll come with you."

At first, Widow wanted to tell her to wait, but the fear of her running away had occurred to him. After all, he still didn't know what the hell she was involved in. It might be in her best interest to sneak away, leaving him with four knocked out mercs.

"Let's go," he said.

They walked out of the room and side by side down the hall.

* * *

AT THE ELEVATORS, they stopped, and Eva looked down. There were small droplets of blood on the carpet, which were also matted down and disheveled and scuffed in several places.

She said, "Let me guess, this is where you fought them?"

Widow nodded.

She followed him over to the stairwell. They opened the door and found both guys still there. Still unconscious.

"Isn't it very bad to be knocked out for this long?"

Widow shrugged and said, "Didn't matter to me then. Doesn't matter to me now."

"Come on. Let's drag them back to the room."

Widow stayed quiet.

They both moved into the stairwell.

Eva shifted from one foot to the other because the concrete was freezing under her feet.

She watched Widow lift the first guy up from under his arms and drag him back to the door.

She went around and grabbed his legs, tried to pick him up like a wheelbarrow.

"Never mind that," Widow said. "Just get the door and then be the lookout. We don't want someone walking out to the hall now."

"You sure?"

"Yeah. Go."

She went behind him, passed him, and held the door open. She peered both ways and listened.

"I don't hear anyone."

Widow dragged the guy out onto the carpet.

Eva moved ahead of him and made her way to room nine-twenty-one. She didn't have the keycard to open it, but then realized that she didn't need it. It was still broken from Widow kicking it in.

She opened it and waited for Widow to drag the guy in. He dumped him down on the carpet.

They went back and repeated the process for the other guy.

After a short break, Widow found the supply of sedatives stuffed into a satchel under the bed.

He stopped and stared into it for a moment. He saw something that told him exactly what he needed to know about these guys and what they planned for Eva.

In the satchel, he found a bulky rolled-up sheet of plastic, black like a garbage bag. There was a box of surgical plastic gloves, and two pairs of hacksaws, and one very sharp bone saw that looked so crude it was almost obscene.

Widow took out the sedatives and closed the bag before Eva could see in.

He used the needles and the sedatives and injected each of the other guys, and re-injected the one who had only gotten a small portion earlier in order to equal it all out. He didn't clean any of the needle areas before injecting them. He wasn't concerned with sanitation, only their silence.

They checked around the room again for anything useful, found nothing but Eva's shoes, which she took this time.

"Damn," she said.

"What?"

"I had a bag. It's not here. What did they do with it?"

Widow looked at the pile of sedated guys and said, "We probably should've asked them that before we knocked them out."

Eva smiled and stepped out of the door first, back into the hall.

Widow came next and pulled the door as far shut as it would go, which took some effort. It dragged across the carpet.

Eva looked left and looked right.

Suddenly, she saw shadows and heard voices. Five young guys were walking down the hall toward them. They were talking loud and laughing. They looked like five guys coming back from a night out, clubbing, barhopping, having a lot of drinks on the town.

"Widow," she said.

He looked up and was holding the door shut. It kept jerking back from the hinges.

They were getting closer. Widow tried to close the door. He at least wanted it to shut.

Without hesitation, Eva took action.

She wobbled around, acted a little intoxicated, and scooped up two handfuls of Widow's t-shirt. She nearly ripped it, pulling it and him toward her so hard and fast.

She stood up on tippy toes and kissed him, hard and wet—a distraction.

Her lips were wet. Her tongue was ample, and she wasn't afraid to use it. That was obvious.

If Eva was a day over twenty-five, Widow would've been shocked. And if she had started her seductive spy training a day short of five years ago, he would've been doubly shocked.

She kissed him so hard; he was suddenly worried that even five drunk guys in New York City were going to complain to the hotel's management.

The guys walked, stopped talking for a long minute as they passed by. But they didn't stop and gawk. They kept on walking. Kept on laughing.

Eva didn't stop kissing Widow.

She kissed him hard and long. A good long time after the coast was clear.

She was damn good at her job. No question.

Widow suddenly doubted that the FSB would give her up under any circumstances.

After another long minute of kissing him, she stopped, backed down, and looked in his eyes for a moment. Then she asked, "Are they gone?"

Widow spoke, and for an instant, his voice cracked like he was a teenager all over again.

"Yeah. They're gone."

"Good. Let's get back."

She let go of him, but kept her hand locked onto the bottom of his fingers. She pulled him along, gently, seductively.

Widow wondered if she could even help it.

They walked back down the hall, past the elevators, staying close together.

Back in Widow's room, Eva sat back down on the same chair.

"What now?" she asked.

"Now, tell me what's going on?"

"Can I have something to drink?"

"What do you want?"

"Water, please."

"Of course," Widow said, and he reopened the minibar, took out two bottles of water, and handed her one. He joined her at the table.

Widow watched her screw the bottle open and take two long, deep pulls from it.

He did the same and waited.

"You don't have a cigarette?" she asked.

"I don't smoke."

She frowned, took another drink of water, and then she said, "Listen. I am grateful for your help, but you may not want to know about me?"

It was more of a question than a declaration.

"Tell me."

"My name is Karpov."

He nodded, knew that part.

She said, "I have been in America for three years. Working here in New York."

"Doing what?"

"Officially, I do modeling work and study at university."

"What do you do for the FSB?"

"I date who they tell me to date."

Widow nodded.

"It's not as bad as it sounds. I'm not a prostitute. They don't want me to do that. If I got arrested, it would be the end of my work here. I have a contact here, a handler, who tells me the name of someone and where to go to meet him. I arrange meetings and work my way into their circles. They give me information. I return that information to my government."

"Circles?"

"You know. Social things. Sometimes I date diplomats, lawyers, or whoever, and I work my way into knowing who they know and what they know."

Widow asked, "Married men?"

"Usually. But don't judge me."

"I'm not. Believe me. I'm sure I've done much, much worse for my country."

She said nothing to that.

Widow asked, "So why did these guys kidnap you?"

"They must be trying to stop me."

"From what?"

"My father. He's a submarine commander for Russia."

Widow drank another gulp and waited.

Eva said, "About a month ago, a man approached me. An American man. He is a CIA agent. They took me in and said they knew who I was. But they wouldn't turn me in if I helped them."

"What do they want?"

"I begged for this assignment. Here in America, I mean. Begged for it. Do you know why?"

Widow shook his head, even though she meant the question to be rhetorical.

"I love this country. I want to escape Russia. I hoped I could find a way out."

Widow stayed quiet.

"Of course, we all wondered about trying to escape to your country."

"What do they tell you?"

"Before we are sent here, we are warned not to run. If we run, they will do terrible things to our family."

"Like what?" Widow asked.

"They only pick girls who have parents."

Which was a surprise to Widow. He had heard that the Russians liked to use orphans. Girls who could disappear easily, without notice. No one left behind to worry about them.

Eva said, "They use the parents as leverage over us. If we try to...try to..."

She was struggling over a word.

She asked, "What's it called when a foreign citizen tries to request safety here?"

"Defect?"

"Yes. I want to defect."

"What about your parents?"

"I only have a father. He, too, wants to defect."

"Where is he?"

"That's why I'm here because he is the captain of a submarine."

Widow stayed quiet.

"A nuclear submarine."

25

Eva said, "A few months ago, I made a friend. More than that. He was another student in one of my classes. We hit it off, and I've been dating him."

Widow said, "Don't take this the wrong way."

"What?"

"This guy. He's a friend or a mark?"

"He's a friend. He's not government. Just a regular American guy. A chance meeting."

"Okay."

"We dated. I wanted to. It wasn't related to work."

Widow stayed quiet, listened.

"His name's Edward. He works as a fireman."

Widow noticed her face change as she spoke of him. Something in her eyes.

He asked, "You care about this guy?"

She nodded.

"What happened next?"

"Two weeks ago, he introduced me to this guy he knew, a friend. He said he used to work with this guy. So, I met with him—twice. The guy's name is Frank Farmer. He works for the government. After our first meeting, Farmer told me he was a CIA agent. And he knew who I was."

She stopped talking and looked down at the floor.

"What?" Widow asked.

"I was so stupid. They teach us not to have feelings for a man."

"Edward and Farmer aren't what they seem?"

"No. I trusted Edward and told him who I was. Who I really was. He told Farmer, and they both convinced me they could help me and my father get out of Russia."

"Let me guess. Farmer asked you to set up communications with your father?"

She nodded.

"What else did he promise?"

"Farmer promised he could arrange for my father and me to go under protection for the submarine."

Widow said, "Sounds like Clancy."

"Who?"

"You know. The book by Tom Clancy. The Hunt for Red October."

"Yes! I know this book! It's one of my father's favorites."

"I bet he knew that."

Eva said, "You think so?"

"Of course, CIA guys don't just show up by chance like that. They identified you before you and Edward even met. They knew exactly what they were doing."

She nodded, said, "Those are his guys that kidnapped me?"

Widow nodded.

She shook her head and said, "I feel so stupid."

"I wouldn't. You wanted to have a better life for you and your father. I can understand that."

She looked down in shame.

"You love this guy?"

"Yes. I think I do."

She had said it without hesitation.

Silence.

Widow said, "What exactly was the plan?"

"Farmer told me I was to go about my business for a week. Then I was to tell my father the plan and get his answer."

"He agreed?"

"Of course."

"Then what?"

"I was told to come here and wait. Farmer gave me coordinates to relay to my father. They were supposed to meet."

"Where?"

"The middle of the Arctic Ocean."

Widow said, "So, let me guess, the deal was this Farmer guy gets the submarine, and you and your father get your freedom?"

"Yes. And now I'm here."

"Why?"

"Why what?"

"Why the hell does Farmer want this submarine?"

She shrugged and said, "Because it's nuclear. I guess."

"No. We got nuclear subs. Better than yours. In terms of submariner warfare and technology, the US Navy has the best."

Eva said nothing.

"No offense."

She shrugged.

"Why the hell would the CIA want a Russian one?"

She didn't answer.

"There must be something else. What do you know about the sub?"

"Nothing. I know nothing about them. Just what I told you. It's nuclear."

Widow nodded and stood up. He paced to the center of the room and then over to the window. The drapes dangled and wafted slightly. He peered out and looked down at the courtyard.

"The good news is, no cops. They would've already been here. NYPD is pretty fast."

Eva asked, "So, what do I do now?"

"What about Edward?"

"What about him?"

"You know where he lives?"

"Of course. I've been staying there five nights a week for the last month."

"So?"

"So what?"

"So, where is it?"

"He lives on the Upper East Side."

Widow smirked and said, "Not bad."

"What's that supposed to mean?"

"For a guy who is a college student and a fireman, the Upper East Side is an expensive spot to live. Does he live with roommates?"

"No."

"It didn't strike you as odd that a guy on his dime can afford an apartment on his own?"

"It's a family-owned loft. Lots of people live here who have owned the same apartments forever."

Widow said nothing to that.

"You think I'm stupid?"

"Not at all. I think you had feelings for this guy."

She nodded.

"Love can be a real son of a bitch."

She nodded again.

"What about your handler? Who is he?

"He's a she."

"Who is she?"

"I can't tell you that."

Widow said, "I'm trying to help you."

Eva was quiet.

"Look, I'm not one of the bad guys here. Obviously. You called me. How could I have faked that?"

"Her American name is Sarah Walsman. She's a partner in a law firm down on Forty-Second Street."

"Is she American?"

"What do you mean?"

"Is she like you? She's here on a visa?"

"No. She's Russian born with American citizenship. She's been here most of her life."

"Do you know where she is?" Widow asked.

"Not at this time of night."

"No home address?"

"No."

"How do you contact her?"

"By a secure phone number."

Widow paused a moment, and then he said, "What about this Edward guy?"

"What about him?"

"You remember his address?"

"Of course."

"Then that's our next stop."

"Now?"

"Yes. We can't wait. I'd bet the guys who kidnapped you will probably have to check in with this Farmer guy, and when they don't, he will know something's wrong. We should go."

Widow stood up, finished his bottle of water, and said, "Want anything else to eat? We're not returning to this room again."

Eva drank the rest of her water, finished the protein bar. She got up.

"What about your stuff?"

"Don't have any."

She said nothing to that.

Widow carried both weapons, one still in his pocket and the other tucked in the back of his waistband.

Before they left, he picked up his sweater but didn't put it on.

"Here. You should wear this. It's chilly out."

"What about you?" she asked.

"I'll be fine for now."

She nodded and took it, which was fine with him since she was in a skirt that was barely there, and he still had chinos, boots, and a t-shirt.

They walked out of the hotel room and out of the hotel. No one noticed.

26

Widow stayed close to Eva as they stepped out of a random cab and onto the curb of East Seventy-Eighth Street, her directions to her boyfriend's apartment.

The wind blew between the remaining leaves on a single thin brown tree.

Widow heard sounds of cars whooshing in the distance on FDR Drive. He heard the ambient noises of a busy, dark city night.

"That's it. On the corner," Eva said.

Widow looked, casually, and then glanced around the street.

"Doesn't look like anyone is here, staking the place out."

Eva nodded. She'd done the same thing, only much more anonymously and, probably, with more thoroughness. She was a trained spy, after all.

"Okay. Let me go in first and check it out."

Eva said nothing.

Widow looked around and saw a 7-Eleven type of all-night convenience store less than a block away, toward the west.

"Over there. Come on. Let's go over to that convenience store."

"What? No way!"

"This isn't a time to argue. What if there's someone here some-where? They'll recognize you."

She shook her head.

"Forget about it. I'm not your woman in distress."

Widow stared at her in disbelief. Had he appeared a chauvinist? He hoped not.

But he didn't apologize.

"I'm only trying to do this the right way."

"Look, this is my ass—not yours. If Edward betrayed me, I'm going to get to speak to him about this! Not you!"

Widow held his hands up in a universal "I give up" sort of way.

"Okay. Fine," he said.

"Good."

Although Widow's way was safer, he couldn't say that he blamed her. She had met a man, trusted him, and he had almost literally stabbed her in the back.

If a woman had done that to him, he too would've stepped up and confronted her. No question.

Widow headed toward the building on the corner that she had pointed to.

She followed him down the sidewalk. They stopped at a four-way intersection and crossed over the street.

They stopped at a side alley, too small for a dump truck, but wide enough for him to stretch his arms out and not touch both sides. Almost.

He gazed down it, his hand behind his back, fingers touching the butt of the Maxim 9 stuffed into his waistband.

There was a chain-link fence, about ten feet high, linked up the wall, blocking anyone from strolling into the alley. He saw various pipes and grates. There was one backdoor into the building that they were interested in, but it was padlocked.

The alley was empty.

They walked up the steps to the front door entrance. There was a key code lock—all numbers.

"What's the code?"

Eva didn't answer him. She just brushed past him and entered the numbers in a four-digit sequence.

"That's it," Eva said, and the front door made a loud, grating sound. She reached up and jerked the knob and pulled the door open wide.

Widow grabbed the Maxim 9, again ready to brandish it, but kept it hidden. He figured that the whole building probably wasn't CIA or whoever these guys were.

The inner lobby area of the building had high concrete ceilings and a long, white leather couch and a metal bookshelf, and various abstract paintings hanging on the walls.

There were a couple of thick concrete pillars half-embedded into the walls.

He saw a single thick, brown counter that wrapped completely around a guy sitting in a chair, leaning back like his feet were up on a desktop that wasn't visible from where Widow and Eva were standing.

He was looking down, playing on a smartphone, Widow figured.

Another one, he thought.

Suddenly, he pictured what would happen if one of his guys or team members had been caught playing with his phone back in the Navy.

The guard immediately recognized Eva and sat up straight, like he was at attention, and said, "Good morning, Miss Johannsen."

He knew her.

Another thing surprised Widow.

Suddenly, Eva Karpov spoke. Only any trace of her Russian accent had completely vanished. Her pronunciation of English had improved dramatically. It wasn't perfect conversational American. It still stood out that she was a foreigner, but where she was from was more of a guessing game.

If Widow had known no better, he would've guessed that she was British. Not that she was using a British accent. It was only because out of all the English-speaking people of the world; the Brits were the best at blending in with Americans. He had met a dialect coach once, a guy back in Glynco, Georgia, the NCIS training grounds, who had taught agents on various dialects and how to disguise them. At the end of the course, the guy revealed he was British, and they hadn't realized it the whole year.

When Widow entered the course, everyone in the class had presumed he was from Virginia. He had perfected that deep rural Virginia accent.

Eva said, "Hi, Gerald. How is it tonight?"

"Everything's been quiet. How are you?"

Eva nodded and said, "Good. I'm just going to go on up."

The security guard named Gerald gave Widow a look over, which wasn't the friendliest that Widow had ever seen. But he said nothing to the plus one that Eva had brought with her.

He simply nodded and waved them up.

Widow smiled at the guy and followed Eva around a corner and past several doors, generic and gray, until they reached an elevator.

"This is an expensive-looking building."

"I guess so."

Her accent returned.

"This whole industrial loft style isn't. Not anymore."

Eva asked, "So what?"

"I thought you said that Edward is a fireman? Allegedly."

"I didn't mean he is an ordinary one. He's an assistant deputy in the department. He works out of city hall."

"He's the next guy down from the top or something?"

"I think so."

"I didn't know they paid this well."

Eva shrugged and said, "Believe me. I looked into it. He makes a good salary."

Widow stayed quiet. He didn't know what to say to that. Truthfully, he wasn't sure if he believed it. But anything was possible.

They waited for the elevator. It came, and the doors sucked open. Widow followed her on, and she hit the button for Edward's floor.

27

THE ELEVATOR DOORS OPENED, and Widow and Eva stayed where they were, waiting, breathing.

Widow kept his arm out in front of Eva, blocking her path forward.

He took out the Maxim 9 and kept it back behind his thigh, out of sight of anyone walking past.

Eva whispered, "What?"

Widow said nothing.

After a moment went by, the elevator doors closed. He moved his hand out and blocked them. The sensors picked up the resistance, and the levers and gears turned back, pulling the doors open.

Widow stepped out into the hall. He looked left. Nothing was there. He jerked to the right and saw nothing there, either. No one was waiting to ambush them.

He tucked the gun back into his waistband and motioned for Eva to step off the elevator.

Eva said, "I think you've seen too many movies."

"Just being safe."

"You've done this before?"

"You can say that."

"Don't worry; this isn't Iraq. Or wherever you've been."

Widow stayed quiet.

Eva turned left and walked west.

"Which one is it?"

"The last one. On the corner."

Like the lobby to the building, the hallway had high ceilings, smooth concrete floors, and concrete walls. There was more abstract art hanging on the walls between the apartment doors.

The doors were these huge wooden things. No peepholes. No doorbells.

It was amazing how this industrial look had come back into style. Widow remembered seeing an old bullet factory in Ukraine once. It had been converted to a hotel. He couldn't remember the name, but the whole thing had a ton of roped-off photographs and old tank shells turned into art.

This building wasn't an old ammunition factory, but it had that same industrial look to it.

The major difference being that the old ammunition factory in Ukraine had once been a working factory. It had been designed that way for convenience, and it was cheap.

The owners of this place had probably paid out the ass to have the same look that cost nothing decades ago.

Strange what rich people will pay for.

The thought brought Widow to another conclusion. No way was this Edward guy just working for the fire department. Not with this kind of pad.

They continued on and stopped at the door.

"Should I knock? You stand out of sight?"

"There's no peephole. Makes no difference."

Eva shrugged and knocked on the door, flat-handed, three loud pounds.

They waited.

Widow leaned into the door and listened. He heard nothing.

"Sounds like no one's here."

Eva reached out and pounded on the door again, two more times.

Widow asked, "How can we get in?"

"Can you kick it in?"

"No way!"

"You're a big guy. You can do it."

He said, "Besides all the racket it'll make, this door is solid wood. No one is getting in that he doesn't let in."

Widow reached out and tried the handle. It was locked.

"You don't know where he might keep a spare key?"

She paused, and then she said, "The front desk has one. He could let us in."

"Will he do that?"

"It's doubtful. But maybe."

"We could wait for him to get home."

"No. I can't wait. What if Farmer has already contacted my father?"

Widow thought for a moment, looked over her head, down to the end of the hall.

He said, "He probably has."

Eva said nothing, but a look of fear came over her face.

"You've been sedated for two days, right?"

She nodded.

"Then I'd say whatever this guy's plans were with your father; he's already well ahead of us."

"So, how are we getting in, then?"

Widow took stock again. He turned and headed back to the elevator.

"Come on," he said.

"Widow?"

"We'll convince the guard to let us in."

"How?"

* * *

BACK AT THE FRONT DESK, Eva stood and explained to the guard at the desk exactly what Widow had told her, a simple plan that usually worked.

"I have to get in there. We knocked on the door, and we heard him ask for help."

The guard looked at her. He was standing up.

Widow heard his fingers tapping on the desk behind the counter. He was waiting, listening hard for any sign that the guard was going to press a hidden security call button, like a hidden distress call he had seen in banks.

It was very doubtful that they had one that called the police. Why would they?

But if the security for the building was outsourced to a local agency, which it probably was, then they might have a call center, like a headquarters. They might have such a switch installed at all their building locations.

This was New York City.

The guard had a look of concern on his face. He seemed to buy the lie, but there was one problem.

Widow realized he was that problem.

The guard said, "I don't know."

Which was blurted out, like a reaction to the whole situation.

"Please! We have to get in there!" Eva said. She was good. She was really selling the whole concerned girlfriend bit.

The guard looked Widow up and down, fast.

"We should call the ambulance. I think."

Eva said, "No! We need to get in there!"

Silence. He wasn't buying it—not quite.

Widow thought of backup plans. He could just pull the gun on the guy and make him produce the key. They could lock him up in a broom closet and take away his cell phone. Or Widow could just knock the guy out. A swift, not-too-brutal punch to the face would do the trick.

However, he hated the thought of it. A security guard staying up all night on a long graveyard shift probably made minimum wage. He probably already had an inner resentment about having to guard a property that he couldn't even afford to live in, not even if his salary had been doubled or tripled.

Then Eva said something brilliant.

"Gerald, Edward is diabetic! He probably had an attack! The paramedics won't get here fast enough!"

Gerald stayed quiet, but the expression of disbelief in his eyes completely faded away, and the look of concern overtook him.

Eva said, "I know Edward! If the ambulance is called, his insurance will go bullets."

She had meant *ballistic*, not bullets, but Widow got it, and the guard named Gerald had as well.

Widow half-smiled.

She was good.

The thought made him terrified of what else she could convince a man to do. He figured with her training and mannerisms, plus her looks, she probably could convince a four-star general to leap off a ledge.

Suddenly, he wondered if she had ever done that.

Gerald said, "Oh, man! Come on! Let's go!"

Which wasn't the response that Widow had hoped. He had hoped that Gerald would turn over the key without going up with them. But he figured that was a long shot.

Gerald turned around and pulled a long drawer open.

Widow heard clanging metal, like a drawer full of keys would make.

Gerald pulled out a key fast, like he knew which one it was. It must've been organized into cubbies.

He put the key into his pocket and pulled his coat off the back of the chair.

Widow and Eva started walking to the elevator. Gerald came up behind them and slid his jacket on. The back of it said "Security" in generic lettering. There was no name of his company labeled anywhere.

Gerald had also scooped up a Maglite, which Widow figured was because of him. Maybe it was out of caution or simply second nature. Either way, it was a good clubbing weapon.

They all got on the elevator and rode up.

28

THE SECURITY GUARD SAID, "Did you call him? I should've tried that first."

Eva said, "Of course we did. No answer."

Widow said, "We're already here now."

Gerald nodded and pulled the keys out of his pocket, held them in his hand.

He tucked the flashlight under his armpit and held it there. He used his free hand and knocked on the door twice.

"Mr. Daniels? Are you in there?" he called out.

He listened. Widow and Eva pretended to.

No sounds.

He knocked again and again. He called out.

Eva said, "Come on! We've got to get in there!"

Gerald retracted his knocking hand and pulled up the keys. Widow noticed he trembled, which was a natural reaction when you think you're about to walk into an emergency where a guy might slip into a diabetic coma.

Quick and without hesitation, Widow reached his right hand back and grabbed the Maxim 9, ready to draw it. He placed his other hand out and just behind the security guard, in case he had to jerk the guy out of the way.

There was no telling who was on the other side of the door, waiting for him.

The door was heavy, and Gerald had to push it open. He did this slowly and knocked on the door.

"Mr. Daniels?" he called out.

No answer.

Eva moved her eyes side to side, scoping out the place. She had the advantage over Widow because she knew exactly the layout of the apartment. She knew where all the furniture was placed, where the bathrooms and closets were.

It turned out not to be that hard because continuing with the industrial design of the apartments, this unit was completely open and very spacious.

The door opened to a kitchen to the left. All stainless steel appliances. All new.

There was a large bar top that doubled as a cooking island. Three white stools were tucked in on the right side and cutting utensils and a stack of cutting boards and bar glasses were neatly placed on top.

Straight ahead of them was an open living room area with a twenty-foot ceiling and a metal stairwell that led up above them to a loft, which was probably the bedroom.

To the immediate right was a small half bathroom. The door was wide open, and the light was off.

With a quick glance, Widow saw the sink and the toilet. The room was empty.

To the right, past the bathroom, was the living room area. There was a huge television placed on top of a modest entertainment center, with a coffee table and two white leather sofas with three yellow leather chairs.

The apartment was dimly lit.

The television was on, but not to a program or a movie. It played a screensaver that kept changing between different earthly backgrounds.

There were two good-sized speakers on the floor.

Low lounge music that Widow didn't recognize hummed from them.

There were huge glass bay windows on the wall, with the best view of a combination of cityscapes and some of the East River that Widow had ever seen.

There was a glass door that led out onto a balcony. Edward Daniels wasn't out there. That was clear.

Nor was he upstairs, hiding, or simply asleep.

He wasn't in either of these places because he was lying on the flat of his back on the floor, near the back of one sofa. And he was dead.

His face stared up at the ceiling above, and his eyes were wide open. His skin wasn't white as a sheet, as was often written in books or seen on TV.

He was as blue as the afternoon sky.

At least his entire face and head were.

The cause of death hadn't been diabetes; even Gerald could see that.

The cause of death had been strangulation and with a garrote. That was obvious.

Widow had seen a lot of deaths and murders in his career. Next to a gunshot wound, strangulation by a garrote was one of the most obvious ones because of the damage left behind.

Edward's neck was black and blue, and there were severe up and down lines left on his skin like he had struggled with a sharp piano wire, while someone who knew what he was doing nearly sawed his head off, trying to choke him.

29

"OH, MY GOD!" Gerald said.

In a mad dash, he ran straight for the body. Maybe he had never seen a dead body before. Maybe he thought the guy was still alive. Maybe he even still believed that Edward had an attack from diabetes and was only in a coma.

Running to the body wasn't Widow's first instinct. He had seen dead bodies before. His first instinct was to make sure that no one else was there, waiting to ambush them.

No reason to keep up the charade anymore. Widow drew his weapon.

Eva saw it first. She was smart. She didn't run to the body.

She stayed back in Widow's line of sight.

He took out the other gun and reversed it, one-handed, and offered it to her.

She took it, left-handed, and held it down and out that way. She clicked the safety off and racked the slide back, chambering the first round.

Widow shouted, "Gerald!"

He shouted, just to stop Gerald in his tracks.

The guard stopped and flipped around, saw the guns, and froze. He dropped his Maglite so fast and moved his hands straight up in the freeze position Widow was certain he had definitely seen a gun before. No question.

"Holy hell!"

"Keep calm," Widow said.

"What's going on?"

Eva motioned for Gerald to stay quiet, one finger over her mouth.

"Come back this way," she commanded.

Gerald moved back to them and stopped.

Widow said, "I'll check out the rest of the place."

Eva nodded.

Widow didn't wait to hear what she told Gerald about what they were doing. He imagined it was some kind of lie involving them being law enforcement or undercover cops.

Although a pair of undercover cops with high-tech, expensive handguns with built-in silencers was a stretch. Still, the guy would probably buy it. Why not?

Widow moved out into the kitchen and stopped. He saw a hand towel hanging off the oven door handle. He reached out and pulled it off. With the dead body there, it would be a good idea not to leave fingerprints, although the building had security cameras. But clear images of a person from a camera feed weren't the same as fingerprints or DNA. With an image, the only way to identify someone was actually to recognize his face.

He was pretty sure that his face wouldn't pop up anywhere to be identified.

He continued on, passed the body, but didn't look down at it.

He swept the corners of the room, which were shrouded in dark shadows, quickly. Then he pointed the business end of the Maxim 9 at the stairs, checked the darkness underneath. Nothing there but rows of sneakers and sealed moving boxes.

He looked up the stairs, followed the metal railing above. The room above him was black, but he figured that if anyone had been there, waiting, then they would've made themselves known with a bullet if they had a gun.

Widow stepped on the bottom step, which clanged like a rung on a metal ladder.

Luckily, he wasn't worried about being silent. They had already destroyed that tactic.

Widow climbed the stairs with giant steps, two at a time. Within seconds, he was at the top. He crouched, gun out.

It was one quick sweep, checking the corners, checking the bed, and checking the open doorway to the bathroom, which had a low ambient light on. It was one of those plug-in nightlights. Maybe it doubled as an air freshener, because there was the smell of factory-made lavender in the air, like a burning candle purchased from any grocery store or low-cost department store found all over America.

The dim light from the bathroom cut a cone of light out onto the bed.

It was a king platform thing. It was made. Unlike the cheap-smelling lavender air freshener, the sheets and the bedding and the bed itself looked expensive.

There was a modern-style headboard up against the wall. No footboard.

The thing about the headboard that Widow noticed, without trying to notice, like a reflex, like an involuntary instinct had looked for it, were the bruises on the wall behind the headboard. He had seen those kinds of scuffs before.

In the Navy, Widow had to room with guys, lots of different SEALs and sailors, and even Marines. Over the years, whenever he had been stationed dockside or wherever, it was rare that he got a hotel room all to himself.

Suddenly, he could recall all the socks that he had seen left out for him, tied around door handles. A universal indicator from one guy to another that the room was occupied for a while.

Widow was struck with a little jealousy. He didn't know Eva, and the feeling wasn't warranted, not on a logical level. She was basically a stranger and a foreign agent at that. But they had shared an intense first meeting. And there was something about her he felt drawn to.

Widow shook off the jealousy and checked the other side of the bed. No one was there hiding.

He flattened himself up against the wall, slid down to the corner of a massive walk-in closet. No door, but lots of darkness.

He saw a light switch, flipped it. He waited.

No gunshots. No one reacted to the light being switched on. No breathing.

There was no one there.

Instead, Widow looked on in awe at the collection of suits and ties and dress shoes, polished and neatly stacked on wooden shelves.

The bathroom was next to the walk-in closet, making it easy for him to take a peek inside, which he did.

He flipped on the light, but he didn't need it.

The bathroom was a big, square box room. There was a huge glass shower that looked more like an empty aquarium than a shower. There were towels neatly folded on metal shelving above the toilet.

The vanity was a plain, white thing with decent counter space for a single man, but not big enough for a woman to use effectively.

There was a single large mirror hanging above the sink and rising higher than necessary toward the ceiling, which made him think it was designed for a tall guy like himself.

There was a small, cube-shaped wastebasket, lined and half-full on the floor next to the toilet. Widow looked in and saw a red toothbrush tossed in. Underneath it was a woman's shampoo bottle, an empty pack of pink razors, and a crushed tampon box.

Widow lowered the Maxim 9, but kept it in hand, moved away and out of the bathroom. He returned to the closet and checked it.

There was a pair of matching suitcases on rollers pushed up to the inside wall.

On a shelf, next to a shelf with folded ties, was a good amount of expensive-looking jewelry. All for a man, he guessed. There were watches and bracelets and gold chains.

There was one empty shelf, which Widow wondered might've once been for Eva.

He left the closet and left the lights on for a moment.

Then he took a towel and wiped the switch, walked back to the bathroom and wiped that switch as well.

He hadn't touched the handrail on the way up the stairs, so he didn't wipe it on the way down.

At the bottom of the stairs, he saw Gerald was seated on the armchair, facing the kitchen and the body.

Eva stood near him.

She asked, "Anyone there?"

"No. It's empty. Whoever killed him is gone."

"We know who killed him."

Widow said nothing to this.

Gerald asked, "What the hell is going on?"

Widow said, "It's a need-to-know thing. Basically, we're the good guys. And the bad guys did this."

Gerald said nothing, but he didn't have to. The look of fear in his eyes said it all.

Widow walked close to them, kept the Maxim 9 down by his side, and the hand towel in his other hand.

Widow asked, "Who was the last person to come out of here tonight?"

"No one. You guys are it."

"He didn't have any other visitors tonight?"

"I saw no one."

Eva said, "He smells. Maybe he was killed yesterday?"

"Could be," Widow said. "You don't remember anyone coming in and out of here yesterday, either?"

Gerald shook his head, said, "I'm not the only desk guy. I mean, there might've been someone come out, and I wouldn't know. This ain't a bank or nothing. People come and go."

"Someone was here."

Eva asked, "What now?"

"Now, we leave."

"Go where?"

"Not sure, just somewhere else."

"What about him?"

Widow looked at the guard. He said, "Gerald, when's your shift over?"

"Four hours."

"I'm really sorry about doing this to you."

"Wha...What are you going to do?"

"Sorry, but we have to put you somewhere. We can't have you calling the cops when we leave."

"I won't! I swear!"

Widow cocked his head at him, but he said nothing.

"Is there any duct tape in here?" he asked Eva.

"Under the sink. There's a toolbox."

Widow nodded, tucked the gun into the back of his waistband, and went to the sink.

He used the towel as a glove, and opened the cupboard, pulled out the box, set it on the floor.

He popped the top and took out a roll of duct tape. He took Gerald to the downstairs bathroom without incident since he was terrified, and Eva still had her gun out.

He taped the guy up, bound his wrists and feet together, and then put one strip over his mouth. He checked the guy's pockets and pulled out the contents. He placed them on the vanity while he ran another series of tape strips around the guy's feet to the back of the toilet piping, to hold him in place.

Widow scooped and then carried the guy's possessions out to the kitchen and dumped them in the sink. He took the cellphone and held down the home button until the thing went off. He left it on the kitchen countertop.

He returned to the bathroom and shut the door.

Before shutting it, he said, "Don't worry. You'll be safe."

Eva asked, "What do we do?"

"Let's take off. And we can decide somewhere else."

"What about the guard? What if they come back?"

"They won't."

"How do you know that?"

"Would you?"

She shook her head.

They stepped out into the hall. Widow wiped down the doorknobs, both sides of the front door, and tossed the towel back inside the apartment.

He used the guard's key to lock the deadbolt behind them, slid the key into his pocket so he could keep it until he found some place safe to ditch it.

30

CAPTAIN KARPOV's feet were killing him because he had been zip-tied with his hands out in front of him, and told to stay on his feet.

The submarine dove deep and would remain there for the rest of its mechanical life, right after they surfaced once more, but the captured crew on board didn't know that much.

They were nearing the time when they would surface soon, in a few hours.

Frank Farmer stood still, leaning over a console on the bridge of the submarine. Green lights reflected at him, washing over his face. He stood behind the only member of this team who spoke perfect Russian, as well as knew the controls of the submarine like the back of his hand.

Farmer had never even been onboard a submarine before. He wasn't even sure if he'd be able to handle it because of a slight concern for claustrophobia, but if he could overcome the fear of death, he could deal with a little claustrophobia. No problem.

Farmer stood back up and swiped his brow of sweat as relief overcame him. Which it had—tenfold, if he was honest with himself.

He had been feeling extreme stress because only a moment ago, they'd navigated deep under the surface of the North Atlantic through a cluster of US ships.

At this depth, and without breaking silence, he waited until his go-to submariner gave the all-clear from the scanning equipment of the US ships. Then he walked back to the captain's chair and dumped himself down.

He said, "Mister Kegler, you may take us back on course. We need to get there within the next few hours. Can you manage?"

"Why else would you have brought me along?" Kegler, the man at the screen, asked sarcastically. Sarcasm was a trait of many sailors that he had known in a past life.

Farmer had never been a sailor. He wasn't pleased with the sarcasm, but he ignored it anyway.

"Good. I'm leaving the command to you," Farmer said.

It really had been up to Kegler, to begin with, since Farmer's knowledge of helming a submarine was limited to what he had seen in movies.

"Where are you going?"

Farmer didn't answer him, not directly. Instead, he sat back in the chair for a moment and then got up. He waved at the redheaded guy to follow him.

They walked over to Captain Karpov and stopped.

Karpov had one black eye, swollen shut. Not from a fist, but from the butt end of the redheaded guy's MP4 stock. Two vicious blows to the face. Same eye. Within the same minute. All because Karpov had refused to instruct his crew to follow their orders over the intercom system on board the boat.

But like many of the enemies that Farmer had made in the past, the captain eventually gave in.

It surprised Farmer that it took them shooting his second-in-command and then beating him with the rifle, and then threatening his third-in-command. Who had been identified by Kegler, not just their submarine expert, but also their expert on all things Russian military.

Karpov, giving in to this threat, told Farmer everything that he needed to know about the captain. The way to get him to comply with demands was simply threatening someone else.

How noble! Farmer thought.

He was excited about the next person who he would threaten to Karpov—his own daughter.

"Let's go," the redheaded guy commanded.

Karpov stayed quiet but moved away from the wall where they had put him and walked ahead.

"Stop," the redhead ordered.

Karpov stopped.

Farmer said, "Take us to your quarters."

Karpov didn't argue or speak. He started walking, and they followed.

31

Outside on the sidewalk across the street, the man in black sat on a motorcycle, not one of those known as "hogs" from Harley David-son, but a faster model from a Japanese brand.

The man was dressed in bikers' attire, no leather, but all black. A cotton-polyester blended jacket, black slacks, and a biker's helmet, with a tinted shield, pulled all the way down. It wasn't used for blocking out the sun, as there was no sun, not in the late-night hours.

The man in black also had a brown satchel that didn't match his fashion ensemble. It hung tight with one strap around one shoulder; the satchel part draped down the small of his back.

The satchel didn't match because he had taken it from Edward's apartment. Only because he needed to take Edward's laptop and smartphone and various memory sticks he'd found lying around.

Perhaps they contained records or notes leading the police, or whoever else, to Edward's connections to the CIA and, eventually, to the man in black and the person he worked for.

The bike's engine hummed and purred underneath him. The low, deep vibrations rattled through his thighs and bones. The bike was well made, but it wasn't made for idling. It was made for driving fast.

Right now, the bike was like a horse showing its rider that it was ready to move, that it was getting restless.

The man in black ignored the bike and waited, but he also felt the restlessness. A major part of his job was waiting. He didn't like this part, but it was necessary.

He was anxious because he had taken the stairwell in and out of the apartment building, disabling the security camera at the bottom of the stairs before he entered, of course. This wasn't a hard act to do, since the damn security was a joke.

Normally, he might've killed the guard behind the desk, but only if there was a threat of the guard being an eyewitness. Here there hadn't been.

The man in black kept his eyes on the entrance to the apartment building and his hands on the bike's handlebar, gripping the clutch, waiting.

He was about to take off after he walked out of the stairwell, because the stairwell's ground exit led straight to a fire door that opened out onto the other intersecting street, perpendicular to the entrance.

On his way out, he noticed a couple standing around the corner, chatting near the entrance to the apartment building.

He only glimpsed them. He stuck around and see if they came back out.

More than just the coincidence of their being there at that late hour was that he saw a bulge in the small of the man's back, a bulge that indicated a gun. Nine times out of ten, anyway.

Under the man in black's coat, in an inside pocket, was an expensive, simple piece of equipment that he used in his job from time to time, a razor-sharp wired garrote with two stainless steel cylinder handles.

It was a tool that was built for only one purpose, murder, and not just any kind of murder. The garrote is a stealth weapon. It's not as fast as a sharp knife to the throat or a bullet to the head or heart, but to the man in black, it was a hell of a lot more satisfying than a gunshot to the temple from a silenced gun, like the one he had in his pocket.

Normally, it was a shiny, clean weapon. At that moment, it was wiped clean, but still had stains of red, thick blood dotted along the wire and some spray on the handles. It needed a deeper cleaning, which the man in black would give it.

This wasn't that time.

He had only been given one target so far to take care of this time, but it had been relayed to him that there were to be no witnesses left alive. This gave him carte blanche to remove the couple as he saw fit.

Just then, he saw them step out, which made their presence more than a coincidence. However, they didn't qualify as eyewitnesses, not the kind that could identify him. So far, they hadn't seen him.

They may have discovered the crime scene. Not cause for panic, not to his mission. After all, it was going to be discovered, eventually. He intended for it to be found.

Edward was dead, and there was no trace of his involvement or sign of who Edward worked for in the apartment. He'd made sure of that.

The first thing that the man in black noticed about the couple who came out of Edward's apartment building was that the man was pretty tall, taller than he had noticed before, probably because the man in black's first instincts were to check for weapons on anyone and everyone new who came across his path, a call back to his training.

Even if this guy had no weapons, he still would be hard to take down, at least in a fair fist fight. But the man in black wasn't accommodating of the rules of engagement in fighting. He wasn't a fighter. He was a killer, which isn't the same thing. Snipers aren't trained to engage in hand-to-hand combat. They're trained to shoot and kill their targets with one shot from a distance. Sure, they're trained to fight up close if need be, but that's a last resort.

The man in black wasn't only an assassin, but this had been the focus of most of his training, which was why he felt pretty stupid that he'd failed to notice the woman first.

His instincts had led him to be a little misogynistic because, naturally, he thought the man was the threat. However, he realized that this wasn't the case after he got a good look at the woman.

The man he had never seen before in his life, but he knew the woman. And she wasn't where she was supposed to be.

32

WIDOW STEPPED off the bottom step first and looked right, looked left. He noticed a black van parked across the street. Being black made it suspicious automatically. But what made it stick out to him was that it hadn't been there on their way into Edward's apartment building.

He dismissed the van as nothing more than coincidence as soon as he saw the driver switch on the hazard lights and get out. The lights blinked, red in the back and yellow from the front.

The driver slid the side panel door open, revealing a steel setup with trays of plastic-covered food or baking ingredients, Widow couldn't tell, that were stacked on sliding metal shelves.

The guy was delivering early morning supplies to the back entrance of a corner bakery across the street, opposite the convenience store.

Widow ignored it, checked the rest of the streets and corners.

Steam rose from a sewer grate. A nearby lamppost hummed with electricity from the bright light above. Small groups of pedestrians walked on both sides of the street.

He saw a black shape in the shadows off on the next street. A dark silhouette that looked like a man on a horse to him, only for a moment, until he realized it was a guy riding a bike. Only the bike wasn't being ridden. It was stopped at the intersection—nothing to raise the alarm in Widow's head because the traffic light was red for the guy.

Even with the distance between them, Widow heard the foreign engine buzz and purr, ready to go, impatient by design.

The light turned green, and the guy on the motorcycle paused a long beat, stared at Widow, or so it appeared. Widow couldn't tell because the guy had a black motorcycle helmet over his head, with the shield down, which was the part that made Widow a little uneasy.

The primate part of Widow's brain didn't sound the alarms, but it was just below a code red. Caution was strictly enforced.

Widow kept his eyes on the guy. Even though he couldn't see the guy's eyes, he was certain that the guy was looking back at him as well.

After another long second, the light was still green, and the motorcyclist was still there, staring. Then he looked right, looked left, and turned left, headed away from Widow and Eva.

Eva asked, "What now?"

Widow watched the motorcyclist ride away and turned to her. Looking at her, it hit him why the guy on the motorcycle was staring so hard. Eva was still in that little dress, shivering, even with Widow's sweater over her. Although there was no way the motorcyclist could see the display on top, it was all covered. But he could see her legs. And these were no bony stumps.

Eva's legs looked as if they were strong enough to allow her to leap over parked cars. If she had been taller, she could dunk a basketball easily.

So, of course, the motorcyclist was staring at them. There was something to see.

Widow said, "We need to get some new clothes."

"New?"

"Different. Anyway. You're shaking."

"I'm fine."

"You're shivering."

She said nothing to that.

"Besides, the guys from the hotel will more than likely describe us from what we're wearing. Best to change out of these clothes."

Eva looked him up and down and said, "You think they'll describe you by what you're wearing?"

"No. But for you, they will."

Just then it seemed to dawn on her. She was noticeable. She knew that.

"Where are we going to find clothes at this hour?"

Widow shrugged.

"We could go to my apartment. It's far, though."

"Where?"

"Brooklyn."

Widow thought for a second.

"Nah. We can't go all the way to Brooklyn. Besides, whoever killed Edward probably knows where you live. We should avoid that for now."

"I wouldn't have any clothes for you, anyway."

Although Widow didn't know the exact time of night, he knew it was late, or very early, depending on your point of view.

"What time will your handler be in her office?"

"Probably, eight a.m., at the latest. But why?"

"I think we should have a talk with her. We can do it in the morning. We can stop and buy some clothes on the way. There's bound to be a department store opening somewhere by then."

"Widow, I can't go to her."

He stayed quiet.

"I've been gone for two days. Don't you think she'll want to know why?"

"Then, we tell her."

"I can't tell her I was held against my will."

"Why not? It's the truth."

"I am trying to defect, remember?"

"You don't need to tell her that part."

"What exactly do I tell her?"

Widow said, "We can figure that out. At least I don't see any other choice. Unless you know where to find Farmer, I think we are out of options. Edward is dead."

Eva shook her head and said, "I don't know where to find him."

Widow nodded, changed the subject, and asked, "You like coffee?"

"American coffee?"

He shrugged.

"Not really."

"I'm sure they'll have coffee from south of the border."

A confused expression came over Eva's face.

"South of the border? New Jersey?" Widow smiled and said.

"I like Turkish coffee."

Widow thought back to the last time he was passing through Istanbul. It had been a mission, like so many others. Undercover. And it included a stint sharing a hotel room with a pair of SEALs that he'd never met before, never seen since. They were doing something and waiting for something and passing the time with small talk, deep enough to be interesting, vague enough to keep their anonymity. All three had used names that were aliases, but Widow couldn't be sure about that. He knew for a fact that he had given them a fake name. He figured they had done the same.

He wasn't there to investigate them, but they all had the same mission. And they were told to keep it a secret.

While in Istanbul, he had the local coffee. He remembered they had to boil it in a pot. That was how it was made at home.

It wasn't bad. It wasn't good. To him, it was okay.

Maybe it was better at a café. He wouldn't know, because he never made it to any local cafés.

"Not sure we'll find that at this hour, but we should find somewhere. Get some breakfast and some coffee."

Eva shrugged.

"Let's get away from here."

"Lead the way."

Widow turned inward, left foot first, right foot followed.

Three paces forward, and Eva reached out, took Widow's hand. Hers was cold. He felt that and immediately figured she was trying to warm up. But he wasn't sure. Maybe she was trying to blend in. Her training might've kicked in and told her they should act like a couple.

By the end of the block, he was more confident that was her reasoning because she lifted his arm and ducked underneath it and came up on the other side. His arm draped over her, thick and hanging too long, like a gorilla hugging a spider monkey.

33

THE MAN in black sat on the motorcycle, a couple of blocks away from where he had driven after he had seen the large stranger that he didn't recognize and the woman that he did.

His helmet was off and under his arm. The bike's engine still hummed idly, and he was still sitting on it. It was on the side of the road in an empty parking space with a meter that still took quarters. Not something that was found too much in the city anymore because New York had pulled up those old metal meters and replaced them simply with a sign and a five-digit number intended to work with a smartphone application that allowed the commuter to open, type in the number and the time that he wanted to purchase. Then the app would charge a preset credit card for the amount.

The man in black didn't use such an app, nor did he have quarters for the meter. Nor did he intend to park there.

But he could see the couple walking together in the distance. He was close enough to see them, but far enough back to avoid detection should they look in his direction.

During normal business hours in New York City, he would've lost them easily. But during this time of night, on this side of town, he could keep up with them with little effort.

He set the helmet down on the fuel tank of the bike in front of him and unzipped his jacket. He reached in—right hand. He brushed past a gun in a shoulder rig, no silencer attached, but he had one squeezed into a tight pocket on the chest strap of the holster rig, in case he needed to be silent.

The jacket had two inside pockets. One was velcroed shut, made to hold a cell phone.

He unzipped it and jerked out his phone.

It unlocked as he pressed his thumb down on the home button and called the only number that he had used since he'd arrived in New York.

The phone rang and rang. The person who owned the number was asleep. So he knew it would take a minute before he got an answer.

On the fourth ring, he heard a groggy voice answer.

"Yes?" the voice said, not upset about being woken up, but calm and collected. Still, with surprise, because the call was unscheduled and the man in black was known for being punctual and methodical. He was a by-the-book sort if there was a book on killing people in a cold-blooded fashion, and one existed. He knew because he had been taught from such a book, back in his days of training and statecraft.

The man in black said, "Sorry to wake you."

"What's happened?"

"I'm not sure, but she's out."

"What do you mean?"

"Karpov."

The voice on the other line paused a beat.

"She's out? Freed?"

"Yes."

"You're sure?" the voice asked.

"I'm staring at her. Right now."

"Where?"

"Edward's place."

The voice asked, "What about him?"

"Eliminated."

"Does she know?"

"I'm sure she does. I watched them go in and come out."

"Them?"

"She's with some guy."

"What guy?"

The man in black breathed heavily over the phone, leaving an air of menace. The Listener, on the other end, heard him.

The man in black said, "I don't know. Just some guy. A big guy. Tattoos all over his arms."

"Russian tattoos?"

"Don't know. Don't think so. But I wasn't close enough to see them."

The voice on the phone said, "I don't know who that is. Must be some friend of hers or something."

"I don't know."

"How the hell did she get out?"

"Maybe her friend helped her."

"Maybe. That means she might know about what Farmer was planning."

The man in black stayed quiet.

"Where are they now?"

"Upper East Side."

"You know where they are going?"

"Only one place I can think of," the man in black said, and then he told the person on the other end with only two words.

"Eva's handler."

The voice said nothing.

"Want me to kill them?"

"No. Not yet. We need to know more."

"Want me to intercept them?"

The Listener said, "Not yet. Wait for now. See where they go. They may lead us to her handler. A bonus. Call me if anything changes."

The Listener hung up the phone, and the man in black slipped his phone back in his inside pocket, near his gun. He pulled down the visor on his helmet and watched the Russian spy and the stranger.

34

Eva HELD a coffee mug of cheap hot tea as if her life depended on it. Even with Widow's sweater pulled over her, the tight dress underneath didn't provide much warmth. Greasy spoons are notoriously cold all day, all night. Widow figured it had something to do with a happy staff over happy customers. The wait staff, the kitchen staff, and whoever else worked back there moved around a lot. They brought this out and took that back. They hauled heavy items from way back in the walk-in cooler and stocked items and took out heavy trashcans. Naturally, they were always hot.

Widow and Eva had originally gone on the search for a bakery or a doughnut shop that was open early enough for them to grab a doughnut and some coffee. Their search took them to an all-night greasy spoon first, which was just fine with Widow. He liked these places.

Nowadays, lots of doughnut shops and bakeries are parts of franchises. They were restaurants designed to look quaint, but truthfully they had bigger corporate faces—not all of them, but many, and many here in the city.

Widow was glad to find a diner locally owned instead.

Eva wasn't interested in coffee; she said it wasn't her thing. She asked the waitress for some kind of herbal green tea crap with three different names. All were plants that Widow had heard of before. All sounded healthy, in that overboard kind of way.

It was the last nail in the coffin of a fantasy that was birthed in his head about him being her kind of guy.

Eva was a refined woman and a Russian spy, which Widow wasn't sure meant that she had been trained to be refined or if she had been born that way, reared that way.

Either answer didn't matter, because she was refined now. And a refined woman wouldn't be interested in a man like him.

Widow said, "You sure you want nothing to eat?"

She looked up from her tea, and he stared into her eyes. There was something there. A sense of desperation, Widow figured. Like she was part scared, part worried, and part completely confused, all of it adding up to utter desperation.

She said, "No, thanks. I have no appetite."

"You really should eat something."

She stayed quiet.

"In the SEALs, we say if you want to eat an elephant, eat it one bite at a time."

She stared at him blankly, which was a better expression than her desperate look. He guessed.

"What does that have to do with eating?"

Widow shrugged and said, "Nothing."

"What the hell does it mean, then?"

"It's a metaphor."

"You mean idiom," she said.

He shrugged again, his shoulders fell, and he took a pull from his coffee.

"Same thing. I suppose," he said.

"So what does it mean? Idioms are strange to me. English has too many."

"I guess we have a lot of them."

"What's it mean?"

"It just means that if you want to achieve something, something huge, like an elephant, then you have to take small steps toward it. I guess. That's what I always thought it meant."

"Makes sense."

Widow took another large pull from his coffee and finished it, and put the mug down on the edge of the table. An old trick Widow had learned years earlier. Put the mug down on the edge of the table, and the waitress thinks it's empty, and she comes by to refill it, like a white flag of surrender. He figured.

Eva stared at him and looked away, toward a group of four older ladies who walked in from the cold. All white, grandmotherly types. All wore their Sunday best, which made sense because, to them, it was early morning. And old ladies across the globe often go to church on Sunday morning.

Right then, Widow realized something that he should have thought of an hour earlier when they were standing in Edward's apartment. He literally face-palmed himself.

"What is it?" Eva asked.

"Today's Sunday."

"Yeah?"

"Sunday."

Widow explained what he was thinking, but he didn't have to. She got it.

Eva said, "She won't be there today."

They had planned to go see her handler, a lawyer who worked near the United Nations building, but law firms aren't normally open on

Sunday. That was basically true all over the world, not just in New York City.

"Shit," she said.

"Do you know where she lives?"

"Nope."

"She doesn't trust you very much."

"She doesn't trust anyone. She's been in America for a long time. I guess there's a reason for that."

"I guess so."

"What now?"

"Do you have a phone number for her?"

"Of course."

"I guess we call her then. Have her meet us somewhere."

"Okay. When do we call her?"

Widow looked over Eva's shoulder, searched the room for a wall clock, but didn't see one.

He saw a waitress look over at him while he looked around. She saw his empty coffee mug, and she stepped back behind the counter, picked up a pot of black coffee, and walked over to their table.

She stopped and poured coffee into his mug. Then she stepped back and picked up the empty plate that Widow had eaten a breakfast meal off. The plate looked licked clean, which he hadn't actually done, but he had used a fork to scoop, scrape, and shovel up every drop of eggs and hash browns.

The waitress asked, "Ready for the check now?"

Widow said, "We are. And what time is it?"

The waitress pulled a handwritten check out of her apron, placed it upside down on the tabletop, center edge. Then she fidgeted with a loose wristwatch and stared at it.

"It's almost five in the morning."

"Thanks."

The waitress walked away, and Widow took the check, studied the amount, and shoveled out the correct bills for it, as well as an additional five-dollar bill as a tip.

"It's too early to call now. Let's wait a little longer and call her."

"She's probably still not going to be awake."

"Doesn't matter. We'll wake her up. This is important. Besides, you're not going back."

"What do you mean?"

"You can't go back to your old life now. She's gonna figure out what you were planning, whether or not you tell her."

The look of worry overcame her other facial expressions.

She said, "Widow, they'll kill me. I can't tell her."

"You're safe now. Don't worry. You're not going back with her. She won't tell Moscow that you were planning to defect. Trust me."

"How do you know?"

"If she's been here for twenty years, then she won't want to be exposed. We threaten to tell that she's here. That she's a Russian spy."

She nodded and listened.

"And I don't mean we tell the Feds. We threaten to tell the *New York Times*. Her law firm must have a website. I bet she has a profile there with a headshot. She's probably got a LinkedIn profile too. We take her information and her photos and threaten to give them to the *Times*. They love stories like this. Her face will be blasted all over the place. The Feds will deport her. She'll be forced to return to Moscow, where she doesn't want to be."

Eva nodded, said, "That could work. I know for a fact she's terrified of losing her life here. She loves her status. In Moscow, they'll have her sitting behind a desk. If she's lucky."

"See. We can do this. We can figure this out."

"I'm not worried about me that much. I'm worried about my father. What if they have him?"

Widow said, "We don't know that for sure."

But he knew it for sure. If she had been abducted for two days and this Farmer guy was supposed to arrange a meeting with her father on board his submarine, it had probably already happened.

Farmer had already shown that he had the manpower. Four well-trained guys with high-tech equipment had revealed themselves to Widow already, back at the Plaza.

Plus, the dead guy that Eva had been dating, the turncoat. Whoever had killed him wasn't an amateur. Widow pictured Edward's dead body in his mind. The guy was shorter than Widow, but he had been no kind of slouch. He could pass as a New York firefighter, as he had pretended to be. His dead body showed that he had spent some time in the gym.

The killer had used a garrote. Widow was sure about that because of the deep wounds around Edward's neck.

Garrotes weren't the kind of weapons that could be bought at a hardware store or even a gun store or any store. Maybe it could be ordered off the internet. Or it could have been homemade.

Either way, the person who used it was strong and knew exactly what he was doing. Widow figured that the only way the killer could have strangled Edward like that was with a quick snag of the wire over Edward's head, from behind, then a fast turn from the feet and hips and a pull in the opposite direction, taking Edward off his feet.

The killer had wrenched him over his back, facing the opposite direction.

Strangling someone with a garrote is very difficult. Besides taking immense strength and coordination, it also has a huge risk factor when the victim has his hands and feet free.

Edward would've been flailing around and struggling to fight back. That's not what you want when using a garrote.

The killer would want him immobilized, and the only way to do that was to tie him up or to twist and hoist him over the killer's back like a guy with a meat hook towing a heavy chunk of beef.

Widow imagined the entire scene, and it was brutal. Edward had gone out with a violent death that Widow didn't want to experience.

Eva asked, "What are you thinking about?"

"I think we gotta get you into warmer clothes soon," he lied.

"I'm okay for now. I've worn less in colder places."

Widow smiled, and they sat there, waiting for the dawn.

35

THE WATERS off the Eastern Seaboard were cold, but the crew inside Karpov's hijacked Russian submarine hadn't known that by the sense of touch. They knew it from being educated about it because not one of them had ever been this close to the United States before.

Technically, they weren't breaking international law, which stated that the boundary between a nation's shores and international waters was universally accepted as twelve nautical miles. They weren't in violation of this law. However, the United States Navy was known for suspecting any foreign vessel that came anywhere within double that amount. And for Russian submarines, with nuclear-tipped missiles on board, the number of nautical miles was triple, if not more.

Farmer waited for his man to give the go-ahead, and then he climbed the ladder, past the tower, and up to the surface.

Karpov was still standing against an unmanned station on the bridge. The redheaded soldier had assigned one of his guys to watch over Karpov.

Karpov remembered the redheaded soldier saying, "If he flinches, shoot him."

Ever since then, the soldier watching him had done nothing else but blink a few times. Karpov knew for sure that's all he had done because he watched the soldier in exchange. He studied the man's patterns, trying to discern a rhythm to his standing there, breathing, and guarding Karpov.

Farmer had taken away Karpov's gun and his bridge crew's weapons as well. And of course, Travkin had gone overboard and was dead. But there was one last handgun that Farmer and his men didn't find. It was in Karpov's quarters. It was an old black-and-brown US Army issued Colt 1911. Supposedly left in Eastern Berlin by a US paratrooper on some covert mission that Karpov didn't know the details of.

The gun had been given to him as a gift by a now-dead Russian commander that he used to know.

He had the gun encased in a box with a glass lid. It was on display in his quarters, on the back wall. There were seven bullets lined up at the bottom of the case on the red velvet behind the gun.

Colt made good-quality guns. He knew that. If the origins of his Colt 1911 were true, then it was over seventy years old. Would it even fire after all this time? Under normal circumstances, probably not. But one of his favorite stress relievers was to take out that 1911 and polish it and clean it and oil it.

Although he had never fired it, not with live ammunition, he had dry fired it before—plenty of times. And it seemed to work.

If only he could get to it.

36

FARMER LOOKED AT HIS WATCH, which luckily was waterproof because the waves ripped and collided with the bow of the submarine, splashing over it with powerful, quick gushes of white-capped water.

In one wrong moment, a wave could have swept him and the redheaded soldier off the bow and into the Atlantic.

They both held onto the railing above the hatch that led down to the bridge. The water splashed hard enough to send droplets beating across their faces.

Farmer's blue windbreaker rippled around him from the intense icy wind blowing off the ocean surface.

He took several deep breaths, trying to adjust his lungs to the cold air.

Then he pulled a sat phone up from a long cord that hung around his neck. The cord secured it so that it wouldn't get blown away. With one hand on the rail and one hand on the keypad, he dialed a number from memory, starting the call that was slightly early.

Still, the recipients of the call would answer because they were already in play. And they worked for him. They had better be awake and waiting, even though in New York City it was early in the morning.

Farmer listened as the satellite phone whirred and rang. The connection was there, but the sound quality was closer to a CB radio than a ten-thousand-dollar phone stolen from the US military.

The phone rang and rang and rang. No one answered.

Farmer waited, looked at the redheaded soldier.

No one answered.

He hung up.

"What?" the redhead asked.

Farmer shrugged and said, "No answer."

"Try again."

Farmer tried again. Same result. Same frustration.

"They are supposed to answer. They know that."

"What now?" the redheaded guy asked.

Farmer didn't answer. Instead, he dialed another number and put the phone to his ear, listened to the ring.

A voice answered that wasn't asleep. The voice sounded rested and awake, but frustrated as well.

"We have a problem," Farmer said.

"The girl is free," the Listener answered. The Listener already knew the circumstances.

"What?"

"She is free. Your boys messed up."

"How do you know that?"

"My guy. He saw her. On the street, outside Edward's apartment."

Farmer asked, "Why was he at Edward's?"

"Why do you think?"

A pause and a cold breath exited Farmer's lips.

He said, "You didn't need to kill him."

"Apparently, I did. I'm tying up loose ends. Your loose ends."

"How the hell did she get free? My guys aren't answering."

"She escaped."

"Impossible. She had four former Special Forces guys with her."

"She got away from them."

Farmer repeated the same protest of disbelief.

The Listener said, "She had help."

"What help?"

"I don't know. Some stranger."

"Who is he?"

"I just told you. He's a stranger."

Farmer said nothing.

The Listener said, "Don't worry. My guy is watching them."

"He needs to retrieve her. Now."

"We can't do that. She's out in the open, and we don't know who this guy is. What if he's FBI? We need to know who knows what first."

"Have your guy pick them both up. Interrogate him."

The Listener said, "Not that simple. It's New York City. There are witnesses everywhere."

"So, what then?"

"Don't worry. He'll get them both soon enough. They're bound to go somewhere more private."

"What about the operation? We need her to make Karpov cooperate."

"Does he know that we have her, yet?"

"I'm sure he's put it together. I wanted to have him hear her voice before I threatened him. Better impact that way."

The Listener said, "Time to change your tactics. Make the threat so we can stay on schedule."

"Karpov is a tough man. A smart man. He won't give up the launch code without proof of life."

The Listener said nothing to that. Instead, he said, "Just do it. My guy will have them soon, and we'll prove it to Captain Karpov if he so wishes. We have little time left. I want that missile in the air on schedule, Farmer."

"I'll have it done."

"Good. Don't give me your location over the line. But are you within the preferred striking distance?"

"Almost."

"Good. Get moving then."

"I'll call you back later."

Farmer hung up the phone.

The Listener clicked the cell phone off and laid it down on a desk, tried to relax. A yawn. A stretch. And the Listener was more alert again.

The operation had had a couple of hiccups, but it was going to happen. And no stranger or Russian was going to stop it.

37

WIDOW AND EVA ended up walking around for over an hour. They had left the diner, and Widow had taken a full cup of coffee to go. He'd finished it long ago, and they had to stop once more at an early morning coffee stand on the side of the street to get another coffee for him.

Eva kept her hands free but had them wrapped up inside Widow's sweater.

She stayed close to him as they walked, partially for warmth, and partially for other reasons that he didn't completely dismiss, but also wasn't ready to believe were true.

The sun had come up, and usual morning activities had begun.

First, they saw the early risers hitting the streets. They saw the morning joggers coming out of their apartments. They saw the first shifts of first responders coming on and then the third shifts signing off. They saw fresh-faced cops driving their routes, getting coffee, preparing for the day.

They saw twice the number of stores and diners opening up. The streetlights switched off all at once, and the birds chirped.

Widow and Eva found themselves in the East Village, walking in circles after a while.

"Widow, I don't think department stores are open on Sunday morning. I think most of them don't open till noon, maybe eleven, but not this early."

"I'm sure we'll find something. Have faith."

Eva said, "You know we've walked this street before?"

"I know. See that van right there?"

She looked. There was a rented yellow panel van, parked in front of a small clothing store that looked half empty.

"What about it?"

"That's what we're looking for."

"What is it?"

They were coming up on the parked van from about ten yards away.

"It's an opportunity."

Widow led the way, and they walked over to a small store that was about the size of the First Lady's closet and not much bigger. The windows were tinted black enough to be the shades on a Secret Service agent's sunglasses. There was no visible sign for the store, only where it used to be above the door. There was the sun-bleached outline of letters. It was a name that Widow couldn't completely spell, because some letters were undecipherable. Not that he was trying too hard.

The name of the store wasn't important to him. What was important was what they sold.

"Widow?"

He pointed at a handwritten paper taped to the door and read it to her.

"They're going out of business."

"Do you think they'll sell us clothes?"

"I'm sure of it," Widow said, as they both saw stacks of open boxes with folded clothing hanging out.

They were greeted by a young couple. Both tattooed. Both had huge smiles on their faces. Both were busy moving things and packing things and telling two other guys to pack this or move that to the van. Hired help, Widow figured.

* * *

THE MAN in black circled past the parked van and the stranger and Eva twice. They had been in the store for almost an hour.

They were shopping for something. He knew that. But he was confused as to why?

He ended up parking down the street and waiting.

Finally, the stranger appeared first, and then Eva. And he knew exactly what they were doing because they both came out with new clothes on, which he figured was only a tactical decision for the girl. She hadn't been wearing any kind of field clothing, after all.

He watched them shake hands with a young couple, and then they left, headed for First Avenue and moving north.

The man in black started up his bike and followed as slowly as he could, staying back, staying way back because he knew the Russian was trained and obviously, the stranger must have been as well. At least he must have been dangerous.

He stayed as close to them as he could without being spotted until they came to the entrance to a metro station and ducked down the stairs into New York City's underbelly, which meant he had to follow them on foot.

He parked his bike, abandoning it in front of a fire hydrant. Illegal he knew, but what choice did he have? This was New York City. Sunday morning. The weather was crisp, but warming up with the sun, and early morning pedestrians were coming out to enjoy it. There was no parking available, and he would lose them if he searched for some.

He followed them down the steps into the tunnels of New York's subway system.

38

Eva wore all black.

They had told the couple that they needed some very comfortable clothes. When asked how comfortable, Widow had responded that it should be durable, comfortable, warm, and good for "night work."

The man had chuckled out loud to this comment, even though Widow was serious.

They played it off, and the guy helped Widow, while his wife helped Eva. It had turned out that the couple had moved to New York City with a dream of expanding their little shop into a franchise and a clothing brand.

The woman designed the clothes, and the man had obviously been in love with her about as much as Widow had ever seen in a married couple.

It also turned out that she was three months pregnant, and sales weren't going according to plan. However, the new addition to their family meant that neither of them was sad that they were being forced to close the shop and move back to Kansas or Indiana or wherever they had said that they were from.

Widow ended up in all black as well. Black jeans. Black t-shirt under a black hoodie that zipped up and had space in the pockets for one of the Maxim guns. The other he gave back to Eva, who stuffed it into a black bag that she had purchased.

The bag slung over her back like a backpack; only she had informed Widow it was a purse. He didn't argue.

They purchased their metro passes from a machine and entered the underground system.

"How do we get to the right street?" Widow asked.

She shot him a questionable look.

"What?"

"You don't know?"

"I'm not a local."

"Still, doesn't everyone know the metro in New York?"

"I don't. I've only used it once."

"What do you use, Uber?"

"I've used that once."

"How? You don't have a phone?"

"Someone else's phone."

"Old girlfriend?" she asked, and led him into the small crowd of commuters as they crisscrossed people going either.

"No. An FBI agent actually."

"FBI? Were you FBI?"

"I said it was someone else's Uber. She was an FBI agent."

Eva said nothing else about it and pointed down the tunnel.

"We're taking the sixth train. To Grand Central Station and then we'll transfer to head toward the United Nations."

Widow nodded and felt her warm hand take his. She led him farther, which distracted him, and he didn't see the man in black following behind them.

39

THE LISTENER SAT behind an office desk in a building that wasn't as busy as it was during the week because it was Sunday. The plan didn't include being in the office today. The plan had been to deal with everything from home since that was a quiet place with no family members around. No distractions. No significant other.

The Listener had no real friends here, anyway. Although there were plenty of colleagues who thought they held the title of friend. But to the Listener, that's all they were, colleagues—nothing more and nothing less.

It had been time for Russia to return to the good old days.

The Listener, the man in black, and Farmer, and the men at their command were dedicated to this.

The Listener had military training and counterintelligence training, and experience to boot. Most Americans that came and went throughout the Listener's daily life had no idea what it meant to live back when the Soviet Union was strong and powerful. Back when it and the United States were great enemies. That was when everything was great. That was the time to be alive. That was when it meant something to be a warrior, fighting for good, fighting for your country.

Today, globalization had changed everything. In today's world, the enemy was also your friend.

Russia and the United States were allies, who covertly waged war against each other, all at the same time. What the hell was that? What kind of state of affairs was this?

The Listener and the man in black and CIA agent Farmer were all on the same page on this front.

They were all tired of the world being so weak and gray.

The balance of power was gone. All three of them knew that. They knew that there was no more "balance."

The scales had been tipped in favor of the United States long ago. There was no enemy to fight. No opposition.

Politicians in DC and Moscow went on and on about terrorists. Terrorists were the new enemies. The militaries of both countries must fight terrorists. But what kind of enemy was that? What kind of war can be fought against so-called soldiers, most of whom can't even read?

It was a slap in the face to the Listener. It was a shot to the heart.

Experience told the Listener that most so-called enemy terrorists didn't even know the difference between right and left.

Afghanistan was a country that both the United States and Russia had fought in for decades. The Russians got there first, but both had been there for what seemed like forever. Fighting there was a complete waste of time. Most of the enemies they fought there knew nothing about warfare. They had little technology. They had no grasp of world affairs. They were below under-educated.

To the Listener and the rest of the operation heads, what they were doing was a necessary action.

The Listener looked at the clock and date on a cell phone screen. It was November ninth. It was a Sunday, and the time was nearing eight in the morning.

It was the day of the anniversary. It was the day of a restart of hostility between Russia and the US. It was the day that the Listener had been planning for a long time.

The Listener texted the man in black.

"Where are they now?" The message read.

A moment later, the message was answered with: "Going to subway. Headed to the United Nations is my guess."

The Listener read the message and took a sip of coffee from a mug on the desk. Then responded with, "No. They're headed to a law office nearby."

A moment later, there was another messaged response.

"You sure?"

The Listener typed back, "It's where her handler works. It's good. It means the stranger is a nobody."

The man in black typed back, "How so?"

The Listener responded with, "If he was a Fed, they wouldn't be going to the Russian spy handler for help. He has no backup. He really is a nobody."

And then the Listener paused a beat and sent another text that read: "Get a photo of them."

A couple of moments later, a message came back with three images attached. They weren't the best quality, all from a distance, with people moving in and out of frame. And all were taken with the zoom on a cell phone, which isn't the best resolution to begin with.

The Listener studied them. He looked hard at the stranger's face. A feeling of partial recognition, a stir of familiarity, and a sense of the kind of man the stranger was—came to mind. But he had no tangible memory of the stranger.

The Listener got more of a feeling of déjà vu. The Listener had never met the stranger. But something was identifiable about the stranger.

The Listener knew exactly what it was. The stranger had a long military career, possibly more.

Another text came through. It read: "Want me to retire them?"

The Listener typed: "Yes," but paused a beat and then backspaced and typed over it. The text read: "Forget them. We know where they're going. Go to the hotel. Wake up Farmer's men. We might need them. Be careful."

A moment later, the man in black responded with: "You too."

40

WIDOW AND EVA got off at the Grand Central Terminal, and Widow pointed out a payphone and reminded Eva that they should call her handler and get her to meet them. At first, the handler protested because it was a Sunday. In the end, she gave in and agreed to meet.

Afterward, Eva hung up the phone, and they exited the terminal and walked east down Forty-Second Avenue toward the river, where they turned at the United Nations building. Widow took in the row of flags and admired the building that had been built with good intentions. He was suddenly reminded of the cliché that the road to hell is paved by them.

Eva ignored it, probably because she had been there and seen that.

The temperature was warming up a little from light jacket to long-sleeve weather.

Widow asked, "Do you normally meet with her at her office?"

"No. I've been there before. People think she helps me with my green card. She helps a lot of Russians. She's an immigration lawyer. It's a perfect cover."

"Are all of her clients Russian spies?"

Eva smiled, said, "Of course. All of them are just like me. Beautiful seductresses here to take over your country."

Widow tittered but embraced the thought, anyway. He realized that if there were thousands of Russian spies that were just like her, the men in this city were in deep trouble.

They pressed on until they were close, but Widow never stopped checking the surrounding buildings, windows, entrances, and sidewalks. He looked at as many faces as he could of pedestrians, both on foot and on bicycles. He looked at the drivers of cars and at people sitting on benches, reading newspapers. He took particular interest in anyone using a cell phone. There was no one who stood out to him as out of place. No detectable surveillance. No men with earpieces. No dark, unmarked vans. Nothing.

Of course, in a place like New York City, Widow couldn't be sure. No one could. It was too crowded. Too many faces to vet. Vetting everyone that you come across on the streets of New York as a non-threat was impossible.

They came to the law offices, which were in a building complex with other firms and offices. The building was ten stories of brushed steel and shiny glass.

"This is it," Eva said.

"When is she going to get here?"

"Soon. She said twenty minutes."

"She must live nearby then."

"I guess. We wait then."

"Is there a café in the lobby?"

"There's a little cart thing."

Widow smiled, said, "Let's get some coffee."

"You drink a lot of coffee!"

He shrugged.

"Aren't you scared of a heart attack?"

"No. A beating heart isn't likely to have a heart attack."

"But isn't that coffee making it beat faster?"

"Better to beat fast than slow."

"Or not at all, I guess," she said.

They walked through a set of automatic doors and waved at a guard sitting behind a desk. This one was more alert and friendly than the one from Edward's building, which reminded Widow of the guard that they'd left duct-taped inside Edward's apartment. He wondered how long it would be before someone found him. He would have to remember to make an anonymous call to the NYPD about him when this was all done, if it was ever done.

They waved back at the guard, who seemed to recognize Eva, and smiled at her.

"He remembers me," she said.

"How could he ever forget?" Widow muttered under his breath.

"What was that?"

"Nothing. Where's the coffee?"

Eva pointed to an offshoot of the lobby, and they walked down it to grab a coffee and wait for her contact to arrive.

41

THE MAN in black kicked the guy that he knew to be in charge of the babysitting mission. The guy didn't budge. He lay on the floor, unconscious.

"Wake up!" the man in black said.

No movement.

One snored loudly. Another tossed and turned. All four of them had rapid eye movements, like they were in deep dreams.

The man in black went to the bathroom to find the team's black kit, which was where they kept the sedatives, needles, and smelling salts.

It wasn't in the bathroom. But he found signs of where the Russian girl had been kept. He wondered why they didn't have eyes on her at all times.

They were amateurs. For the first time, he questioned the Listener's logic in hiring them. Then again, the operation that they were running didn't lend itself to having a variety of options. They couldn't just ask any old mercenary to take part.

He searched the rest of the room and found the kit and, in it, the smelling salts.

He cracked the bottle open and shoved it under the nose of the man in charge of this group.

A loud gasp, followed by violent wrenching and coughing, erupted from the guy. His eyes darted open, and a look of utter confusion spilled across his face, which lasted for a whole minute. Then the realization hit him.

He sat up.

"Where is she? There was a guy. Some guy came in. He took us all down."

"Forget about that. I know all of it."

"Where are they?"

"At her handler's office."

The leader looked up at the man in black and didn't know him.

"Who are you?"

"I'm the one to set you straight. Now wake up the others. We don't have a lot of time."

"I'll make this up. We'll make it up."

"Don't worry. You'll have your chance. Now wake them up."

The man in black handed the rest of the smelling salts bottle to him. The guy took it and stood up, wobbly.

The man in black asked, "Where are your guns? Did he take them?"

The leader nodded.

"You got backups?"

"There are MP5s under the bed."

The man in black bent down and pulled out a large carry-on case. He unzipped it and found a stack of silenced MP5s. Right off the bat, he was embarrassed that they had them stacked inside the case with nothing holding them down. They looked used and worn and not very well maintained.

How unprofessional, he thought.

It took about twenty minutes to get all the men awake and on their feet and standing up straight.

The man in black messaged the Listener, "They're ready."

A moment later, the Listener messaged back with only an address and the name of a law firm. Then one more line of text. It read: "Take the girl alive. No witnesses."

42

THE INSIDE of the lobby was too cold for the weather outside the building, in Widow's opinion, but lobbies in emotionless steel office parks were like that in a lot of cities. They were faceless and callous and unremarkable. The management liked to keep them cold, so the workers didn't fall asleep. Office park management was like any other corporate management; it was all about productivity.

Suddenly, Widow didn't miss having a job.

Eva left him in a tight corner, near a generic plant and a small coffee table, to enjoy his coffee alone. She went to the restroom down the hall. So far, he hadn't enjoyed his coffee at all because it came in a little paper cup, and the damn thing was four bucks. That was more expensive than the Tall at Starbucks, which was the standard for overpriced coffee.

Whatever, he thought, and took a swig. Might as well drink it before it gets cold.

Eva was gone for more than five minutes. He'd nearly finished the coffee before she finally returned.

She stopped at the same café and bought a doughnut, which was a far cry from her previous statement of not being hungry. Apparently, she had been starving because she scarfed the entire thing by the time she sat down.

Widow smiled and asked, "Hungry?"

She laughed and smiled at him, mouth open. He saw nothing but white powdered sugar and her teeth.

"Was that a doughnut?"

"Yeah, a powdered sugar doughnut."

"Isn't that a lot of sugar?" he asked.

She shrugged and smiled so widely that powder was tumbling out of her mouth.

He reached over and handed her the napkin that he had been given.

"Here."

"Oh. Sorry." She took it and wiped her mouth.

Widow said nothing.

Eva finished chewing and swallowing, but kept the napkin handy. Then she asked, "So, Jack Widow, you married?"

"No way."

She made an audible, "Hmm." And a gesture like she was trying to think or make a life decision.

"What?"

"Why did you answer like that?"

"Like what?"

She said, "No way." Only she said it theatrically, like she was doing a dramatic reenactment of the whole thing. Then she reached across and poked him in the abdomen.

Widow didn't wonder if she was flirting with him. That was obvious, even to the one-tracked mind that he considered himself to be. What he wondered was if she was doing it on purpose, or if it was Russian seductress training.

He stayed quiet for a moment, and then he said, "I didn't mean it negatively about marriage. It was just a reaction."

"So, have you ever been married?"

Widow shook his head.

"Me neither."

They fell silent for a moment. Widow finished his coffee. He thought about a refill but saw a sign that said: "No Refills. Or Refunds."

He wouldn't shell out another four bucks for another little coffee that wasn't very good to begin with.

Just then, a woman a little older than Widow walked in. She wore a sweater that had a Russian university written on it, one that Widow couldn't pronounce because it wasn't in English. He knew it was a university sweater by the typical design. Although he supposed he could have been wrong. The sweater was red with gold piping and a single stripe.

The woman had thick, long hair, dark with thin gray streaks. It was pulled back. She had a dark complexion. No jewelry. No rings. No necklaces. The only piece of jewelry was an expensive-looking watch with a plain black leather band and silver face that might have been real silver.

She looked straight at Eva and then right at Widow and waved them to come over.

Eva said, "Come on. That's her."

Widow stood up after Eva and stayed several feet behind to throw his coffee cup away. He caught up to them after the women hugged like old friends.

They spoke to each other in Russian, something that Widow didn't catch, nor would he have understood anyway.

Then Eva turned back to Widow and introduced him. She introduced the lawyer as Mina Putin, and then she insisted that there was no relation to the president of Russia.

Widow didn't doubt her claims, nor did he rule out that she was lying either. Putin was a common surname in Russia.

After a quick moment of shaking hands and smiling, Putin asked them to follow her up to her office. Before they could go to where the elevators were, Widow stopped dead in his tracks.

Eva asked, "Widow, what's wrong?"

He glanced at her and then at a large plastic doorframe that was hooked up to wires that vanished into the guard desk. It was set up between them and the elevators that they had to walk through in order to get there.

He stepped up and leaned into her and whispered, "Metal detector."

"Oh. Step over there. One second, Mina."

Widow stepped back to the lobby, and Eva followed. Then Eva passed him and headed back toward the bathroom, out of the line of sight of the guard at the desk. She surreptitiously drew the Maxim 9 out of her jeans and slipped it to him.

She said, "Take them to the bathroom and hide them behind a toilet tank. Then come up and meet us on floor six. It's the last office down the hall."

Widow nodded and left her and stepped into the bathroom to hide the weapons as instructed, which reminded him he was taking orders from Eva and not questioning them.

43

THE MAN in black stepped off his motorcycle, which was in the parking garage underneath the Russian lawyer's office park, alongside a white panel van. The doors to the panel van opened, and the four mercenaries working for Farmer hopped out. They were armed with four MP5SDs. They were cocked and locked and ready to go. A sight that the man in black was glad to see.

Even though that might have all been a little overkill, they had all been defeated by one man, so he could forgive their eagerness for redemption.

The leader of the mercs nodded at the man in black, and he led them toward a set of elevators. They almost made it to the elevators when a voice from down a few car spaces called out, "Hey. Who are you guys?"

The man in black turned to see a young security guard walking toward them. He had a flashlight in one hand. It was switched off, and the man in black wondered why he was even holding it. He must have intended to use it as a club if need be.

The man in black said nothing. He didn't talk their way past him. He simply reached in his coat and drew his SIG Sauer P220, not silenced, and he took aim, slowly and carefully.

The guard stopped and stared on.

"Wait! Wait!" he called out.

The man in black paused, closed one eye, and aimed down the sights. He wondered if he could still make a shot from that distance.

The young security guard dropped his flashlight and turned and ran, his boots stomping down hard, echoing in the underground garage.

The man in black waited until the last second and squeezed the trigger—one shot.

The bullet missed the bullseye, but not his target. He had aimed for center mass, an easier target from that distance with a handgun, but he had hit dead on the back of the guard's head. He knew that because a red mist erupted and brain and skull fragments exploded out from the other side. The bullet went clean through.

Not a bad shot, he thought, even with mediocre odds.

He pulled the gun back, wisps of smoke coiled out of the barrel. He paused for it to clear and holstered the weapon.

"Let's go," he said.

Farmer's mercenaries followed him to the elevator. He saw the security camera above the elevator. It was the only one.

He shrugged at it. It was no concern. He figured that the building was probably empty except for minimal staff and the targets.

He pressed the button to call the elevator and waited.

After the bell dinged and the elevator doors opened, and they all stepped on, he said, "Shoot to kill. Everyone but the girl. We need her back. Got it?"

Farmer's mercenaries all verbally acknowledged the order, and the man in black studied a sign behind a plastic panel with a list of all the offices in the building. He found the Russian lawyer's name and pressed the button for the sixth floor.

The doors shut.

44

WIDOW FINISHED HIDING the weapons and stopped to use the bathroom, since he was already in there. *Always take advantage of any situation*, he thought.

He washed his hands and dried them and headed back to the door. He stepped out of the men's room and turned the corner, back to the lobby. As he made eye contact with the guard behind the front desk, they both paused a beat because they heard a loud *BOOM!* that echoed from somewhere in the building.

Widow asked, "What the hell was that?"

The guard shrugged and said, "Car backfiring. There's a parking garage below us."

Widow nodded and stepped up to the desk.

"I'm going through now."

The guard looked at him, cockeyed, and said, "Okay. Go through. They're on six."

Widow nodded, stepped through the metal detector. It didn't buzz.

He walked over to the elevator and heard the motors humming as one elevator ascended the floors.

He clicked the call button and waited for the next one.

45

Eva remained standing in Putin's office, which she had been in a dozen times before. Usually, she sat across from her at the desk, without batting an eye. But this time, she stood because Putin kept a small silenced SR1MP pistol in her top desk drawer. The SR1MP was a lightweight pistol, popular with some Russian forces. It was good for covert operators because of its size and power.

Eva told her what had happened, but Putin stopped her with a hand up.

She said, "Eva. What have you done?"

Eva stayed quiet, and Putin sat alone.

"Yesterday, your father's submarine went dark and hasn't been heard from since. You have vanished for two days. I have tried to call you. I'm getting distressing questions from Moscow. What the hell have you done?"

Eva said, "I'm sorry. I had to help my father."

"What's happened?"

Before Eva could speak or explain, the door to the office slammed open like it had been kicked in by a SWAT team. Eva assumed it was Widow. She turned, and Putin stood up, fast.

"What is this!" she asked.

Five men came pouring into the office. They were armed with MP5SDs.

Like they were in sync, both women felt surprise and then terror. It wasn't the men with guns that scared Putin. For her, it was the fact that the MP5SDs were silenced. She had been in the US for twenty years, working successfully as both a lawyer and as a spy for the Russian government. She had been trained long ago. But one lesson that she knew for sure was that men with submachine guns and suppressors didn't have the best intentions. The local police didn't use suppressors. Neither did the FBI or any other law enforcement agency that she was aware of. Only two types of people would have them: soldiers and mercenaries. And soldiers wouldn't be barging into her office.

The reason Eva was terrified wasn't the guns or the suppressors. What terrified her was that she recognized the four men who had kidnapped her.

The man in black stepped forward and spoke.

He was a short man, not tiny, but for the type of men that she normally found herself in the company of, he was short. Maybe he was five foot eight, but he looked taller because he wore boots with significant heels. He wore all black, which made her think he was some kind of biker, only missing a helmet.

He had graying hair with black weaved in. It was thick and curly. He was white, but there was something else there. Maybe Latin. Maybe some kind of Native American, but whatever it was made up a small percentage of his ethnicity.

Even though the man in black was the shortest of the five, he looked amazingly strong. His chest was wide, but not overdone. It was like a cinder block, not a barrel.

Eva had never seen him before. But she recognized he was some sort of leader here. It wasn't Farmer. There was another man in charge. Right off, she recognized he wasn't the brains. He couldn't have been. He came off more like a weapon than a leader.

The man in black said, "Ms. Karpov. Ms. Putin. It's a pleasure to meet you both. Ladies, please sit."

The women glanced at each other and sat uncomfortably.

Putin asked, "Who the hell are you? How did you get in here?"

"Ms. Karpov, you've caused us grief. I've been chasing after you all damn night."

Eva said nothing.

The man in black looked at her. He looked at her fingertips. They rested on her lap. They trembled, which made him smile. Then he looked up at her arms; he noticed her muscular build. Then he traced the outline of her breasts inside her shirt.

She noticed and cringed, which was visible to everyone in the room. But the man in black didn't comment on it. He didn't falter from his staring.

Then he moved up to her neck. He stared at it. He savored the hint of veins and crinkles and flesh.

The man in black asked, "Where's your friend?"

Eva said, "What friend?"

The man in black smiled. He reached into his jacket and drew the SIG Sauer P220 out. He held it down by his side, one-handed. More like a threat than anything else. It was there to say, "I won't ask twice." But he did.

He asked, "Where's your friend? The big guy?"

"I don't know."

Just then, Putin bolted up from her seat. Back straight. Shoulders apart. It turned out that she had a gun under her desk, only it hadn't been in the top drawer. It must have been in a hidden compartment under the top, just above her lap. And it wasn't the SR1MP pistol. It was a Glock 17, unsilenced, which surprised Eva.

Time slowed down. Eva reacted as she had been trained to do. She leaped off her seat and ducked down in the back corner. There were no good options for cover in this situation. The office had one way in, and one way out, and the way out was blocked by the five armed enemies.

Eva wasn't sure if Putin was a good shot or not. She didn't know how much training Putin had with the Glock 17. All that didn't really matter much because the man in black was only seven or eight feet away, ten at the most. And even if Putin missed, she was bound to hit one of them.

It turned out not to matter how much training Putin had with a firearm. It didn't even matter how good she was, because the man in black was better.

Before Putin's Glock 17's firing line could near her target, he had raised his P220 like an experienced gunslinger from out of the pages of an old western novel. He didn't fully extend his arm like some kind of amateur.

In a gun duel between two cowboys, squaring off in the middle of town at high noon, the first mistake he always noticed in movies was the actors extended their arms all the way out. This was a mistake.

The proper way to be quicker, to be deadlier, was to practice firing from the hip, which the man in black had done a lot.

He drew from the hip and squeezed the trigger. Eva had missed that because she was staring at Putin, her friend.

The room filled and echoed and boomed with the sounds of dual gunshots.

The first was from the man in black's P220. The second one was from Putin's Glock.

Next, two things happened. The bullet from the P220 blasted through the air and blew a hole the size of a quarter straight through Putin's forehead. Red mist sprayed out behind her and splashed on the window and blinds with thick redness. She fell back into her seat and was dead. Eyes open, staring up and lifeless.

The man in black was faster than her. But Putin had squeezed off one shot. Only she didn't hit the man in black, as she had hoped.

Instead, one of the other guys who came with him had been hit square in the side of his neck. He fell back against one of his friends and clung to life. He wrenched his fingers on his friend's coat and pulled at it, taking the friend down to the ground with him.

The others all stood around, setting their weapons down. They stood around, not knowing what to do. At least, that's what they wanted their buddy to think, even though he knew the truth. They had a procedure to follow if one of them received a life-threatening wound in the field. The procedure was simple. Let the man die. If there was nothing they could do for him on their own, without a hospital, then he was as good as dead. That didn't mean that they didn't care about each other. They were all friends. But that was the cost of doing business. They were involved in a highly illegal operation. There were nukes in play. They couldn't take him to the hospital.

By this point, the man was bleeding out profusely.

He knew he was going to die. He didn't cover his wound as he bled out, which was difficult for about thirty seconds, but after he lost a few pints of blood, facing death became much easier.

Within minutes, their friend was dead.

The man in black never took his eyes or the barrel of the P220 off Eva.

Finally, he asked once more, "Where is he?"

46

GUNSHOTS ECHOED above him as he rode the elevator up. This time, Widow was certain it wasn't a car backfire. Not unless someone had parked a forty-year-old muscle car on the sixth floor.

He didn't have his guns anymore and had no time to get them, not if Eva's life was in danger. He couldn't make the elevator go back down to the lobby anyway, not until after the doors opened on six.

He was sure that he had heard two distinct handguns being fired. He wasn't sure about the make or models, but they sounded close to being simultaneous, which was only possible with two weapons. And one of them was louder than the other. It sounded like a .45 ACP, maybe. The second one was a nine-millimeter, no doubt about it.

Widow had enough experience to know that it was never a good idea to walk into a potential gun battle, unarmed and completely cold. He had to help Eva. That took priority over his fears.

Instead of riding up to six, he hit the fifth-floor button just in time as the elevator passed the fourth.

The elevator registered the change in the journey and stopped on the fifth floor. The doors shot open, and Widow stepped off.

He looked left and looked right. He prepared himself to dodge and roll back onto the open elevator if there had been a danger on that floor as well, but there were no signs of life.

Widow searched the signs above the doors in the hall until he saw the fire exit stairwell. He charged at the door and ripped it open in one heaving motion that would have torn a cheap door off its hinges. He took the stairs up, two at a time, and darted up two flights. He rounded the corner and stayed alert for sounds. There was nothing but the loud hum of the elevator, moving on to six without him.

He stopped outside the door to six and hugged the inside wall. His heart was racing. His blood was pumping hard. He stayed still and concentrated on his breathing. He breathed in and breathed out. He watched as his chest heaved up and then down. He waited, tried to slow his breathing, and thus, his heart rate. He needed to slow it all down so he could be as quiet as possible. He needed to recon the situation before making a move.

After a few moments went by, he knew the elevator was stopped because the humming had stopped.

He paused one last time, and then he turned and faced the door, crouched down and pushed the door open. He pressed the open bar slowly and then followed that with the door just as slowly. He cracked it open and looked down the hall. The elevator was behind him. But that was okay because what he was looking for, he saw a second later.

The door to Putin's office opened up wide. And there was Eva. She was alive, but she was bound. Her hands were out front, zip-tied together at the wrists. The look on her face was shock and terror all at once. She was being forced forward by four men, three of which Widow recognized from The Plaza Hotel. The fourth, he didn't.

The fourth man wore all black and seemed to be the leader. He was the only one who looked from side to side like he was checking the doors, checking the corners.

Widow heard him bark an order to the others.

He said, "Elevator!"

Widow slipped back and pulled the door with him, making sure not to click it shut. He didn't want the door to register a loud sound like most fire doors do when they are closed all the way.

He left it with a hair crack, just enough to make it look closed. He pushed his back to the wall and listened.

He heard footsteps, quick. The men were checking the open elevator. He waited until they had all passed. He heard Eva's footsteps and then those of the man in black. He knew Eva's because they were the lightest and sporadic, like she was being half-pushed forward.

Widow heard them pass and stop near the elevator.

The man in black asked, "No one there?"

The other said, "No. Nothing."

Silence for a long moment. Widow backed away and went up the stairs to the seventh floor. He stepped three at a time this time and tried to keep his footsteps silent.

He went up and not down because if they were going to check the fire stairs, most people looked down. Not up. It was stupid for an attacker to go up. Up was the roof.

Widow stopped two flights up on the seventh floor and crouched down out of sight, and listened.

He heard nothing, and he waited longer. Then he heard the sixth-floor door jolt open in one violent swing. He heard the clicking sound of a submachine gun being aimed around haphazardly.

He peered down with one eye over the edge of the cement. He got a glimpse of one of The Plaza Hotel guys, staring over the railing, looking downward.

Widow saw the back of the guy's head, and then he saw the MP5SD in his hand.

Widow slipped back slowly, in case the guy checked upward.

He paused and waited. The guy wasn't all that bad. He stayed there for a long minute until he gave up.

Widow heard him say, "There's no one here."

The words trailed off as the guy from The Plaza Hotel walked back through the fire door.

Widow waited until he heard the fire door shut. He descended back down the two flights until he was back at that door. He paused another beat, listening until he heard the elevator engine crank back to life and the cables humming somewhere behind the wall. They were on the move back down.

Widow charged through the fire door and checked the hall, fast. He swung right toward Putin's office, and then he swung left toward the elevator. It was indeed closed and moving down.

Widow ran back down the hall to check the office. He hadn't seen Putin leave with them, causing him to presume that she had been the recipient of one bullet he had heard fired.

The office door was open. Widow snapped in and snapped back out in case someone shot at him. But there was no one there to shoot him. Not alive anyway.

The first thing he saw was a dead guy on the floor. Blood still oozed out of a neck wound. The wound was so dark and covered with blood that Widow couldn't even see where the hole was.

He passed over the guy and saw the blood splatter on the window and the blinds. He saw Putin. She was definitely dead. There was a hole in her forehead, and Widow could see brain fragments on the window.

Shit, he thought.

He didn't wait. There was nothing else to see. He went over to the desk and saw that Putin had fired a Glock 17. He scooped it up, didn't need to test fire it. It looked like it fired just fine.

Then he turned around, but stopped because he saw that the dead guy on the floor was blinking.

Widow set the Glock down on the carpet, away from the pool of blood, and shoved his hand over the guy's neck, tried to stop the bleeding.

He asked, "Can you talk?"

The guy blinked.

Widow's hand found the hole in his neck, and he pushed hard.

"Speak!"

The guy said, "Don't wanna die."

His voice was weak, and his skin was cold, growing colder by the second. Widow was certain that his voice wasn't speaking with its normal tone because the bullet had scraped his voice box. It had to have because of the location. Widow was surprised he could even utter a recognizable word.

"Where did they take her?"

The guy said nothing. He just blinked.

"Where?!"

"Strike."

"What?"

The next word sent cold chills down Widow's spine.

The guy said, "Nuclear."

Widow heard: "nuclear strike." He changed course and asked, "When?"

"Today. The anniversary."

Anniversary, he thought.

The guy was dying faster and faster by the second.

"Where?"

The guy said something inaudible. Widow didn't understand. The guy's eyes rolled back in his head. Widow only had seconds left with him.

"Where did they take Eva?"

The guy coughed up blood. It splattered onto Widow's clothes and face. Then it trickled down the guy's cheek and mouth.

"Where is she?"

"Moreau."

Then he was gone.

Where the hell was Moreau? Widow wondered. But there was no time for that.

He picked up the Glock 17 and ran after them. Widow pressed the elevator button and watched for a second to see what floor it was coming up from. The second elevator answered the call. It was coming from the lobby, slowly.

He gave up on that and turned to the stairwell again. He ripped the door open just as hard as before, and he leaped from the flight of stairs down to the next landing. On the way down, he barely touched a stair. He was going as fast as he could. He knew they hadn't taken her back through the lobby. They had come from the parking garage below.

Widow went as fast as he could. But it hadn't been fast enough.

He burst through the door to the garage and caught the taillights of a white panel van traversing up the ramp to the street.

47

FARMER STARED AT KARPOV, who stood upright, mostly, with his hands behind his back. He was being held tightly by one of the guys who'd come on board with Farmer. The redheaded leader was standing behind Farmer.

Farmer held a roll of quarters in one hand. He stared at Karpov's bloody face and said, "Captain, I can keep hitting you, but we both know you're going to give me that passcode."

The Listener had clarified that the operation was going to go according to plan no matter what. He didn't need to say it. Farmer knew well enough.

Without Karpov's daughter, threatening him to give up a passcode was proving impossible.

The Russians had gotten smarter. Like the rest of the nuclear club with submarines, they equipped their nukes with not only two required turnkeys but also a failsafe passcode. It was a word that was required to arm the nuke. The missile could be fired without it, but the nuke wouldn't be armed without it. And a nuclear missile without the "nuclear" part is about as dangerous as dropping a Buick from the sky. Sure, someone could get hurt, but the damage was reduced to almost nothing compared to a nuclear blast.

Farmer had brought the roll of quarters just in case. One of the oldest tricks in the book. Can't afford brass knuckles? Use a roll of coins.

He stared down at his hand, which was turning red.

They had already tried to threaten the captain by shooting his men. That proved useless because they had shot one in front of him, and nothing happened. He didn't give up a thing.

Farmer had suspected that much. Submariners swear an oath, just like any sailor. They won't give up such a dangerous thing as a nuclear passcode to the enemy. Not even for the lives of their fellow sailors. They had all sworn an oath, too.

They were prepared to die.

Farmer turned back to the redheaded leader and whispered, "This is getting us nowhere."

The redheaded leader nodded.

"We need to surface again. Call the Listener. We need Karpov's daughter. It's the only threat that seems to faze him."

Farmer left, and the redheaded leader followed but stopped to instruct the other guy to bring Karpov.

They returned to the bridge.

Farmer went over to his submariner and said, "Bring us to the surface."

The guy said, "Are you sure?"

"Do it."

"But we are likely to be seen? At least on sonar."

"Do it. I gotta call him."

The submariner did as he was told and barked orders at the crew in Russian. They followed his commands, all while the redheaded leader and one of his guys swept behind them, pointing and poking the backs of their heads with their MP5s.

48

WIDOW WALKED up the ramp to the street, pausing for a moment because he saw a dead security guard. He was sure the guy was dead because he could see the bullet hole in his head. It looked to be like the one in Putin's head and probably was. Probably the same gun. Probably from the man in black.

Widow continued out onto the surface street. He continued walking briskly in the direction that he had seen the van turn and moving away from the building. He was just in time to hear police sirens in the distance—screeching, blaring, and growing louder.

He figured that the guard at the desk must have called the police.

The white panel van was a far speck on the horizon, and then it was gone from sight.

Widow stopped dead on the sidewalk.

Pedestrians stared at him, avoiding him. Most moved to the other side of the street, or they turned around and walked away.

That was when he realized he still had the Glock out. He stuffed it into his waistband and then realized there was blood on his shirt and face. His shirt was black, but his face was white. Therefore, the pedestrians weren't staring at his shirt.

He turned away from the street and faced the buildings. He walked toward one, stared at a sign out front. It was one of those "You are here" maps of the office park. He waited for the sirens to pass.

A moment later, he looked over his shoulder and saw three NYPD spec cruisers pull up and stop dead on the street in front of Putin's building.

Widow saw himself faintly in the glass's reflection that encased the map. He pulled his shirt up and licked the tip of it and wiped his face.

Then he turned and walked casually, but hurriedly, away.

49

BREACHING the surface took a lot longer than Farmer and his men had thought, because they found out that there was a battle group nearby. Not on top of them, but within radar and sonar distance, for sure. It looked to be a US destroyer, along with an aircraft carrier and a couple of cruisers. They had also picked up a submarine coming toward the group from the south.

Farmer wasn't worried about it like his men were. But the reason he wasn't worried was that they were a part of the plan. He had known about the ships long before.

Still, they weren't ready to expose themselves just yet. So, he ordered them to move slowly away and out of range enough to surface.

The submarine was coming up, and the engines slowed. The waves broke over the bow.

"Let's go," Farmer said to Karpov.

The redheaded leader gripped Karpov by the elbow and hauled him onto his feet and over to the ladder and up it, staying behind Farmer, who climbed first.

On the deck of the boat, water sprayed in white and gray snarling waves. Karpov wasn't told where they were, but he knew just by listening to Farmer's commands and by the color of the water and the temperature. He knew they were near to the legal point of invasion into US waters. If he had to guess a more precise location, he would say that they were in striking distance of the major US targets, including New York City and Washington DC. The first target would certainly mean an all-out war with the US. But the second target would mean the crippling of the United States' centrally based federal system and, therefore, the nation's response time to the attack.

A nuclear strike on the US would mean a return strike on Russia. Probably from NATO, which meant a quick attack, which would mean the end of Karpov's friends who mostly lived in Moscow.

Karpov swallowed as he stared up into the blinding daylight above him.

Farmer was dialing a satellite phone and holding onto the guardrail near the hatch they had emerged from.

Farmer and his guys had already gotten the two turnkeys from Karpov and the political officer, who held the other one. That part was easy. The political officer had done little to hold out from volunteering it.

Karpov knew they needed the passcode, which wasn't widely publicized information—a secret code word that is entered a separate keypad on the bridge's computer. It had to be issued before the launch in order to arm the nuke.

There was no way Karpov was going to give up that code. But then he thought about why he was meeting Farmer in the first place—his daughter.

They had her. That's how they were going to get that code from him. The only person who he would give it up for was her.

He squeezed his eyes tight as he faced the sky. It was time to take away their upper hand.

In a fast spin, he turned and ran for the side of the boat. If he could make it to the edge, he could jump off. He could drown. He could save thousands of lives, maybe even millions. They might kill Eva, but at least he wouldn't have given up to the threat.

He shoved Farmer out of the way and ran to the edge of the boat.

The blinding light from the sun grayed a bit from the fast-moving cloud cover, making it almost impossible for Karpov to distinguish the exact edge of the submarine's bow, which was slightly curved anyway and painted to blend in with the ocean.

He neared it and ran at full speed. He didn't need to jump. He only needed to keep running. Eventually, he would fall right in.

As he neared what he thought was the edge, he heard a quieted *PURR!* It was a familiar sound. It was the sound of suppressed gunfire.

And suddenly, the metal deck in front of him sparked, and bullets ricocheted, and his instincts for self-preservation kicked in, overtaking him. He froze solid.

Funny how many suicides wind up being aborted at the last minute because of every animal's natural need to stay alive.

Karpov froze, and before he could force himself to continue forward, he felt strong arms grapple him and haul him backward.

The redheaded leader had wrenched him back off his feet and slammed him onto the hard, cold steel deck. The breath was knocked out of him.

The redheaded leader jabbed him once, hard, straight in the face.

"Don't try that again!" he shouted.

50

WIDOW HAD CONTINUED WALKING ABOUT AS FAR as he could go until he felt he was safely out of the reach of the NYPD's net, at least for now.

The lawyer was dead. There was a dead bad guy, who would probably come up as a John Doe for the low-level computer database of the NYPD, which might cause them to investigate with Homeland or the FBI, which might provide some better results.

Widow had no intention of being a part of their investigation. He had had his fair share of police lately. And there was a more pressing matter. The bad guy had said, "Nuclear Strike." Now the stakes were much, much higher, and Widow had to skip ahead. With such a threat out there, a credible one, there was no time for red tape and half-measures. He had to go over the heads of local law enforcement. And unfortunately, he had to set aside Eva's safety for the time being. A nuclear strike was more important. She would understand. But he intended to get her back alive.

Where should he go? Where to start?

The boyfriend, Edward, was dead as well. He couldn't start there. He had only the name Farmer, who was supposedly a CIA agent. No reason to doubt that was the truth.

But with the threat of a nuke, the thing to focus on for now was the stolen Russian submarine.

Widow walked back the same path that he and Eva had come, back to Grand Central Terminal. He had seen a payphone there.

Once he got there, he went underground and back to the phone. It wasn't being used, which wasn't a surprise. Most people had their own personal phones on them.

Widow picked up the phone before he realized he had no change. No quarters.

He didn't want to go searching around for a place to get change. So, he simply dialed one of those call-collect services he had seen advertised somewhere.

He waited and got the operator and requested to call collect. He gave her a number that he had used before that he knew from memory.

She asked him to wait while she tried to connect the call, and then he heard Rachel Cameron's voice answer. He was given a chance to say his name, which he did. Then he listened as Cameron was asked if she accepted the charges. She did.

"Widow? What the hell is going on?"

"I need your help."

"Okay?"

"There's a situation. A Russian submarine has been stolen. It's nuclear. I believe that they have a US target."

Cameron paused a beat, and then she said, "I heard about it."

"What? You know about it?"

"Why do you think I'm at the office on a Sunday? The whole unit is here. We've been working overtime with Norfolk and COMNAVAIRLANT, trying to get hold of the sub's location."

COMNAVAIRLANT stands for Commander Naval Air Force Atlantic.

Widow asked, "Did you send me to The Plaza Hotel on purpose?"

"What? Of course I did. It was your birthday gift."

"No, I mean to get involved in this?"

"What? I don't understand?"

Widow took a breath. He was a believer in coincidences, only because he had been the victim of wrong place, wrong time, many times before. But this seemed suspect.

"You didn't send me there because of Eva Karpov?"

He could hear Cameron kind of snarl over the phone.

"Who? Widow, I don't know who the hell that is."

Widow said, "She was kidnapped while I was at the Plaza. She was being held for two days by a group of armed men. Supposedly they were part of a bigger operation."

"What operation? What's this girl gotta do with it?"

"I believe they wanted to hijack this sub."

"You know who's responsible then?"

"Yeah. Some guy called Farmer."

"Farmer? Never heard of him."

Widow said, "There's more. You already know that the Russian sub is nuclear, but do you know who the boat's captain is?"

"No. Who?"

"A man named Karpov."

"I've never heard of him either," she said, but then he heard her sigh. And she said, "That's someone related to Eva Karpov?"

"Her father. She says."

"This guy Farmer kidnapped her to get her father to turn over the boat?"

"Supposedly Farmer convinced her he'd help her and her father to defect. I don't believe that Karpov thought he was going to be turning over the sub to a bunch of terrorists."

"Wait, defect? Like in that movie? The one with James Bond?"

"Sean Connery, not Bond, but yes. Kind of like that movie. *The Hunt for Red October*," Widow said, and then he paused a beat and added, "It's a better book."

"This Karpov captain, he believed that this guy Farmer wanted to help him? Sounds naïve to me."

"Could have been. But this guy Farmer is supposedly CIA, which explains the manpower and the means and even the location of the hotel where they held her. The CIA love their expensive-ticket items."

Cameron ignored the quip about the hotel and simply asked, "CIA?"

"That's what she told me."

"I think we need to bring you both in. Where are you now?"

"I'm in New York still. At Grand Central Terminal, but she's not with me."

"Where the hell is she?"

"They got her. Again."

"How?"

"Long story. But there's a dead Russian immigration lawyer down near the UN building. We were attacked. They got away with her."

"Immigration lawyer? Wait, what did Eva do here?"

"She was a spy."

"A spy?"

"Yeah, the lawyer was her handler."

Cameron said, "This gets better and better."

Widow decided not to tell her about Eva's cover job as a model. The whole thing sounded more and more like an airport spy novel.

Instead, he said, "Send someone to pick me up, but Cameron, I can't come to you. This Farmer guy intends to use the sub to launch a nuke at us. I'm sure of it. It's the only thing of value on the sub."

"What? Why would he do that?"

"No idea. But we presume that's what they're planning. I need to get to Norfolk."

"Navy command?"

"I knew a guy who should still be there. Nick Ebert. We can trust him. Last I heard, he had been stationed there. He's in counterintelligence. Find him, will ya?"

"Okay. Stay there, by the phone. I'll call you back."

She hung up, and Widow did the same. He turned and looked around and found a bench along the nearest wall, within earshot of the phone. He took a seat and waited.

51

THE MAN in black punched Eva square in the stomach one more time. And she heaved forward as far as she could, tasting the doughnut that she had eaten earlier.

By this time, they weren't at their final destination, but they were already at the tip of Long Island, the northeastern side, on Highway Twenty-Five in Orient. They had pulled off the road and onto a dirt path. They drove for a while. Eva was gagged in the back of the panel van. She felt the bumps and knew that they had gone off road.

After the van stopped, the doors opened, and two of the men who had kidnapped her twice now got out and stretched their legs.

The man in black had hopped into the van with her and the third guy, who held her elbows back.

That was when the man in black punched her in the gut. He didn't speak a word to her, not one. No questions. No requests. He just punched her. And then he punched her again. Same spot. Same pain.

After she caught her breath, he pulled her chin up and ripped the gag out and said, "When I tell you to, you will speak."

She said nothing.

The man in black stepped out of the van, pulled out a satellite phone, and twisted his hand to see his watch. He waited.

They waited a long time, and finally, the sat phone rang.

The man in black answered it and said, "Yes."

He listened.

Said, "Yes," again. And then he listened some more.

Then he turned and walked back to the van, climbed inside, and said, "She's right here."

He reached the phone to her and held it in place for her. He said, "It's for you."

Eva listened and heard the wind blowing loudly in the background. Then she heard her father's voice.

He spoke in Russian, a simple, "Are you all right?"

But then he was struck by someone, she knew by the sound, and she heard a voice order him to speak English.

He asked, "Are you safe?"

She didn't speak in Russian.

She said, "I'm alive. In New York, somewhere."

Then she paused a beat and stared up at the man in black. She said, "Don't do whatever they want you to do, Papa!"

The man in black pulled the phone away and listened.

He heard Farmer speak, "That's enough. Hello?"

"It's me," the man in black said.

"Thank you for cleaning up after me."

"Don't worry about it."

"The Listener told me there was interference. Some guy?"

"Again, don't worry about it. We're back on track now."

"So, same schedule then?"

The man in black looked at his watch, then he said, "Yes. We keep going. Unless the Listener says differently."

There was a pause and a deep breath between both men.

Farmer said, "We're actually going to do this."

"Yes."

"Then, I'll see you at Moreau's in two hours?"

"In two hours. See you."

Then Farmer said, "If Karpov tricks us, kill the girl."

The man in black said, "In one hour, fire the nuke. If I don't see news of it by then, she'll be dead one minute later."

And both men hung up.

The man in black looked at Eva and smiled. Now that she knew they were actually going to fire a nuclear missile, she made that expression that he loved on the faces of his victims as he strangled them. It wasn't the same, but very close. She looked completely terrified.

Eva muttered something that the man in black pieced together. It was something like, "No. All those people."

He slid back out of the van, tossed the sat phone on the ground, and stomped on it over and over, violently until it was only shattered pieces of a phone.

Then he said, "No going back now."

Eva stayed quiet.

"Get her out and onto the boat."

The men who had kidnapped her hustled to it, pulled her out and dragged her along a smaller path between some brush and out onto a secluded beach. A military-looking zodiac was waiting in the shallow water.

She was thrown into it like a bag of bricks. A moment later, the men all climbed in, and the man in black followed.

They left the van where it' was, alongside the man in black's motorcycle.

He sat right next to Eva and ordered one man to go. That guy climbed back out and shoved the boat farther out onto the water, where it was deep enough to use the motor. Then he climbed in, soaking wet.

He fired up the motor, and a moment later they were cruising along at high speed out around Long Island. They threaded through markers along the shoreline and weaved out until they were headed north and east toward nothing but blue horizons.

52

Karpov was hauled back down the ladder and through the communications tower to the bridge, with nothing but defeat on his face.

Eva was his little girl. She was all he thought of.

Farmer said, "Keep him standing."

The redheaded leader did as he was ordered.

"What's the password?"

Karpov looked at the floor panels and said nothing.

"Karpov, I won't ask again."

Karpov looked up, slowly, and stared at the faces of his men who were still on the bridge. They looked at him under gunpoint. Their eyes were all blank. They looked almost as defeated as he did. They looked hopeless. They knew they were probably all going to die.

In shame, he answered Farmer.

He answered with one word, "October."

Farmer smiled. He had the password. He had the keys. He had the nukes. Now all he had to do was wait one hour until the deadline.

53

THE PAYPHONE at Grand Central Terminal rang once, and Widow jumped up and walked over to it, catching it on the second ring.

"Hello?"

"Jack Widow?" a voice from the past asked. The sound behind the voice was familiar. It was a lot of ambient noise, like people talking and machines beeping and making sounds.

"Yep."

"It's Nick," the voice said, and then Widow heard a door open and wind noises.

"Hey, Nick."

"Man, you are all wrapped up in this mess?"

"I guess so."

More wind.

Widow asked, "Where the hell are you?"

Ebert didn't answer that. Instead, he said, "Listen, no time to chat over the phone. I sent you a car. Go out of the terminal back to the street. You should see it."

"What kind of car?"

"Don't worry. They know what you look like."

And with that statement, Ebert hung up the phone.

Widow hung up and turned and walked back out of the terminal and up the stairs to the street.

He didn't know what kind of car he was looking for. He saw a navy blue sedan, which was completely forgettable except for someone who knew better, and Widow knew better. It was a Navy vehicle. No doubt about it.

It didn't look like a police cruiser, but it was armored like one. There was no light bar on the roof, but that was only because sirens and blue lights were embedded in the grille.

There was an array of antennas planted on the back like little steel telephone poles.

The driver was leaned up against the vehicle. He called out from across the street.

"Jack Widow?"

"That's me."

"Hop in. We don't have a second to waste."

Widow scrambled across the street and opened the rear door out of habit. He was about to hop in when the driver said, "Sir, you can sit in the front."

Widow arched his eyebrow out of reflex. He wasn't used to sitting in the front of a cop car.

He shut the door to the back, opened the passenger front door, and dumped himself down on the seat, shut the door, and buckled up.

"Ready?" the driver asked.

"Ready."

And they were off to a destination that Widow didn't know. He assumed to JFK airport because, more than likely, Ebert was far away. Probably at Norfolk.

54

THE LISTENER LOOKED at his watch. Time was running out. Soon the entire world would witness the first and last nuclear attack on the United States, and they would blame the Russians for it.

So far, everyone was buying it. So far, everyone believed that a Russian submarine had gone quiet and was headed into Atlantic waters off the US coast.

They had reacquired the girl. The man in black had texted the Listener's phone and told him the good news that Karpov had given up the password, and now the nuke would be armed.

The Listener had considered pulling back on the operation. After all, many people that he knew would die—people blind to the world, blind to the uselessness of the current military.

They would die in less than an hour now. They would die in a fiery blast of nuclear clouds and sky and radiation.

The bums in Washington would have to listen then. They would have to return the state of the military back to its former grace.

The Listener wouldn't back out. No. He couldn't. Not now. Not even if he wanted to. Farmer was unreachable.

The Listener texted the man in black one last time before the planned nuclear strike and said, "Go dark. I'll reach out to you after the heat dies down. One more thing, wait for the strike, but don't wait for Farmer to make it. Just kill the girl. At your discretion."

The Listener waited, but there was no response. He figured that meant the man in black was already on his way to Moreau.

He stared down at his phone and selected edit in his messages app. He swiped to select all and swiped again to delete all. Then he did the same under call log.

He took his satellite phone, kept it in his hand. Then he slipped a coat on top of his uniform, walked out of his temporary office, and stepped out into the hall. He walked past sailors and other crew members, ignoring their salutes, and made his way to the deck of the USS Washington, which had once been a flag battleship until its decommissioning in nineteen forty-seven. It had recently been constructed once again, not the original ship, and not as a battleship, but a new breed of a high-tech aircraft carrier for the US Navy. They just reused the name, an unconventional approach, but worthy, the Listener figured.

The very existence of the new ship was another slap in the face to him and his cause to reestablish fear in the rest of the world. Why on earth does the government spend all this money on new tech that they never intend to use in battle?

The Listener walked out past flight crew members who worked on deck. Around his neck was a pair of binoculars, very expensive ones. He liked to walk around from time to time and observe the performances of the other ships in their vicinity. The sailors on board were used to it.

No one bothered him as he walked the deck.

He waited until he was out of sight of anyone around. He looked to starboard and back to port. No one was watching him. Casually, he leaned against the railing and held out the sat phone. He dropped it.

It tumbled off the side and was sucked under the water. It vanished just as quickly as it broke through the waves.

The Listener glanced once toward the US coastline in the distance, and then at the placement of Navy ships, which were there under the pretext of war games, but really they were hunting the missing sub.

Then he looked at the causeway between the farthest ship and the carrier. By this time, Farmer had already squeezed past them. The new Russian sub technology had an absorbent outer skin that actually surpassed their own. But that wasn't what made the boat so deadly; it was escaping detection. This new sub wasn't the world's only stealth sub that could escape detection, but it was probably the most advanced, for the moment. And the moment was all that mattered to him.

He couldn't help himself. He looked one last time at the precise location of where the Russian sub was supposed to be at the marked time. He glanced at his watch.

Forty-two minutes to go.

55

WIDOW WAS a little stunned because they weren't going to JFK. They went right back to where he had started recently. The driver took him to the United Nations building. The street was already shut down and closed off by NYPD. Because of the dead bodies in the lawyer's building, Widow was sure. But the driver showed his badge, which made him NCIS and not Navy. The officer controlling the flow of traffic let them pass.

"Where are we going?" Widow asked.

"Helicopter."

And that was all the NCIS agent had said. Widow made no remark to give away that he had once had the same badge. He simply sat back and watched.

They pulled up onto a drive and up to a guard station for the United States Department of State Diplomatic Security Service, which is assigned to guard the UN. The agent re-showed his badge, and they drove past the guards and into the compound.

After a few moments of driving and sweeping around the walls and posted security vehicles, they came to a clearing of concrete, where there was normally parking. The driver pulled to a stop.

"Let's go," he said and parked the car, left the keys in it, but turned off the ignition.

Widow followed him out and shut the door.

The driver walked around the hood and waited. He just stood there.

Widow asked, "Aren't we going in?"

He figured they were headed up to the roof, where there was a helicopter pad.

"No time," the driver called out. He had called it out loud, like he was preparing for it to be loud.

Then Widow looked up and saw a twin-engine Seahawk helicopter flying overhead, maybe four hundred feet above them. He recognized it as probably an MH60 or similar. It was gray and unremarkable as far as appearance, making it more unnoticeable to civilians, Widow guessed.

The chopper came down steadily, but not slow.

Widow looked around the ground and saw guards and diplomats who were outside, he figured, to stare at him like he was some kind of important figure to be getting a helicopter landing right in the parking lot in front of the United Nations.

And suddenly, he felt a little proud.

The Seahawk circled in, and Widow felt the pressure from the rotor wash growing stronger and more intense.

He watched as the machine came in and blew his hair up in powerful waves like blades of grass.

The Seahawk landed on its wheels and bounced once. The flight crew left the engines on, and the blades continued to turn above Widow.

The driver called out, "Come on."

Widow followed him onto the back of the helicopter, and they both buckled in—a Navy crewman who helped them get on banged on the roof twice, and cleared the pilot to take off.

They rose up and up. Once they were high enough, Widow felt the engines running harder and harder, and the helicopter tilted on the Y-axis, and they bolted forward at a much faster speed than the bird was used to traveling.

They headed out toward the Atlantic. Once Widow saw Manhattan vanish behind them, he called out to the driver, "Just where are we going?"

"To see Ebert."

"Yeah, but where?"

The driver said, "The USS Washington."

Widow sat back. It had been a long time since he had been on board a Navy aircraft carrier. A long time.

56

The Seahawk flew under good weather, which made the trip faster and smoother. Widow had flown in helicopters many times before, but this may have been the longest trip on one that he could recall. He wasn't calculating the miles, and he didn't know the speed they traveled, but they had been flying over open water for thirty minutes or more. He didn't know the exact time. He didn't have a clock in his head. What an absurd notion that would have been.

He figured thirty to forty minutes was as good a guess as any.

They were flying to an aircraft carrier, so no need to worry about fuel. There would be plenty onboard.

The Seahawk came in over the Atlantic, and Widow scooted across the rear bench and leaned to see out the side window. He saw the aircraft carrier coming into range, and he saw a destroyer not far off, along with a couple of other ships too far away to recognize. What he did notice was their pattern. They were spread out in different directions but staying within sight range. They were hunting.

The wind picked up as they descended. The helicopter yawed and fell, and the rotors whooped and seemed to get louder.

After another five minutes of approaching, they were coming in over the new USS Washington.

Widow got up off the bench and moved into a position that allowed him to watch through the cockpit. He saw the ship come into view. He saw it grow bigger and bigger. He watched as the ground crew prepared for the Seahawk to land.

The bird landed on a clear helicopter-marked landing zone. Widow braced for the wheels to touch down and bounce, which they did. Not too hard. The pilot was a real pro.

The driver who had picked up Widow unzipped his windbreaker, and for the first time, Widow saw his nameplate. Hardy was his name.

Hardy said, "Follow me, sir."

Widow followed behind him as Hardy swiped open the side door and hopped out onto the deck. Widow did the same and immediately felt the wind blow across his face in slapping gusts. And a far-off, familiar feeling of life in the Navy came back to him.

Parked on the deck were dozens of fighter jets in different corners. They looked like EA-18G Growlers. Widow wasn't an expert on planes. Without checking out the call numbers up close, he simply trusted his gut.

Two of them were in the queue to dispatch at a moment's notice, one after the other.

Widow figured somewhere under the convoy was at least one American Seawolf attack submarine. Also waiting and hunting.

Hardy said, "This way, sir,"

Widow followed him. They weren't headed below deck. They were headed up to the tower and probably to the bridge.

They entered through the bottom, passed officers and crew, and climbed upstairs until Hardy walked through an open hatch and onto the bridge.

The bridge was laid out bigger than the ones Widow had seen before. Normally, they were smaller than one would think. On a ship, realty space is a luxury. This one was huge in comparison. And high tech. There were new pieces of equipment that Widow had never seen, or at least never paid attention to. He washed his eyes over it all with a quick look. Saw everything, took in nothing.

There were up to ten sailors present, give or take, because every few minutes one would leave, and another would step on.

Widow's eyes went right to a familiar face.

"Jack Widow," Nick Ebert said. He was standing, middle of the bridge, facing the portal that Widow came through with his hand held out for a shake. Behind him were two other men, all wearing Navy-blue shipboard uniforms. All three men wore Navy caps. The two behind Ebert looked important. One was tall, lean, and older. He probably considered himself middle-aged, but he was more in his sixties. The man standing a little farther back and to the right looked ancient. He was short, thin, and had a professor's face. Like the kind who refused to retire and sometimes forgot where he was, but was also brilliant, in spurts.

Widow walked straight over to Ebert and took his hand and shook it. He looked at his collar pin. Widow said, "Commander now, huh?"

Ebert nodded.

"I wish we were meeting under different circumstances," he said.

"Me too. What's going on?"

"Cameron told us you already know."

Widow asked, "Any sign of the boat?"

Ebert turned to introduce the other two men.

"Widow, this is Captain Towdez," Ebert said, and the tall, younger man reached his hand out to shake. Widow shook it.

"And this is Admiral Kiley."

Widow paused a beat and took Kiley's hand and shook it.

"Admiral," he said. "I've heard of you."

Kiley reached out his hand in a slow upward movement that felt more like a crane was hauling it up rather than human bones and muscles and motor skills.

"All good things, I hope."

"Mostly good."

"So, what do you know, Widow?" Kiley asked.

Widow had never met Kiley before, but Kiley was the type of career sailor whose reputation preceded him by a decade and a thousand miles. To say that he had been around the block was an understatement. He had been around the block, and around again, and then had the block dropped on him.

The man was more of an institution at this point. He was the last of a dying breed of military man. Widow had figured that the man had retired long ago. Not that he had any prejudices against him. It was just that facts were facts. And the fact was that Kiley was old.

Widow was more than surprised that an admiral was taking part in this endeavor, which told him volumes. Then he remembered something about Kiley being *the* foremost expert on submarines, which was another reason he was probably there and not on a golf course somewhere.

"I think, Admiral, that you already know what I know."

"How do you mean, son?"

"Well, you're here."

"Come again?"

Widow said, "A famous Navy admiral like you rarely takes part onboard an aircraft carrier."

"I assure you that Captain Towdez is the commanding officer here. Not me."

"And yet, here you are."

Kiley smiled, probably because he didn't know what to say.

Widow moved on and said, "There's a hijacked Russian sub out there, and it has nukes. It's somewhere in the quadrant, and you're out here searching for it."

Captain Towdez and Kiley both nodded.

Ebert asked, "We knew that already. Of course. What don't we know?"

Widow asked, "How did you know about it?"

"One of our subs picked up unusual sound patterns two days ago in the Arctic," Kiley said.

"You knew it was a Russian sub?"

"No, but we picked it up again last night and again hours ago," Kiley said.

Ebert said, "And then, one hour ago. Just about."

Widow asked, "How did you pick it up and then lose it again? Weren't we watching it like a hawk?"

Ebert nodded.

Towdez said, "We think it's been surfacing."

Widow nodded and said, "To communicate."

Kiley said, "Maybe."

Ebert said, "That's what our intel guys think."

"Well, intel guys are only guessing. We don't know for sure, but it seems likely. That's why you're here, Widow. We think you might have the missing piece. Who they've been talking to. If they've been talking."

Widow nodded and said, "I know."

Just then, one sailor on-deck stood up from a machine that he had been seated at and walked over to them. He was average height, with a small gut. He looked Middle Eastern. He had a dark complexion, like he had literally just stepped out of the desert.

Upon closer inspection, Widow realized he wasn't Navy, not at all. His uniform was all wrong. His demeanor was all wrong. He didn't belong there.

He was an imposter.

57

THE IMPOSTER STOPPED a few feet from Widow and put his hand out, offered it for a handshake.

Widow asked, "What's this?"

"My name is John Ali, like the boxer Muhammad Ali. Only with John."

Widow stayed where he was.

Ebert said, "Widow, this is a state representative," which in slang terms meant a spook or a CIA officer. Often they claimed to be from the State Department. Which was a terrible cover because everyone knew it, but a great cover because it explained why they were wher-ever they were.

Widow simply cut to the chase and said, "CIA?"

Ali nodded, just a slight nod, but an affirmative, clearly.

Ali said, "I'm here as an observer."

Widow said, "No, you're not."

Ali said nothing.

"You're here because of your boy, Farmer."

Ali said, "You know about him?"

"I know he's the one who hijacked the submarine."

Ali nodded.

Ebert and Kiley and Towdez all said nothing, which told Widow that they all knew.

"So what are we doing here, fellas?"

Kiley said, "We're here to stop a nuclear missile from being fired onto the US."

"But why am I here? You already know about Farmer, apparently. You already know the sub is out there."

Ali said, "Frank Farmer went rogue a couple of weeks ago. He was..."

Widow held out his hand and stopped him. He said, "I don't care. I don't need to know his motivations or his terms or whatever. I get that you're here to represent the agency and to disavow the blame. I don't care about that. All I care about is stopping a strike and finding someone that Farmer has abducted."

"Abducted?" Ebert asked.

"Yeah, a girl."

"Who?" Ali asked.

Widow looked at them and said, "Karpov's daughter."

Towdez asked, "Who's Karpov?"

Which told Widow that things were worse here than he had thought. No one was talking to anyone, or the captain assigned to the ship hunting the Russian sub was a moron not to know the name of the captain of the very submarine that he was hunting.

The answer came to Widow just then—the captain was a moron. Because Kiley said, "He's the submarine captain."

"His daughter's been abducted?" Ebert asked.

Widow nodded.

Ebert looked at Kiley and said, "That means?"

"Farmer has the passcode," Ali said.

"The passcode?" Widow asked.

Ebert said, "The Russians use a two-key system to launch their nukes from their subs, but five years ago, maybe, they installed a passcode failsafe system."

Widow said, "The passcode arms the nuke?"

"Right," Ebert said.

Ali's face turned flush like he was worried for the first time. He asked, "How do we stop them?"

Kiley stayed quiet.

Ebert said, "We don't. Not unless we find them before it's too late. Let's hope they surface again."

One sailor called out, "I found them!"

58

THE RUSSIAN-SPEAKING soldier that Farmer had brought with him said, "They can see us now."

Sweat beaded on his brow as it did for all of them, including Farmer. Red lights flashed on the bridge. Everyone was washed over with the sudden realization of imminent devastation by the alert that the missile doors were opening. It was an automatic effect that Farmer didn't expect, but also didn't care about.

The reason that the soldier who spoke Russian knew the US ships could see their precise location was that Farmer had just ordered him to open the missile bay doors. The action of opening the port and flooding the chamber took some effort and time. Which, when you are about to launch a nuclear missile, can feel like an eternity.

Finally, after the door was open, and the missile prepped and ready, Farmer said, "Prepare to fire!"

The soldier who spoke Russian looked at Farmer and showed him one of the firing keys. He inserted it into the dash keyhole on one side of the bridge, and Farmer stood at the other with Karpov's key. He inserted his key into the opposite keyhole.

Farmer and the soldier who spoke Russian stared at each other.

Farmer said, "Passcode first."

The keyhole was near a computer terminal. The soldier who spoke Russian released his key and placed his fingers over the keyboard and typed in "OCTOBER" in all caps, in Russian as he had been instructed to. The computer whirred for a moment and accepted the code.

Then he called out, "Armed."

Farmer said, "Ready!"

The soldier who spoke Russian placed his hand back on the key and looked at Farmer. Their eyes locked, and sweat doubled on their foreheads.

Farmer said, "On three."

The soldier who spoke Russian said, "Ready!"

"One. Two. Three."

And both men turned both keys for a second that seemed an eternity. Right then, the submarine shook and flailed, and the hull vibrated like train rails singing.

At the top of the boat, near the control tower, they were close to the surface but still submerged.

The PC-28 Сармат or the Russian nuclear ballistic missile designated RS-28 Sarmat in English was more readily known by its NATO name which was SATAN 2. The missile is a liquid-fueled MIRV-equipped, super-heavy thermonuclear-armed intercontinental missile. Not the most efficient missile on the market, but there was a reason it was called SATAN 2. It didn't have to be the most efficient. It was unstoppable enough to get past missile defense systems, usually. And it carried with it a nuclear payload of nothing but fire and death.

The missile fired out of the silo as it was designed to and rocketed out of the water. It ripped into the air and roared high, high into the sky.

59

WIDOW WASN'T under anyone's command. Not anymore. And one perk of not being under command was freedom of movement. He had enjoyed this perk immensely.

But when he saw the RS-28 Sarmat fire from just under the water's surface about two miles away, several of the sailors on the bridge also had freedom of movement because they followed him as he ran out of the portal and onto the deck.

Ebert followed him out as well. Kiley and Towdez remained. True professionals.

Widow hit the deck running, followed by a small horde of sailors. They all stopped behind him like he was their leader. He stood on the deck and stared up as the missile rocketed into the sky. White exhaust smoked behind it. He saw the small fiery propellant at the tail, pushing it up and onward to a target unknown.

Widow was suddenly reminded of the shuttle Challenger. He had seen it explode on television when he was a kid, like the rest of the world. But before it tragically exploded, it looked similar to the RS-28 Sarmat, only bigger.

Widow watched with horror on his face and in his bones.

They actually did it, he thought.

Just then, he looked downward at the deck. Two flight crews of fighter pilots were scrambling for their jets.

Widow could do nothing. He watched until the missile was up, up, and then gone from sight.

60

WIDOW and the rest of the sailors cleared the way, moving back. Most of the crew started heading back to their posts. But not Widow. He had no post. He stood on the deck and watched.

The first pilot and his wingman strapped into their cockpit, fast, and within a minute, they rocketed off the deck into the sky, followed a minute later by a second jet.

That was enough for Widow. He turned and headed back to the bridge.

More fighter pilots and jets lined up and took off.

On the bridge, Captain Towdez was ordering the crew to do this and to do that. The whole ship was chaotic but in a good, old-fashioned sort of way, like ordered chaos. And it dawned on Widow that this was the first time since WWII that an American ship had seen this kind of act of war. Sure, they'd had Desert Storm and Vietnam and so on, but never with these stakes.

Widow looked around in awe at the proficiency of his fellow sailors. Strangely, he missed it.

Captain Towdez turned out to be a lot better under pressure than Widow would've guessed.

Ebert was with him, giving orders and checking over his shoulders.

Kiley stood still, watching, smiling.

61

THE PEOPLE WORKING onsite of the target went about their lives. Late afternoon. A fall day. The trees around were filled with red and yellow and orange leaves that looked more like painted watercolors than real life. Songbirds chirped and flew. The grass was freshly cut and kept as it always was, as was called for by SOP.

The people in the area lived a uniform life. They went to work. They were friendly with each other. They did their jobs well.

The Americans on the East Coast, in the target area, were well-trained and well-prepared. But nothing can ever prepare a community for a thermonuclear ballistic missile.

Although the people in the target area were always prepared, always vigilant, no one is ever truly prepared for what happened next.

Suddenly, the entire community was on high alert because they all heard the raid sirens at the same time. They were under attack.

Dozens of them ran out of buildings. Many of them were armed with assault rifles and handguns. Others, office workers, came to the nearest windows and looked out.

All of them wondered if this was a drill.

They could hear nothing over the sirens.

They couldn't hear the ballistic missile fly down through the clouds and wind. But some of them saw it.

The men and women nearest to the runway saw it best. They saw it best because it was coming crashing, screaming down on top of them.

Some others who could see it ran for shelter. Some piled in vehicles. Others fell to the ground and rolled underneath whatever they could find, thinking that would protect them from the blast. Others scrambled to whatever building was nearby and hugged the wall. Some of them fell to their knees and ducked their heads down.

The ones closest to the missile's likely contact spot did nothing. They just stood there, staring, watching, trembling. They didn't want to die.

None of them wanted to die.

The missile tore through the sky with raw, unstoppable force, and a moment later, it crashed, nose first onto one of the plane hangars on Norfolk Naval Base, crushing through the roof, collapsing it, and impacting with a malfunctioning C130 parked inside the hangar.

The nosecone smashed down into the unused plane first and exploded.

62

KILEY CONTINUED TO SMILE, and Widow saw it.

Just then, Ebert asked one sailor a question.

He asked, "Update?"

"The missile hit Norfolk Navy Base. That was their target."

Kiley said, "An act of war."

Towdez said, "Sir?"

Kiley said nothing.

"It's not an act of war. We know it was Farmer, not the Russians."

"Of course. I'm simply caught up in the moment."

Widow turned to ignore them both and waited for news. He looked at Ebert and nodded like he was psychically telling him what to say.

Ebert asked, "Confirmation?"

"I'm waiting."

Confirmation would have to come from somewhere else. If Norfolk were destroyed in a nuclear blast, they would have to get confirmation from as far away as the Pentagon.

Widow closed his eyes. He thought about the White House. He thought about Secret Service snatching up the president, violently shoving him down to the underground bunker for safekeeping. He pictured all the terrified people in the military and the government and the world, probably.

Then he pictured the missile. He pictured the nuclear blast. He had never seen one, not in real life. Few people had.

He thought about the one he saw on television from the old reel of nuclear testing in the Pacific. The blast from miles away. The shock-wave. The terror of it all. Then he thought about the mushroom cloud—that huge ominous cloud of death.

The mushroom cloud, he thought.

He opened his eyes and ran, full speed, right past a sailor coming in the door, almost knocking him down. He shoved past two others on his way back out to the deck.

Several of the fighter jets had already been scrambled out over the ocean.

He looked west, scanned the sky, waited.

Ebert and Ali both came running after him. Ali was short of breath. He tried to speak, but Ebert interrupted him.

"Widow? What is it?"

"The mushroom cloud," he said.

"What?"

Widow pointed at the southwest horizon.

"That's America!"

"Yeah. It's in that direction."

"There's no mushroom cloud! A nuclear blast would have a cloud! We would see it even from here! Small, but it'd be there!"

Ebert looked at the direction he pointed. They waited. But there was no cloud.

The sailor from the bridge came out after them, a young woman. She breathed in hard, chest panting from scrambling out so fast.

She said, "Commander."

He turned and waited.

"It was a dud!"

"A dud?" Ebert asked.

She shrugged and said, "It didn't explode."

"What?" he asked.

Gusts of cold wind beat across Widow's face.

"It exploded, but there was no nuclear blast. It wasn't much of anything."

Ebert asked, "You're sure?"

"Yes. We got Norfolk on the comms now. They're talking to Towdex. Nothing happened."

Widow asked, "Nothing?"

"The missile hit a plane hangar. It exploded like a normal missile, but it was a weak explosion. Might not even have been from the missile. Might have been from the fuel tank in the jet. They said it was being worked on. I don't know. But there was no nuclear blast."

Ebert said, "Get back up there. Order them to get HAZMAT out there! And clear that base!"

Ebert ordered it, but Widow was sure the base commander, whoever he or she was, had already started evac procedures. And he was sure that Ebert knew it as well. Still, saying it all out loud probably felt pretty good.

Widow smiled.

Ebert asked, "Wait! Any casualties?"

"Not so far. There's a fire."

Ebert nodded, and the woman walked off, back to the bridge. Ebert stayed behind.

Widow asked, "What about the sub? We gotta take it out now!"

Ebert nodded and pointed and said, "Over there!"

All three men turned and watched as two fighter jets flew off in the distance and fired missiles into the ocean. Then, from two hundred yards away, a swell went rushing through the water. It was a torpedo from the American sub.

Widow watched as the missiles and the torpedo collided in the same location. A fraction of a second later, there was an underwater explosion. Widow watched as water sprayed up and out like a volcano erupted under the surface and only shot out water and not lava.

Ebert said, "Looks like a hit. And the explosion means it's sinking. Out of commission."

Then he turned and headed back to the bridge.

Before the missile rocketed away, Farmer and the redheaded leader and the rest of his crew had docked the mini-submarine up to an empty torpedo tube and pressurized the tube to allow them to get into the sub. The fifth man in their crew had piloted the mini-sub to them from Moreau.

All four of them squeezed into it just after the missile was fired and noticed by the Navy convoy, and after they had shot Karpov's crew on the bridge, right in front of his eyes.

The redheaded leader was just about to shoot and kill Karpov when Farmer put his hand up and stopped him.

"Bring him. He may be useful," Farmer said.

Karpov felt nothing but shame for what he had helped transpire.

He didn't fight them. Weakly he had followed them back through the corridors of the sub, down the ladders, and through several hatches. He watched them shoot and kill every man who tried to interfere, and he did nothing. He had no strength left.

They entered the mini-sub and shot it out into the ocean.

Widow grabbed Ali by the arm and said, "Wait."

Ali stared on at him.

Widow said, "You know what happened just like I do."

Ali nodded.

He said, "The passcode. Karpov gave them the wrong passcode."

Widow nodded and said, "We have to do right by him. We owe him that much."

"What do you propose, Mr. Widow?"

"His daughter is still out there."

"You know where she is?"

"I heard something about Moreau? That mean anything to you?" Widow asked.

Apparently, it meant something to him, because Ali's eyes lit up.

"What?"

"It's an old abandoned training facility for us."

Widow asked, "What kind of training facility?"

"It's a small town on an island. Used to be a fishing port a century ago or something. The government took it over after everyone left. The agency used it for different exercises. We're not the only ones either. The FBI used it for a time as well. The little town makes for a lot of cover for firefight exercises or whatever the FBI does for training."

"That's where they took her then."

Ali nodded, said, "What do we do?"

"Let's talk to Ebert."

65

Ebert suggested a SEAL team get her, take out the bad guys. But they didn't have a SEAL team onboard, nor did Widow want to wait for one.

Instead, he insisted on going alone or with a local team of whoever they had, but they had to go now. And like that, within thirty minutes, he was back in the same helicopter, only this time he was with Ali. Hardy came as well, and the same pilot crew. Ebert wanted to accompany them, but he couldn't. And he could spare no one else. Although he tried, either Kiley or Towdez had denied the request. Widow wasn't sure which.

He was sure that they made the same old claims that all COs made everywhere. Something about them still being on red alert, and they still had a mess to clean up, lots of red tape. The real reason being budget constraints or the fact that this was more of a federal law enforcement matter now. Moreau was an island belonging to the federal government, after all.

Widow didn't care as long as he got there. He was grateful for the ride and for the guns and body armor that Ebert insisted they take.

The three men geared up as they rode in the back of the Seahawk helicopter.

Widow figured the deck crew must have fueled the Seahawk up before they took off, as he had suspected, because they flew for even longer than the last time.

They flew north and west. Widow saw a blip of land far to the west, and then it was gone. New Jersey, he figured.

The three men were issued sidearms. Widow was happy to trade because a Navy weapon was always better than some Russian lawyer's weapon. Each of them got a Heckler and Koch .45 automatic. No suppressors. Ten rounds each. This was a fine weapon.

They each also got carbine M4 assault rifles. Widow kept his switched to single-shot. He had no idea what Hardy's was set to. And Ali actually rejected his weapon. He just took the sidearm. He claimed he wasn't much good with an assault rifle. Widow didn't argue.

After about ten more minutes, the pilot turned and called out, "We're nearing the coordinates you gave, Mr. Ali."

"Okay," he called back.

Ali turned to Widow and asked, "It's your show. How do you want to approach?"

"It's an island. There's more than a ninety percent chance we'll be spotted, no matter what. How big is it?"

"Not big. You can jog across it in forty minutes, maybe less. I'd guess like four miles. Not even."

Widow said, "Then let's just get dropped off wherever. Once we hit the ground, we hit it running. And we hunt them down."

Hardy asked, "Know how many hostiles we're up against?"

"At least four."

They both nodded.

Widow double-checked the Kevlar vest Ebert had given him, and then his ammo. He had a spare magazine for the M4 stuffed in his back pocket. That should be plenty.

Hardy had the same, and Ali had a spare for the HK45.

"We're dropping in now, boys. I don't see any hostiles so far," the pilot called out.

The Seahawk swung around the island and scanned it before touchdown. They saw a zodiac on the beach, abandoned, and they saw the abandoned town that Ali had told them about.

No people.

The Seahawk made its way back around to where the zodiac was abandoned and came down and landed on the sand. The rotor wash picked up sand and blew it everywhere.

Widow was the first man out. He ducked and rolled and came up ten feet away and crouched on his knees. Sand was flying around everywhere. He looked through it and scanned the trees and dips in the topography. There was no sign of anyone.

Hardy and Ali followed. They ran off, following Ali toward the town. The Seahawk took off and continued to circle, staying high enough to see them and staying far enough not to get shot at by the enemy.

They trekked through a long path that eventually became a dirt road, surrounded by yellow shrubs and aging trees, with thick branches.

Ali said, "That way. Not far now."

Widow stayed quiet and followed closely. He took note that Hardy seemed to be a good wingman. The guy kept up the pace. He stayed low and held the M4 correctly.

They saw abandoned, rusted-out four-wheelers and one half torn-up boat on the side of the road. They passed a rusty old boat trailer with no tires left. They passed brick walls broken like a tank had driven through the area.

They came to the first structure of a house or just a building, Widow couldn't tell. It was empty.

They moved on, and Widow saw the town. They walked up a hill and could see the whole town. It was basically nothing. There were ten structures. All brick. None of them had roofs left. None of them showed any signs of people. The windows were all blown out. No glass was left anywhere. And there were thick weeds and grass growing all over everything.

Widow gave Hardy signals to go quiet, and they searched each building individually, which didn't take long because there was hardly anything to search.

After they were done, they came back out to the middle of the town.

Hardy asked, "Now what? There's no one here."

He dropped his M4 to his side and held it like he had given up.

Widow said, "Someone's here. That zodiac is new."

Hardy nodded.

"Where else is there?" Widow asked Ali.

Ali shrugged, said, "Maybe they're to the north. There are some rock formations and more trees. I don't know of anything else. I've never been here before."

Widow said, "Let's go."

And they hiked north.

66

THEY RAN out of dirt road about a mile later, and then they ran out of island.

They stood there on the edge of the island, wondering how they had missed the bad guys. Widow stood the closest to the edge of a rock cliff and stared out at the water.

"Where the hell are they?" he asked out loud to no one in particular.

And no one answered him. They just shrugged.

Then he looked down. The rock cliff wasn't that high off the water below, maybe ten feet. But he thought about how this end of the island was high, and the other was low.

"The elevation," he called back to the others.

They looked at him, and Widow turned left and started climbing down the rock cliff, stepping on one rock and then another until he was standing in knee-high water.

He inspected the cliff's wall and smiled.

There was no wall, only a huge opening to a cave.

"Down here," he shouted up.

Ali and Hardy climbed down.

"What is it?" Ali asked.

"It's an underwater cave," Hardy said.

Widow said, "Partially underwater."

Widow looked at the mouth and the ocean water that flowed into it.

He said, "It's deep in the middle."

"Yeah," Hardy said.

"How wide do you think this is?" Widow asked.

Hardy shrugged and said, "I don't know, maybe twenty yards?"

"Yeah," Widow said.

He ducked down and peered in. There was nothing but darkness ahead, and then the mouth opened up wider and curved right.

He stormed through the shallow water, which was the only part that could be walked on because there was a rock ledge. Then Widow realized it wasn't rock.

He said, "Ali."

"Yeah?"

"This walkway is manmade."

Ali looked and saw what he meant. It wasn't rock; it was metal.

"What the hell is this?" Ali asked.

Widow said, "It's an underground dock for a submarine."

67

Hardy said, "A small sub couldn't fit through here and then hope to get back out again."

Widow said, "Not a military one."

Hardy said nothing.

Widow said, "Ali, any chance that Farmer got himself a mini-sub? The deep-sea diving kind?"

Ali said, "Anything is possible."

Hardy said, "Do you think this guy Farmer escaped the Russian sub? Now he's here?"

"Maybe. Not all terrorists are martyrs."

Hardy said, "Those things are slow-moving. No way would he make it this far by now."

Widow said, "Maybe they didn't. Maybe they're on their way. Or maybe he had it retrofitted. They could have gotten their hands on one and dumped all the scientific gear out of it. Put on some extra propellers. Maybe an extra engine. A couple of thrusters. Expand the rotors.

"Hell, they could be here already."

Ali and Hardy said nothing.

Widow said, "Come on. Let's get wet."

They followed him down the metal walkway. Widow led the way and followed the walkway down the upper lip of the cave and on for another forty yards until it dipped up out of the water. They bent around the curve to the right and west, and then they came to an enormous cavern with dim lights strung up along metal rigs.

Off in the distance, about another fifty yards away, there was a platform with stacked equipment and a couple of utility poles. Beyond that was a set of stairs that climbed up and disappeared inside a small structure that could have been some kind of control room or something.

Widow noticed the cables snaking up under the stairs and going to the structure.

On the platform were two men that Widow had never seen before. They were seated on crates, talking.

Widow saw a third one, a redhead, pacing up and down the walkway, standing duty even though his buddies weren't helping.

Widow saw no one else. He assumed they were inside the structure.

The other thing that Widow saw was a black mini-sub, just like he thought. It floated underneath the platform. The headlamps were lit up like bright, glowing orbs. They cast more light on the inside of the cavern than any other light.

The sub looked empty, although he couldn't see into it to be sure.

"What now?" Ali asked.

Widow looked back at him. He said, "I'm not here to take prisoners."

Ali nodded.

Hardy nodded.

Widow led the way. They stayed crouched low in single formation. Widow crept along the catwalk, staying out of the light.

They came upon the redheaded leader first. He was walking the other way. Pacing half out caution, Widow figured, and half out of boredom.

He turned to come face to face with Widow. At about ten feet away, which was a shame because Widow wanted to keep the element of surprise, but he knew in such a limited space, a loud gunfight was inevitable.

He shot first.

Widow had the M4's stock embedded firmly in his shoulder. His butt touched his boot heel. He kept his elbow stiff, reinforcing the grip. He squeezed the trigger twice.

Two rounds exploded through the redheaded guy's center mass. He flew back and rolled off the catwalk and into the water. Dead.

The other two men on the platform turned to see what was happening. Before they could lift their guns, before they even stood up, Hardy dropped them both. Two single rounds.

The guy was a hell of a shot, Widow thought.

Now everything was loud. Widow jumped to his feet and charged up the walkway to the platform.

One guy came clawing up and out of the hatch of the mini-sub—no gun in hand.

Widow didn't care. He fired a round and hit the guy square in the face. Blood burst and red mist sprayed out. The guy dropped back into the sub, lifeless.

That's four down, Widow thought.

Just then, three more guys came running out of the structure above and saw the visitors and were met with a hail of bullets. They dropped as fast as their friends. One fell off to the side and rolled down the ramp, off of the structure, and the other was flung over the side into the water to join his dead friend, the redheaded leader.

The last just slumped back and landed on the ramp.

Widow didn't wait for more to come tumbling out of the structure. He ran up and took cover behind a wall to the opening. Hardy followed, and Ali stayed close.

Widow peeked in. The space ahead was crammed, but empty.

Widow said, "Stay back for a minute. It's small in there. Let me go first."

Hardy nodded.

Widow handed the M4 to Ali and went ahead with the HK45 instead. The space was too close-quartered for an assault rifle.

The space beyond was dark and didn't lead to a control room at all. Instead, there was a small hall that opened up into a large room with sofas and old armchairs, and some radio equipment that looked like the last time it had been turned on was during WWII. Off to one side was a string of long drapes hanging from the ceiling, like they were hiding a stage.

There was a coffee table near the sofas and an ashtray with two cigars still smoking.

A guy was sitting on the sofa. He was in bad shape. His face looked like he had been beaten within an inch of his life.

He wore a ripped-up Russian uniform. He was a submariner, Widow figured.

He stared at Widow, said nothing. Widow wasn't even sure if he could speak.

But his eyes were wide open and flicking to the left.

Widow rolled into the room, turned to the drapes, and paused. He figured someone was hiding behind it. And there was. He saw shoes underneath.

And a man jumped out. He fired an M9 Beretta at Widow. Widow suddenly felt bad for the guy. He was almost sure that the guy had never fired a gun before in his life. Only he was in the CIA; he must have.

The guy saw he had missed completely. He didn't readjust his aim to shoot Widow because Widow was looking back at him with the HK45 dead on target.

The guy dropped his gun, which told Widow who he was. Probably.

Widow asked, "Are you, Farmer?"

The guy nodded and started to speak.

Widow didn't let him. He squeezed two times. He put one through the heart and one through the guy's head for good measure.

Farmer tumbled back into the curtains, moving to one side, grabbing onto the other with his dead hand. His corpse pulled it down and off the ceiling. Widow looked beyond it to a stairwell that led up into the ground above.

Eva was nowhere to be seen.

Widow turned back to the man on the sofa. He walked over to him and asked, "Are you Karpov?"

"Yes."

"Where's Eva?"

Karpov stood up and must have been dizzy because he collapsed back over.

"Don't get up. Where is she?"

"He took her. Up," Karpov said.

"Don't worry. Stay here. My friends will get you. I'm going after her."

Karpov said nothing.

Widow ran to the stairs and climbed.

68

THE STAIRS LED UP and out of the cave to a wooden hatch that was so cracked and splintered Widow could see daylight. He was worried that it was a trap. That maybe the man in black waited for him above with that SIG Sauer he had seen earlier.

Widow took a deep breath, and with one fluid, fast action, he thrust himself upward, shoved the door open, and took aim, scanning in every direction. No one was there.

He saw lots of daylight and broken brick walls.

He pulled himself up and out. He was in an abandoned building. He walked out of it and saw he was back in part of the town. Trees surrounded only this part. There was no dirt road. He presumed it must have been an offshoot site.

He came out of the building, kept his back to the wall.

"Where are you?" he called out. There was no answer.

He looked through the buildings, and then he looked down and saw footprints in the dirt and grass blades stomped down. Widow turned to follow them.

The footprints led into a two-story structure with an old door hanging off rusted hinges. Widow entered and swept from left to right with the HK45. He saw nothing, but there were more foot-prints in the dust leading up the stairs. He followed slowly, care-fully. He checked the nooks and corners. Checking the hidden areas as best he could. At the top of the stairs, there was a hallway with three open doorways. Past bedrooms, he presumed.

He walked down the hallway, following the footprints.

They led to the last room on the right, across from another room.

Widow was no fool. He had spent sixteen years as an undercover cop where bad guys would have killed him if they knew who he really was. So he was a cautious guy. Cautious enough. He checked the other two rooms before entering the last one. They were empty.

He stopped at the wall and hugged it before stepping into the doorway.

Like the other buildings, the roof on this one was mostly blown away. The sun was bright at the angle he was at. It beamed down through huge holes and was almost blinding.

Widow called out, "Eva?"

She didn't answer, not with a reply. Instead, he heard her making all kinds of noise. She must have been gagged. He peered in and saw her seated on a lone old desk chair. Her hands were zip-tied in such a way that it looked like she was stuck to the chair. The zip-ties went between her wrists and one of the chair's metal arms.

Widow looked around fast. No one was there.

He saw an open closet. It looked empty. There were holes in the floor big enough to fall through. He studied them. No one was down there, either.

There was a window behind her. No glass. He saw trees beyond it and nothing else.

Widow entered the room, confused. Where was the man in black?

He walked over to Eva slowly. She mumbled and squirmed. The chair's bottom was jammed into a hole in the floor like it was practi-cally bolted there. She was flailing, trying to get free.

Widow said, "Okay. I'm here. I'm here."

He got behind her and looked at the chair's leg. He reached his free hand around her and pulled the gag out of her mouth.

Eva shouted, "HE'S BEHIND ME! OUT THE WINDOW!"

But it was too late. A second later, a razor-sharp garrote shot over Widow's face and came tightening around his neck.

69

THE MAN in black's garrote was deadly. He had never messed up with it before, and he had no intention of messing up this time. He had stepped out the window to hide on the ledge, but he also wanted the leverage because his target was a big guy.

His plan was to pull back and half drop over the ledge as best as he could to let his weight and gravity pull the target back to the window and strangle him that way—a perfect plan. At least it should have been. But he miscalculated the wire and Widow's neck and Widow's HK45.

The HK45 was jammed between the razor wire and Widow's neck.

Widow saw the wire at the last second and had jerked upward and shoved the gun between the wire and his face and neck.

The HK45 was twisted and turned and pointed left away from his face, which was good because a hair more inward and one shot would have blown a hole in his face.

The man in black was strong, not stronger than Widow, but at this angle and the way the guy was pulling him back and out the window, he had the advantage.

Widow struggled to pull him forward while the man in black wrenched backward.

Widow could feel his legs buckling. He could feel his shoulder muscles cracking and throbbing from pulling forward.

He didn't want to fire the gun so close to his face. And even if he did, what good would it do?

He tried to move, to shift away, and try to get free. But every move he made, the man in black was right there with a countermove.

He struggled and wrenched from one side to the other. The garrote wire was etching through the gun's hard shell. What was he supposed to do?

Eva struggled and bounced and tried to get free. She could help him if only she could get free.

That was when Widow decided the best thing to do wasn't to fight. The best thing to do was to give in. He felt the man in the black push off the wall outside the window with his feet, trying to pull Widow back to get him in a better strangling position.

So Widow shifted to the right and then spun left and jumped backward. His feet pushed off the floor with all of his power, and he took the man in black off guard and plowed into him. The two of them went back into the air, out the window, off the ledge, and into the trees.

They bumped into each other, and both fell to the hard ground below. Two stories. Not enough to kill them, but enough to break bones.

Widow landed on his left hand and felt two of his fingers twist and break. The pain hit him all at once. And instinctually, he let go of the HK45, which went flying into the man in black's face, snapped back at him by the garrote.

They both lay on the ground for a moment. Widow in pain from his broken fingers and the man in black with the wind knocked out of him and a bloody nose that could have been from hitting the ground or from the HK45 nailing him in the face.

Widow didn't care. He just wanted to get up.

He dug down deep and shoved himself up on his good hand and stumbled onto his feet. The man in black was up next, going for his SIG Sauer, Widow presumed, because he reached under his jacket to the shoulder holster. Only he came out with nothing because the SIG Sauer was up on the window ledge. And it wasn't alone.

The man in black and Widow both heard a voice.

Eva shouted down, "Hey!"

She was leaning out of the window. She was free from the chair, only not really because the arm hung off the zip-tie around her wrists. She had pulled the old rusted arm off. She held the man in black's SIG Sauer.

She called down to Widow.

"Are you okay?"

"I'll live."

"What about the missile?"

"Don't worry. It didn't explode," he said, and he looked at the man in black who looked shocked. And it dawned on Widow. They had thought it did. They had all thought they started World War III.

Widow said, "Karpov gave up the wrong passcode. Farmer entered the wrong one. The missile was nothing more than an oversized paperweight."

Eva asked, "Is my father okay?"

"He is."

She asked, "Want me to shoot him?"

The man in black's eyes sprang open. Blood trickled out of this nose.

And Widow said, "Do it!"

Eva squeezed the trigger, and for the second time in a day, Widow had blood sprayed across his face and neck and shirt.

The man in black's face was mostly still there. Mostly.

The corpse dropped to its knees and slumped over forward.

Widow called up to her. He said, "Let's get out of here. My hand is killing me."

70

THREE DAYS LATER, Widow waited outside of Admiral Kiley's office with his assistant, who was Widow's favorite person at the moment because she had brought him two cups of coffee, Styrofoam cup, back to back, as he waited.

The only thing good was the coffee, because so far, he was getting the silent treatment from the admiral, who had been in his office with Ebert for fifteen minutes. Widow didn't answer to them anymore, and they had told him he was a hero. But he still had to wait like everybody else.

Finally, Ebert opened the door and said, "Widow."

Widow stood up. He was in new clothes, black jeans still, but he wore a white sweater over a white t-shirt, which matched the cast on his left hand, also white. The hospital on Norfolk Navy Base was pretty good. They fixed him right up. One day, no waiting there, and they had set his bones and cast them up. He was supposed to keep his left hand above his heart. He had been given a sling to wear, which he elected not to.

Widow stood up from his chair and took his coffee with him. He walked into Kiley's office and shook hands with him, and then with Ebert.

Kiley said, "Widow, you did a fine thing for us. A fine thing. Your country is grateful."

Widow said, "I appreciate that."

"Have a seat then."

Widow looked down at the chair and said, "I won't be here long enough to sit."

Kiley looked at him, confused.

"Of course you will. The medal ceremony is this afternoon."

"Medal?" Widow asked.

Kiley said, "Yes. Don't you want your medal?"

"What medal?"

"The Secretary of the Navy is driving out. Or already has. He wants to shake the hand of everyone involved and present medals. I don't know exactly what yours will be, not a medal of honor or anything. But something you'll want."

"I don't want the medal."

"I'm sorry to hear that."

Widow kept smiling. He didn't want to seem ungrateful for the gesture. He looked around the room.

Kiley had quite a career, like the rumors suggested. The walls were littered with pictures of sailors that Widow didn't know. Some black and white. Some in color. There were awards and commendations and medals strung out neatly all over the place. Everything was chaotic, yet somehow organized, which reminded Widow of the aircraft carrier when the missile broke through the water, when Kiley had a smile on his face.

Then Widow noticed something displayed proudly on the table behind Kiley. Right in the center, there was a big, broken old brick. It was polished but was still worn and timeworn. Underneath it, there was a plaque with writing etched in gold.

Widow said, "You love this Navy stuff, don't you?"

Kiley said, "Of course! Don't you?"

Widow shook his head.

"I did once. But that was a lifetime ago. Not me anymore, Admiral."

Kiley said nothing.

Ebert broke the silence and said, "Widow, are you sure you don't want to stay?"

"No."

Kiley said, "One more piece of information that you will like."

"Oh? What's that?"

"Eva and her father will get asylum for their contributions to stopping Farmer."

Widow nodded.

"We offered to send them back, but they begged to stay. It wasn't up to me, of course. It was up to the State Department. But I'm sure that Ali had something to do with granting their request."

Widow thought of Eva. He asked, "Where is she?"

"I don't have the faintest idea. Their names are probably changed by now. They're being treated as if they're in witness protection. They're probably halfway to Oklahoma."

Widow stayed quiet.

Kiley asked, "Sure, you won't stay for the ceremony?"

"No."

Widow turned and walked back to the door.

Ebert walked with him.

Widow turned and said, "I should salute you, sir. After all, I was a SEAL, once."

Kiley seemed to like that statement. And Widow stood proud, head high, shoulders back, and saluted with his good hand. Ebert saluted as well. And Kiley saluted back.

Widow looked past him at the brick. The inscription read: Berlin Wall, November 9, 1989.

Widow dropped his salute and walked out.

Ebert followed and walked him back to the front of the building, and shook hands and said goodbye.

71

AFTER THE CEREMONY, and the shaking of more hands, and the salutes, and the drinks, and the cigars, there was dinner. And after all that, Admiral Kiley was exhausted. He said his goodbyes to Ebert and Towdex and the Secretary of the Navy, and God only knew how many other high-ranking officials. He lost track from all the pats on the back for a job well done.

He got in his car with a smile on his face and drove home.

On the way, he thought about McConnell, his friend. He hated that the man had to die. He hated that the man's wife had to die. Kiley didn't regret the man in black or Farmer.

He deeply regretted that the mission was a failure, really. War wasn't ignited. The nuke didn't go off. He had already been prepared to see it through. Destroying America's greatest Naval base would have done the trick. But it didn't happen.

It wasn't all a loss, though. There seemed to be a new surge of duty in the Navy now. He was proud of that. He could find another project to start things moving, to reignite honor and fight back into the Navy that he had loved.

He could find some warlord in the Middle East, to help or in Asia, perhaps.

Kiley pulled up into his driveway and killed the engine in his American-made Ford Taurus. He got out and clicked the button on his keys to lock the vehicle. He walked to his front door and opened it.

He stepped over to the alarm pad to switch off the alarm like he did every day. Only the pad wasn't counting down fifty seconds like it usually did. In fact, the pad looked totally different today because it was ripped halfway out of the wall. Wires dangled, and the plastic cover was in pieces.

He stared at it, dumbfounded.

Then he heard a voice from behind him in the dark in the doorway to his den.

Widow said, "All those people, Admiral."

Kiley spun around to see Widow standing there with one hand in a sling. And the other down by his side.

"Widow? What are you doing here?"

"You know you almost got away with it."

"What are you talking about?"

Widow said, "Come on into the den. I want to chat."

Kiley walked into the house. The den was where he needed to go. He kept his sidearm in the top drawer of his desk.

He walked past Widow and nodded politely, like some sort of English butler.

Widow walked behind him and sat down in a comfortable armchair across from the desk.

"Take your coat off," Widow said.

Kiley took off his coat and pulled a huge, leather-backed chair from his desk and sat in it.

He slid his drawer open.

Widow said, "I gotta know. Why did you do it?"

"Do what?"

"You know what."

"Indulge me."

"You orchestrated this whole thing. Farmer. Karpov. All of it."

"How did you know?"

"When I saw the brick from the Berlin wall in your office, I was sure. It told me you missed the glory days of war. Or some such nonsense. But the smile on your face when the nuke was fired. That told me first."

"This country doesn't appreciate its military," Kiley said, his tone changed to one full of confidence.

Then he thrust his hand into the drawer and grabbed for his Colt 1911 forty-five, only it wasn't there. And he looked up, terrified.

It was in Widow's good hand.

"How many people were going to die?"

"They're all nothing! They need to know what real war is like! They need to know honor!"

Widow stood up, pointed the 1911 at Kiley.

"Wait! Wait! I'm a patriot! I've saved lives!"

"You're not a patriot! Those men and women out there fighting every day! They are the patriots! You're a washed-up nobody!"

Then Kiley's face turned to one of something pathetic. And he begged.

"Please, Jack! No one has to know! No one really got hurt! The nuke didn't even explode! Remember?"

"No one got hurt?"

"Right!"

"What about Karpov's men? They're dead!"

Kiley shrugged and said, "So what? They're the enemy! They're Russian!"

Widow shook his head and said, "They aren't the enemy. You are."

He squeezed the trigger and watched as the familiar red mist exploded out the hole left in the back of Kiley's head. Blood and brain sprayed behind him across books on a bookshelf.

Widow saluted Kiley one last time with the 1911 still in hand. Then he walked over to the corpse and spit on it.

He turned and went to the kitchen, left the lights off. He found a dishtowel and grabbed it. Used it to pop on the light above the stove. He found a dishwasher and opened it, tossed the gun on the rack. Then he found soap and loaded the machine and started it on a heavy clean cycle, and left it.

He had touched nothing but the front doorknob and the alarm pad. He wiped both on his way out.

Widow walked down the driveway and out of the subdivision without being seen.

Thirty minutes later, he was back on a major interstate. The thumb from his good hand was out.

A semi-truck slowed and pulled over to the side of the road about twenty yards ahead.

Widow jogged to the passenger side, and the driver asked, "Where ya headed, guy?"

Eva and her father weren't sent to Oklahoma like Kiley had joked. Not that far away. But they had been given new identities and sent to Vermont, which Widow knew because Ali had told him.

Widow said, "Vermont."

FIRE WATCH: A PREVIEW

Out Now!

FIRE WATCH: A BLURB
A BLURB

She's on the run.

He's passing through.

With a kill squad after her, can Jack Widow can protect her?

Molly DeGorne is a woman on the run. She's wanted for murdering her abusive husband in a raging fire. Scared, alone, and with no one to trust, she runs to the only place she thinks is safe, her summer post as a fire lookout. Only it may not be as safe as she suspects.

The only hope that she's got is a drifter that she only just met—Jack Widow.

International bestseller Scott Blade fires up the page with thrills, passion, and explosive action in the eighth book in the Jack Widow series.

Fans of **Lee Child's Jack Reacher, Tom Clancy, Vince Flynn's Mitch Rapp, and Mark Greaney's Gray Man** will enjoy the **Jack Widow Action-Thriller Series**.

Readers are saying…

★★★★★ An action-packed mystery that will set your pages ablaze!

★★★★★ Fire Watch has to be the best of the series, and that's saying a lot!

CHAPTER 1

A PRESCRIBED fire is a fire set deliberately. The fire that burned Molly's house to the ground was set deliberately.

Right then, her husband burned up in it, and she watched it happen. And she couldn't help but think about the raging California wildfires happening right then, farther south.

From outside the two-story, dark coastal house, she saw it all. The engulfing red-hot flames. The dark backfire. The plums of white smoke. And the clouds of black. It fumed together, killing off the oxygen in the air.

The smoke rose, blotting out the stars.

DeGorne's husband had been there. In the house. When it all started, she heard his screams. She would never forget. But that was all over now. He was dead.

She had packed a bag the night before—two of them. One was the same bag she packed every April 30th, every year, for the last five years.

Every year she packed a bag with what she needed for the next six months. She packed two pairs of hiking shorts, five pairs of short-sleeved tops, three pairs of cargo pants, five pairs of socks, five pairs of underwear, two pairs of long-sleeved tops, one raincoat, one warm denim coat, two knit sweaters, her basic hygiene and feminine products, two knit caps, two baseball hats, and a foldable toothbrush. Everything that she needed.

She had packed them all in one canvas backpack. It was packed tightly, but it was filled just enough to close. After five years of packing it every April, she knew exactly how to do it. A man wouldn't have been able to pack so much so efficiently. She was much smaller than most men. Therefore, her clothes were more modest, more lightweight, and much easier to pack.

The second bag she had packed was a blue duffle, no bigger than her backpack, but a hell of a lot heavier. Heavy because it was packed with something else. Something that didn't belong to her. Something that she had found just the day before. The contents were the reason she had one black eye.

Neither packed bag was in the fire. Each was stowed away safely in the back of her truck. It was parked in a disconnected garage. It was away from the fire, directly behind her.

DeGorne stood shivering just off the gravel driveway. Out of sight. Off toward the woods. Out in front of the home that used to be hers half the year, she stood and gazed upon the life that used to belong to her. She wore her single black eye like it had always been there. He had done it to her. She wouldn't deny it. Not anymore. No more telling the neighbors that she tripped—no more telling the nurses and the emergency room that she had fallen down the stairs. No more lying for him.

Luckily, she hadn't had to lie to her parents for a long time now. They were already dead. Her father would never have stood for the abuse if he had known about it.

He was retired Army. Following in his footsteps, she had done four years herself, from eighteen to twenty-one. That had made him proud until she decided not to reenlist, until she married to start a family life instead. But family life never came. She never had children. Something about infertile eggs. Something about irreversibility, which was the news that started the abuse—the first time.

It was all around the same time, when her father got sick after her mother died, that she convinced her husband to transfer his job to Seattle. Part of which was so she could take care of her father. And part was to try again—a fresh start.

She threatened to leave her husband if he didn't go with her. She threatened to expose his secrets if he didn't transfer. Why? She couldn't honestly say.

Everything was fine for a while. She had gotten a great job, which allowed her space away from everything, which allowed her to run away from her husband once a year. It allowed her to run to the woods and hide, literally.

Last year was the hardest because that was when her father died. She had been away. Off in the forests of California for the summer. Doing her job, but missing her father's last moments of life.

When she came back from her job, she had to deal with her father's passing, his burial, and his estate. That was also when the abuse from her husband had started up again. Not as bad as before, but it was there.

Last night, it had gone on as it always had gone on. A drink too many. A push into a wall. A shove into a counter. Then a jab to the gut. And then a right hook to the face. Just like what he had done to her before. This time wasn't the first time, but it would be the last. This time she planned to do something about it.

However, last night turned out to be her husband's last time to do anything.

This time hadn't been the worst that she had ever had before. She had no broken nose. No broken cheekbones. No fractured ribs. She didn't need stitches to close torn eyelids. She didn't need to reset her teeth.

There was no dentist's appointment tomorrow. There was no emergency room visit—no paperwork to fill out. No lies to tell. She'd had worse. He had given her worse. But no more.

Her toes sunk into the gravel. She had thick, wavy blonde hair that cascaded down over her shoulders. It caressed her soot-covered body. She looked like she had woken up in the middle of the blaze. Her favorite t-shirt for sleeping hugged close to her small frame. She had no pants on. Just panties. Just the t-shirt and panties, and the soot, and the ash.

She had barely escaped the fire.

Goosebumps scuttled across her skin. The night was cold. Not winter cold, but cold enough. Stony and callous winds blustered off the Puget Sound.

Ashes wafted out of the fire. She thought about her bags. She had only packed the two, and both packed full enough—everything she needed and nothing she didn't.

Then her mind shifted. She thought about where she would go or what she would do, or how she would get through this. She couldn't go on to her job. Could she?

Her mind returned to nothingness, and she watched in horror as the house she had called home for five years burned to the ground, along with the marriage that she had known inside it.

She hadn't planned on burning her house to the ground. None of it was premeditated—none of it but the packed bags.

The flames rose into the night sky like a phoenix rising from the ashes. Fiery steeples jetted up and waved and sparked out like deadly solar flares rocketing off the surface of the sun. The heat was intense. She felt it on her face, even from fifty feet away. A three-thousand-square-foot house will do that.

The house was nestled in the woods, twenty miles north of Seattle. The closest neighbors were miles away. They would see the yellow-red torrents of blaze soon enough. They'd be calling the police and the fire department.

Within ten minutes, the nearest firehouse would receive the distress call of someone reporting the fire. Two minutes later, they'd dispatch a truck. And twenty minutes after that, the fire trucks would barrel down the dirt road onto the gravel driveway that led to her house.

The police would be there sooner.

The nearest police were actually the county sheriff, a pudgy, older guy named Portman. She knew him well. He had been a friend of her family her whole life. He and her husband weren't friends. He suspected the abuse. He had gotten a few reports from the hospital —nothing he could ever do about it because she always lied to him, too.

DeGorne stepped back off the driveway and planted her toes in the cold grass, barefoot. She did nothing. She said nothing. She thought nothing. She just watched and listened.

Trees surrounded her. The wind swayed the leaves in the same direction as the waving flames. She stood there until thoughts returned to her.

She thought. Her husband had been in the house. He had been in the fire. He was dead. But she was not. She was still here. She was still alive.

She froze in place, asking herself one question.

Should I run?

A WORD FROM SCOTT

Thank you for reading THE MIDNIGHT CALLER. You got this far—I'm guessing that you enjoyed Widow.

The story continues in a fast-paced series that takes Widow (and you) all around the world, solving crimes, righting wrongs.

Sometimes, a purging fire is necessary to destroy the past. This is how FIRE WATCH starts for Molly DeGorne who is standing in front of her blazing home and her DEA husband, who is still inside and dead. What looks like murder may be more heinous as she goes on the run from a group of armed mercenaries. She goes back to her summer job as a fire lookout in a California National Park where she meets the one man who can help her—Jack Widow.

The next book, THE LAST RAINMAKER, pulls Widow out the hospital after a train wreck, where he is discovered by an old frenemy, CIA Agent Tiller wronged Widow in the past in a secret mission to North Korea that got Widow's team killed at the hands of the deadliest sniper who ever lived. Now, Tiller needs Widow's help to stop the same sniper, known as a Rainmaker. The sniper has reemerged taking out his victims from great distances. His target list: the world record holders for longest confirmed kills.

The tenth book that follows is THE DEVIL'S STOP, which refers to all the places in the USA named after the devil like Hellbent,

New Hampshire, a small town that time forgot. First day there, Jack Widow meets a beautiful former Air Force MP who's desperately seeking her husband all while being nearly nine months pregnant. Widow being the man he is means that he's got to help. What starts as a simple missing person soon turns deadly when they uncover that the missing husband was involved in a top-secret government nuclear program and the evil team of dishonored mercenaries who are after it.

Book eleven is BLACK DAYLIGHT (coming November 2018). Jack Widow walks a lonely, snowy road at night when he witnesses a heinous crime. The only glimpse of the culprit he gets are taillights that fade into the mist. Widow does all he can to help, but when he does the local South Dakota police and the FBI see him as suspect number one.

What are you waiting for? The fun is just starting—once you start Widow, you won't be able to stop.

THE SCOTT BLADE BOOK CLUB

Building a relationship with my readers is the very best thing about writing. I occasionally send newsletters with details on new releases, special offers and other bits of news relating to the Jack Widow Series.

If you are new to the series, you can join the Scott Blade Book Club and get the starter kit.

Sign up for exclusive free stories, special offers, access to bonus content, and info on the latest releases, and coming soon Jack Widow novels. Sign up at www.scottblade.com.

THE NOMADVELIST
NOMAD + NOVELIST = NOMADVELIST

Scott Blade is a Nomadvelist, a drifter and author of the breakout Jack Widow series. Scott travels the world, hitchhiking, drinking coffee, and writing.

Jack Widow has sold over a million copies.

Visit @: ScottBlade.com

Contact @: scott@scottblade.com

Follow @:

Facebook.com/ScottBladeAuthor

Bookbub.com/profile/scott-blade

Amazon.com/Scott-Blade/e/B00AU7ZRS8

Made in the USA
Columbia, SC
03 October 2023

23844446R00207